Swan for
the Money

OTHER MEG LANGSLOW MYSTERIES BY DONNA ANDREWS

Six Geese A-Slaying

Cockatiels at Seven

The Penguin Who Knew Too Much

No Nest for the Wicket

Owls Well That Ends Well

We'll Always Have Parrots

Crouching Buzzard, Leaping Loon

Revenge of the Wrought-Iron Flamingos

Murder with Puffins

Murder with Peacocks

Swan for the Money

A Meg Langslow Mystery

Donna Andrews

Minotaur Books
New York

A THOMAS DUNNE BOOK FOR MINOTAUR BOOKS.
An imprint of St. Martin's Publishing Group.

SWAN FOR THE MONEY. Copyright © 2009 by Donna Andrews. All rights reserved. Printed in the United States of America. For information, address St. Martin's Press, 175 Fifth Avenue, New York, N.Y. 10010.

www.thomasdunnebooks.com
www.minotaurbooks.com

ISBN-13: 978-0-312-37717-5
ISBN-10: 0-312-37717-7

First Edition: August 2009

10 9 8 7 6 5 4 3 2 1

Acknowledgments

Swan for the Money would never have been written if I hadn't arrived early for a signing at a bookstore and decided to pass the time by browsing in the gardening section, in the hope of finding some new techniques for repelling the deer and Japanese beetles from my roses. I stumbled across Aurelia Scott's *Otherwise Normal People: Inside the Thorny World of Competitive Rose Gardening*, and after half a chapter I knew that Meg's future had to include a rose show. I recommend Scott's book not only to readers who would like to learn more about rose shows, but to anyone who enjoys a nonfiction story told with grace, intelligence, and humor.

I also owe special thanks to Kathy Harig of Mystery Loves Company, who first introduced me to fainting goats.

Thanks to all the folks at St. Martins/Minotaur: Andrew Martin, Pete Wolverton, Hector DeJean, Lauren Manzella, Toni Plummer, and especially my editor, Ruth Cavin.

I'm grateful to my agent, Ellen Geiger, and the staff of The Frances Goldin Literary Agency, who take care of the business side of things so I can focus on the writing, and to the staff at Curtis-Brown, especially Dave Barbor, who helps make Meg international.

Thanks to the members of my writing groups: Carla Couple,

Ellen Crosby, Laura Durham, Peggy Hansen, Valerie Patterson, Noreen Wald, and Sandi Wilson of the Rector Lane Irregulars, and Erin Hooper Bush, Meriah Crawford, M. Sindy Felin, Barb Goffman, and C. Ellet Logan of the Hellebore Writers. And to the other friends who read drafts, listen to me brainstorm, and generally provide moral support: Chris Cowan, Kathy Deligianis, Suzanne Frisbee, David Niemi, Dina Willner, and all the Teabuds.

The members of the Potomac Rose Society patiently put up with my questions and lurking at one of their rose shows. To the extent that the rogue, non-ARS-affiliated, rose show in this book bears any resemblance to a real rose show, they are responsible, but any ghastly errors are mine alone.

A special thank you to my family, who put up with the cranky me when the book is going slowly and are always ready to celebrate when it's going well. They are, as my nephews Liam and Aidan are so fond of saying, "Awesome!"

Swan for
the Money

Chapter 1

"Dreadful news!" Dad said.

He collapsed into a chair at the foot of the breakfast table, as if no longer able to bear the weight of his dire tidings, and wiped his balding head with a pocket handkerchief. The head, the handkerchief, the hand holding it, and nearly every stitch of his clothing were so encrusted with mud and garden dirt that Mother would probably have ordered him off to take a shower immediately if she weren't so visibly curious to hear his news.

"Yes?" she said, one hand clutching her throat in a gesture that would have looked artificial and old-fashioned on anyone else. On her it merely looked elegant.

"We've lost Matilda," Dad said.

"Oh, no!" she exclaimed. From her expression, I could tell that she found this news genuinely heartbreaking.

Faint murmurs of sympathy arose from the dozen assorted friends and relatives seated around the table, but I could tell from their uniformly puzzled faces that they were all mentally asking the same question I was: who the heck was Matilda?

We used to have a Matilda in the clan, my Great Aunt Matilda. But she'd been dead for years, and I couldn't recall anyone else gracing a recent arrival to the family with such an unusual name.

1

Nor could I remember any friends or neighbors named Matilda. There was a time when I would have assumed Matilda was one of Dad's patients, but he was semi-retired now, and his medical practice consisted mostly of those same family, friends, and neighbors, whose names I would recognize. Not a Matilda in the bunch.

"And what's more," Dad went on, sitting up and frowning fiercely, "it was foul play. No question. I only suspected it with Adelaide, but I'm sure of it now."

"It's the Pruitts," Mother said. "I've suspected them all along." Not surprising. The Pruitts were an old local family who used to own most of Caerphilly County and often behaved as if they still did. Most locals were quick to blame the Pruitts whenever anything sneaky or underhanded took place. Mother and Dad only spent weekends here in Caerphilly, in the old farmhouse they'd dubbed their summer cottage, but they were quickly picking up many local attitudes.

"You suspect the Pruitts of two murders?" my brother, Rob, asked. "Have you told the police?"

"Murders?" Dad echoed. "What murders?"

"This Matilda and Adelaide you're talking about," Rob said.

Dad burst into laughter. I suddenly realized what he'd been talking about.

"It's not murder," I said. "Because Matilda and Adelaide aren't people, are they? They're roses."

"Meg's right, of course," Mother said, sounding slightly cross, as if baffled at how long it took us to figure this out.

"Sheesh." Rob returned to his food. "Roses. That's all we talk about these days."

"Now you know how I feel," I muttered, though not loud enough for anyone but Michael to hear. For the last two months, ever since Mother recruited me to organize the Caerphilly Garden Club's annual rose show, roses had taken over my life. Normally I'd be asleep at this hour, not trekking to my parents' farm to collect boxes of rose show equipment and haul them to the farm whose owner, Mrs. Winkleson, was hosting tomorrow's show. And normally the gala breakfast might have made up for the early hour, but today my stomach was wound too tight to enjoy it.

"Can't we talk about something else for a change?" Rob was saying.

"Peonies, for example," my husband, Michael, said. "Much more practical for our yard. They don't require a lot of cosseting, like roses, and the deer don't seem to eat them."

I could tell from Rob's face that he didn't consider peonies a conversational improvement over roses, and Mother and Dad ignored the interruption.

"Meg," Mother said to me. "Your father needs coffee." She managed to give the impression that only with an instant infusion of caffeine could Dad possibly survive this new horticultural tragedy.

"I could use some, too," Michael said, and shot out to the kitchen before I could even push my chair back.

"Matilda and Adelaide were two of my most promising black roses," Dad said to the rest of the table.

"And two of our best chances for winning the Winkleson Trophy," Mother said. "Which will be given out this weekend at the Caerphilly Rose Show to the darkest rose," she added, on the off chance that any of the assembled relatives had managed to escape hearing about the Langslow household's new hobby of breeding and showing roses.

"Is there a big prize?" Rob asked.

"No money involved," I said. "Just the thrill of winning."

"Big thrill," Rob said, through a mouthful of scrambled eggs.

"And a trophy," Mother added. "Quite possibly a lovely engraved Waterford bowl. That's what I suggested." Yes, that sounded like Mother's kind of suggestion. She was a confirmed human magpie, easily seduced by anything that glittered, and a sucker for anything that had ever come out of the Waterford factory.

"Well, if the winning rose is bred by the exhibitor, there's always a remote possibility that a commercial rose company might want to buy it," Dad said. "Of course, that would only happen if it were a significant advance toward the creation of a truly black rose. All the big commercial breeders have their own black rose breeding programs."

"And ridiculous programs to begin with," put in my grandfather. "A genuinely black rose is a scientific impossibility."

"Oh, I hope not," put in my cousin Rose Noire, née Rosemary Keenan, to those who had known her before she'd become a purveyor of all-natural cosmetics and perfumes and adopted a name to match. "I do hope one day to greet one of my namesakes!"

She probably would. Talking to plants wasn't even unusual in my family. Although Rose Noire was one of the few who expected the plants to answer.

"Useless things, roses," my grandfather said. "Had all the vitality bred out of them, so the poor things can barely survive without massive applications of chemicals all the time. Environmentally unsound." A typical reaction from my grandfather, Dr. Montgomery Blake, the world famous zoologist and environmental activist. Of course, he could merely be vexed that Dad's rose growing was preventing him from working full-time on the Blake Foundation's latest animal welfare campaigns, whatever they were.

"Getting back to Matilda and Deirdre——" I said.

"Adelaide," Dad corrected.

"Sorry," I said. "It's no wonder I didn't recognize the names—last time I got an update on your rose-breeding program, you were just referring to them by numbers."

"But that's so dehumanizing!" Rose Noire exclaimed.

"Don't you mean deflowering?" Rob asked, with a snigger.

"How can you expect a living creature to thrive when all it has is a number, not a name?" Rose Noire went on.

"That's why we decided to name them," Mother said.

"Unofficially, of course," Dad added. "I haven't yet registered them with the ARS. Officially, Matilda is L2005-0013."

"But we're going to name them all after family members," Mother said.

"No shortage of names there," Dr. Blake muttered. He was still getting used to the fact that when he claimed Dad as his long-lost son, he'd found himself allied by marriage with Mother's family, the Hollingsworths, whose numbers exceeded the population of some small countries.

"I hope you stick to dead relatives," Michael said, as he emerged from the kitchen with a pot of coffee. "Otherwise we'll have no end of confusion. And imagine if it got around the county that Rose Noire was suffering from black spot disease, or that Rob had thrips."

"What are thrips?" Rob asked, looking alarmed.

"Getting back to Matilda and Adelaide," I repeated, "what happened to them, and what makes you think it was foul play?"

"They were eaten," Dad said. "Undoubtedly by marauding deer. And I found this in some bushes nearby."

He held up a small brown glass bottle with a neatly printed label proclaiming that it contained "100 percent Doe Urine."

"James!" Mother said. "At the breakfast table?"

"Someone obviously sprinkled this near Matilda," Dad said. He tried to pocket the bottle discreetly, out of deference to Mother's sensibilities, but Dr. Blake held out his hand for it. "In fact, they probably sprinkled the stuff in a path leading from the woods straight to Matilda."

"Yuck," Rob said, making a face. "If I were a deer, I'd steer clear of roses some other deer had already peed on."

"But you're not a deer," my grandfather said. "To a deer, especially a male, doe urine would be an irresistible lure. Hunters have used deer urine for centuries to cover up their human scent and attract deer to their hunting areas. It's particularly effective if the urine is—"

"Dr. Blake!" Mother exclaimed. I wasn't sure whether she was objecting to his words or to the fact that he had opened the bottle and was sniffing it curiously.

"So hunters use the stuff," I said. "You're sure that bottle wasn't just discarded by some passing hunters?"

"We hadn't given anyone permission to hunt our land," Mother said.

It took a few seconds for the grammatical implications to sink in—the fact that she said "hadn't" rather than "haven't." Did her use of the pluperfect tense mean that now, after Matilda's demise, they *had* given hunting rights to someone? But by the time that thought struck me, Mother and Dad were deep in a discussion of which surviving black roses were likely to produce a prize-worthy bloom by Saturday's contest. Everybody else appeared to be listening attentively, or as attentively as possible while consuming vast quantities of bacon, sausage, country ham, French toast, waffles, pancakes, cinnamon toast, croissants, and fresh fruit. Were the rest of the family really that interested in rose culture, or did they just figure they'd better come up to speed on the subject in self defense?

"Meg," Dad said, "I'm leaving this in your hands."

He gestured to my grandfather, who ceremoniously handed me the empty doe urine bottle.

"Yuck," I said, dropping the thing on the table. I wasn't normally squeamish, but my stomach rose at the thought of the little bottle's former contents. "What in the world to you expect me to do with it?"

"Find out who used it on Matilda," Dad said. "And help me figure out how to stop it. I'm counting on you!"

Chapter 2

I was opening my mouth to suggest that thanks to the rose show, I already had more than enough to do today, things that were a lot more important than tracking down the owner of a bottle of deer urine. But I thought better of it. Matilda was important to Dad. And if someone had sabotaged his entries in the rose show, wasn't that rose show business?

Better yet, wasn't it a crime?

"Maybe you can get the chief involved," Michael said, as if reading my thoughts.

I shook my head slightly. Yes, Chief Burke would probably understand why Dad was so upset. His wife was going to be one of tomorrow's rose exhibitors. But that didn't mean he'd be willing to drop real police business to hunt for the elusive user of the doe urine.

Not unless someone brought him some actual proof that the doe urine was evidence of a crime. And clearly as the organizer of the rose show, I was the best someone to find that evidence.

Ah, well. At least the prime suspects were mostly people like the Pruitts, whom I didn't like and would be just as happy to see getting into trouble.

My fingers hovered over the wretched little bottle.

"Allow me," Michael said. He picked up the bottle and stepped into the kitchen with it.

"Don't throw it away!" Dad called after him. "It's evidence."

"Not very useful evidence," I said. "Do you expect the perpetrator to be carrying around a sales receipt for the doe urine, or perhaps another few bottles to use if the opportunity arises?"

"We could have it tested for fingerprints.'

My grandfather looked at the bare hand with which he'd been holding the bottle, then at Dad's equally ungloved hands. He cocked one eyebrow at Dad.

"Or something," Dad said. His shoulders sagged as if someone had begun deflating him.

"Here you go." Michael emerged from the kitchen holding a zip-locked plastic bag containing the doe urine bottle.

"An evidence bag!" Dad exclaimed. "Excellent! How remiss of me not to have thought of it."

I grimaced and tucked the thing in a side pocket of my tote.

"You've been under a great deal of emotional stress this morning," Rose Noire said. "I could fix you some herbal tisane."

"A little more time in the garden," Dad said. "That's all I need."

He helped himself to more bacon, no doubt to fuel his gardening.

Of course, I didn't see what good bagging the evidence would do, since Dr. Blake and Dad—and who knew how many other people—had been handling it, mingling their own fingerprints and DNA with whatever useful trace evidence a forensic examination might have found on the bottle.

Still, while I doubted the chief would be interested, maybe I could turn the bottle over for analysis to my cousin Horace, who was a crime scene technician back in our home town of Yorktown. Not that he could necessarily find anything useful by analyzing it, but at least it would be out of my hands, not to mention my tote bag. And Horace was one of the volunteers who'd promised to come out and help me set up for the rose show, so I could rid myself of the vile vial in an hour or so.

"Thanks," I said to Michael.

"My pleasure," he said. "And now I really should be hitting the road."

He folded his napkin and stood, pushing his chair back.

"You're going to miss the great rose show?" Rob exclaimed.

"He's going up to New York with several other drama department faculty members," I said. "One of their former grad students is in an off-Broadway play—"

"Way off Broadway," Michael corrected. "Somewhere in the Bronx, I think. But it's legit, and he's not just in it, he wrote it, and we all promised to come up and see it."

"But does it have to be this weekend?" Mother said, with a long-suffering sigh.

"Meg and I were originally going next weekend, after the rose show was over," Michael said. "But the inside scoop is that the play won't last till next weekend. In fact, there's an even chance we'll get there and find out that last night was the last performance, but we have to try."

"As long as you're back by Sunday," Mother said. "Remember, I'm having the family tea then." And as I knew, she fully expected to have several trophies to show off by tea-time.

"Don't worry," Michael said. "It's just an overnight trip.

We're driving up today, seeing the play tonight, and we'll probably be up late, letting the kid cry on our shoulders and rebuilding his confidence. But we're heading back tomorrow morning."

"Unless they all give in to the temptation to see a few more plays while they're up there," I said, just to tease Mother a little. "Important to keep up with trends in the field they're teaching about."

"If the others decide to stay over, I'll catch a shuttle back," Michael said, seeing the stricken look on Mother's face.

I followed him outside to say a more private good-bye. I'd come over to Mother and Dad's long before he got up, to get a start on my rose show–related tasks, so we hadn't had a chance to talk yet today and wouldn't again until tomorrow evening. Okay, it was only thirty-six hours, but I wasn't looking forward to coping with the rose show without Michael.

Outside it was raining. Barely more than a drizzle at the moment, but since it had been either drizzling or flat-out raining almost continuously for the past five days, thanks to an unseasonably early tropical storm stalled off the Carolina coast, the whole yard was a sea of mud. We stopped on the front porch where it was merely damp and clammy.

"More rain," I said. "I hate to think of you driving all the way in that."

"Good for the roses, though."

"Actually, right now it's not," I said. "The rain can cause spotting on the blooms, and if we get more high wind it will blow all the best blossoms to bits, and if this damp weather keeps on much longer I think there's some kind of fungus that could take hold. This close to a show, all a rain does is cause the growers extra work and heartache."

I gestured toward a nearby rose garden, which might have been beautiful if every single bush hadn't had a trash can or plastic bag over it, to protect the blooms from last night's wind.

I noticed that Michael's face was twitching, as if he was fighting the urge to laugh.

"Good grief," I said. "I'm starting to sound just like them, aren't I?"

"I think it's quite commendable that you've become something of an expert in such a short time," he said, with a chuckle.

"I'm not an expert," I said. "I've just had to learn a few things, in self defense. I was so relieved when they both got involved in this rose hobby. It's taken Mother's attention away from the whole idea of opening a decorating business, for one thing."

"I still don't quite get why you're so worried about that," Michael said. He leaned against the porch railing at my side, and I had the comforting thought that it wasn't just the rain making him delay setting out to meet his fellow faculty members.

"Because you know if she starts the decorating business we'll be the guinea pigs," I said. "She'll want to come over and do rooms in our house as show pieces, probably in styles neither of us can stand, like French Provincial or Louis Quatorze, and then she'll expect us to keep them in perfect order so she can drop in at a moment's notice with prospective clients."

"Potentially annoying," he said, but I could tell he didn't really believe me. He'd see, if Mother ever did launch her decorating career.

"I think she'd already have opened that shop if she hadn't

been bitten by the rose show bug. And it's something she and Dad can share. Frankly, I've been a bit worried about how much time and energy Dad has been spending on Dr. Blake's projects."

"Worthwhile projects, all of them."

"Yes, but I'm getting tired of having to bail them out of jails all over the East Coast when their protests tick off local law enforcement," I said. "Not to mention how dangerous some of their schemes can be. Did you hear Dr. Blake's plan for infiltrating a dogfighting ring?"

"Considering how familiar his face is from all those *Animal Planet* shows and *National Geographic* specials, I doubt if even he can pull that off."

"And even he realizes it. That's why he wants Dad to do the actual infiltrating, while he stands by with a camera crew."

"Ouch," Michael said. "I can see why you're worried."

I didn't mention the fact that my grandfather had been planning to recruit Michael as his undercover agent until I convinced him that Michael's face was almost as well known as his, thanks to reruns of the various TV shows and movies Michael appeared in before he'd abandoned his acting career to take up the less precarious life of a drama professor at Caerphilly College. I was exaggerating a bit. Most of Michael's leading roles had been in soaps, which didn't do reruns. Fortunately Dr. Blake despised television in principle and only turned his set on to watch himself, so my scheme had worked—and then backfired, when he recruited Dad instead.

"That's the great thing about this new rose obsession," Michael was saying. "It may be a little annoying for the rest of us, but it's harmless."

"You haven't met the other competitors," I said. "I've been to a couple of the rose society meetings, remember, since Mother stuck me with this project. I've met most of them. They're all very nice, but they make Mother and Dad seem positively sane on the subject of roses. But yes, at least rose growing isn't dangerous or strenuous. A suitable hobby for people who have reached maturity."

"Maturity?" Michael echoed. "Is that the new euphemism for people well over sixty-five?"

"Yes," I said. "Ever since several cousins began snickering when Mother referred to herself as 'in late middle age.' Though if they show up for the rose show, the cousins will laugh just as hard at 'maturity.'"

"Then I'm even sorrier to have abandoned you to the mercies of the parents who have managed to reach maturity without becoming at all sedate," Michael said. "Sounds as if today and tomorrow will be tough."

"They'll be hellacious, but you'll be back to help with the cleanup on Saturday afternoon, and I can survive till then."

"You're sure you don't want me to pretend to go all Neanderthal and insist that you accompany me to New York?"

"Tempting, but no," I said. "Mother would forgive you, but she'd never forgive me. But there is something you can do. Could you pick up—"

Just then Rob popped out onto the porch where we were standing.

"You're really coming back tomorrow?" he asked Michael. "Don't be a masochist. Stay the weekend. Come back when the town's sane again."

"I enjoy a bit of madness now and again," Michael said.

"Then don't you need someone to go along with you? Would your student's play make a good computer game? Maybe I need to check that out."

As founder and president of a Caerphilly-based computer gaming company, Rob did need to keep an eye out for promising game ideas, but lately he'd developed an annoying habit of going off on game scouting expeditions whenever there was useful work to be done at home.

"It's a four-hour play in blank verse about the political downfall of Millard Fillmore," Michael said. "Not my idea of a hot game property, but—"

"The rose show is sounding better and better," Rob said.

"What was it you were going to ask me to pick up?" Michael asked, turning back to me.

Damn. I had been about to ask him to drop into a drugstore and pick up a pregnancy test. Not that the Caerphilly Pharmacy didn't carry them, but a few months ago, when I'd bought one there, I'd been spotted by several of the most incorrigible gossips in town. By the end of the day, I'd received seven congratulatory phone calls and a dozen e-mails full of pregnancy jokes. Not to mention the three hand-knitted baby sweaters that arrived in the mail at the end of the week. I still wasn't sure whether the elderly aunt who sent all three had heard a rumor that we were having triplets or if she was just clearing out a surplus of knitted goods.

Then there was the outpouring of sympathy we'd received when word got out that no, there was no pregnancy, just a false alarm. We'd only been married a little over a year, so I thought it was early for people to start feeling pessimistic about our chances of having a family, but in the weeks since the false alarm, I'd heard about every couple who had ever experienced fertility problems not only in my family but also in the whole of Caerphilly County. I wasn't eager to start all that again. And much as I loved my brother, I knew better than to trust his discretion.

But what could I pretend to want Michael to bring me from New York? My imagination didn't usually wake up this early, even after a good breakfast. And I'd been too anxious to eat much.

Breakfast.

"Bagels," I said. "Bring back a bag of bagels."

"Bagels?" Michael echoed. He sounded puzzled.

"You can't get really good bagels here," I said.

"Yeah, but I don't think anyone knew you were such a big bagel eater," Rob said.

"I'm not, mainly because you can't get decent ones here," I said. "I've been thinking how much I'd like to have some bagels. Authentic ones."

"Bagels it is," Michael said.

"Not a bad idea," Rob said. "Bring me some, too. And maybe some lox and cream cheese and—"

"I don't think the lox and cream cheese would survive the trip all that well," Michael said. "But I'll bring back authentic New York bagels for everybody."

I'd find a moment later in the day to call him and tell him my real request. For now, I settled for kissing him good-bye, hand-ing him his umbrella, and waving as his convertible jounced slowly away on my parents' muddy unpaved driveway.

"Lucky dog," Rob muttered.

"You think the tragedy of Milliard Fillmore is preferable to the rose show?" I asked.

He tilted his head as if thinking.

"Well, no," he said finally. "But he did say there was a good chance the play would die before they got there, and I can't think of anything that could derail the rose show."

"I can," I said, with a sigh. "A lot of things. And it's my job to see that none of them happen."

Chapter 3

As I turned to go back into the house, I reached into my pocket and pulled out my notebook-that-tells-me-when-to-breathe, as I called my trusty spiral-bound to-do list. I briefly considered adding an exciting new action item that would read "resign post as rose show coordinator." Tempting, but again, Mother would never forgive me. Instead, I jotted down a more practical item, to be done when the show was over: "brainstorm list of potential victims/volunteers to chair next year's rose show."

I'd agreed to organize this year's show before I knew what a big deal it would be, back when I'd thought roses were a sweet, harmless hobby. But I was determined not to get roped into next year's event. Even if I had to—

"Hey, Meg,"

The voice seemed to come from directly above me. I leaned out into the rain and looked up to see the familiar figure of Randall Shiffley, one of our neighbors, standing on the porch roof, leaning against the side of the main house, a crossbow in his hand. The weapon wasn't pointed at me, but it still gave me the willies. One of Randall's many cousins was perched on the chimney, peering down into the front yard and he, too, appeared to be holding a crossbow. They were both wearing blaze orange rain ponchos over blaze orange overalls. That might have made them hard for the deer to spot, since supposedly the deer don't see orange as well as we do, but they stood out quite distinctly as festive splashes of color against the house's freshly painted white wood siding—the one bright spot in a drab, rain-smeared land-scape.

"Hey, Randall." I waved back as nonchalantly as possible.

"Any more news about Mrs. Winkleson's missing dog?" Randall asked.

"I didn't even know she had a dog," I said. "Much less that she was missing one. Though if I were Mrs. Winkleson's dog, I'd try to be missing as much as possible."

"Missing as in dognapped, according to my cousin Epp," Randall said. Since Epp was a Caerphilly County deputy, odds were Randall was passing along real information, not a wild rumor. "She had the cops out there about 4 a.m. this morning when one of the maids found the ransom note."

"How did the maid know it was a ransom note?" I asked. "I've been out there a dozen times in the last few months, and I haven't met a single maid who speaks English."

"Dunno," Randall said. "That's all Epp told me. Maybe the butler read it. But you're going over there, right? Keep your eyes open."

"I will. What kind of dog was it, anyway?"

"Expensive pedigreed dog, according to her," Randall said. "Maltese, I think she said. Some kind of little furball, anyway. Sounds a lot like your Spike from the description, except that I think Epp said it was all white instead of black and white."

To my astonishment, his words brought tears to my eyes.

Completely ridiculous. I didn't feel particularly sentimental about the Small Evil One, as Michael and I both called our dog. Technically he wasn't even our dog. He belonged to my mother-in-law. I still resented the underhanded way she'd foisted Spike off on us several years ago, by pretending her allergist wanted to see if dog-free living improved her health. But today, for some reason, the thought of someone else pining for a beloved missing pet affected me deeply.

Get a grip, I told myself. I couldn't imagine Mrs. Winkleson pining for anything. Having a temper tantrum that someone had stolen her property, yes. I felt a twinge of anxiety at the thought. Mrs. Winkleson in a tantrum could easily decide to rescind her invitation to the Garden Club to hold the rose show on the grounds of her farm.

"Thanks for warning me," I said as I headed back inside.

"Has Michael already taken off, dear?" Mother looked up as I reentered the dining room.

"Yes," I said. I decided not to mention the dognapping, or my private worry that it would derail the rose show. "Dad, why are there armed Shiffleys on your roof?"

"Armed?" Dad said. "Oh, no. It's not rifle hunting season yet. They're only using bows and arrows."

"I think that still counts as armed," I said. "It's a weapon. What are they doing up there?"

"Protecting the roses, dear," Mother said.

"Protecting the roses?" I echoed. "I thought you were against letting the Shiffleys hunt on your land."

"They're not hunting, dear," Mother said, with a touch of annoyance in her voice. "They're not going to do anything unless they see a deer attacking our roses. Didn't you hear your father say that he thought deer could be responsible?"

"Eating roses isn't exactly attacking them," I said. "It's just what deer do. And I could have sworn I also heard Dad say that it was the Pruitts who were responsible."

"I think they're the ones who discarded that disgusting little bottle," Mother said. "After sprinkling its loathsome contents over our poor roses. Deliberately."

"It could be," Dad said. "You never know."

He was using what Rob and I called the "humor your mother" voice.

"So the woman who gave me a hard time for buying a deer-skin leather jacket is now allowing the Shiffleys to slaughter deer just because they're eating her roses?"

"They're not going to shoot the deer," Mother said. "Just scare them off. Along with any conniving Pruitts who try to lure them to our roses."

Behind his back, Dad put his finger to his lips and shook his head.

"Randall's going to send a few of his cousins over to do the same at your house," he said aloud.

"No way," I said. "I can live with your using our yard to expand your rose-growing area, at least as long as someone other than me does all the pruning and spraying and mulching and whatever else they need. I like roses as well as anyone else. But I draw the line at giving them their own private army. What if the Shiffleys shoot the llamas?"

"I think the Shiffleys know the difference between a deer and a llama," Dad said.

"After dark, which is when the damned deer tend to show up for dinner? I'm not betting Ernest's and Thor's lives on it. Not to mention all of Seth Early's sheep, who spend at least half their time lolling around in our yard with the llamas."

"Heck, the sheep and llamas could be going after the roses for all we know," Rob said. "I say shoot to kill! You reach for a rose and you're history."

Mother gave him a withering look, and the rest of us ignored him.

"I doubt if the deer will come into the yard with the llamas there," I said. "I'll make sure the llamas are in the yard with the roses at night, instead of in the pasture. But I don't want any Shiffleys playing William Tell on our roof."

"If you're sure, dear," Mother said. From the tone of her voice, I fervently hoped I was right about the llamas being good deer deterrents, or I'd never hear the end of it.

"Let's go see the remaining candidates," she said to Dad, and swept out the door, Dad trailing in her wake.

I picked up my untouched orange juice glass and then thought better of it and put it back down beside my equally neglected plate. I didn't usually bother with breakfast anyway, unless someone else made it, and this morning my stomach was too tied up in knots over all the work ahead.

Unless, of course, my stomach woes were unrelated to the rose show. Could this be morning sickness? Could my tearfulness at the thought of Mrs. Winkleson's missing dog be due to hormones rather than sentiment? Even if it wasn't, I didn't dare let any of the busybodies see me turning up my nose at breakfast. So I picked up my still-loaded plate, put the scrambled eggs and the bacon between two slices of toast, sandwich style, and wrapped them in a napkin to take with me.

"I'm running late," I said. "See all of you later. I'm heading over to get the show barn set up."

"May Caroline and I come along with you?" my grandfather asked. "She should be here any minute, and she's as curious as I am about this whole rose show thing."

I stared at him in disbelief. Caroline Willner was the owner of a nearby wildlife refuge and, like him, a passionate animal welfare activist. I doubted that either of them knew a tea rose from a floribunda, or cared. When the two of them joined forces, they were usually planning to tackle some egregious case of animal abuse or defend an endangered species. If they wanted to go to the rose show, I suspected an ulterior motive, but I couldn't for the life of me think what it was. As far as I knew, there were no wild animals on Mrs. Winkleson's estate, where we were holding the rose show. The farm animals seemed so sleek and glossy that I couldn't imagine their welfare was in question. Could this have something to do with the dognapping? It seemed unlikely, since Dr. Blake disapproved of the existence of very small dogs, calling them overbred yuppie toys. And if he was investigating the dognapping, I could see infinite possibilities for conflict with Chief Burke, the head of law enforcement in Caerphilly town and county.

But I had embarked on a program of trying to build a better relationship with my eccentric and irascible grandfather. For that matter, building any kind of relationship with him. He'd only appeared in our lives a year ago, when spotting a picture of me in the newspaper had led him to suspect—correctly, according to the DNA tests—that Dad was his long-lost son. Integrating him into our family life hadn't been easy for anyone. So if he wanted to see the rose show or use it as cover for some project of his own, maybe I should cooperate.

"You're welcome to come along, but I'm going to be swamped with show preparations, and might not be able to drop everything to bring you back when you're finished," I said.

"Don't worry," Dr. Blake said. "Clarence said he'd be glad to come out and get us whenever we want." Clarence Rutledge, the local veterinarian, was another of their animal-welfare allies. Yes, definitely a plot of some sort.

"That's fine," I said. "As soon as—"

Mother strode into the room with a dripping, half-furled umbrella in her hand. She looked upset. Very upset—what new disaster threatened the rose show?

Chapter 4

"Meg, dear," Mother said. "We'll be having the garden club fete at your house this evening."

"Our house?" I exclaimed. "No way! What's wrong with here?"

"It is presently unsuitable," my mother said. The last time she'd called anything unsuitable with that same icy precision, she'd been talking about a distant cousin's arrest for indecent exposure.

"What's so unsuitable about it?" I asked, looking around in bewilderment. Everything was neat as a pin and shining with cleanliness—well, except for the spot where Mother's umbrella had dripped rain, and that was an easy cleanup. If I were hosting a party, I wouldn't hesitate to hold it here—well, as long as I could explain that all the ruffled gingham in the kitchen was Mother's taste, not mine.

"You must have a head cold, dear," Mother said. "Otherwise you couldn't possibly miss that ghastly odor."

I sniffed the air several times. Lavender potpourri. The bacon, eggs, and coffee we'd had for breakfast. And from outside, a faint whiff of manure.

Uh-oh. After over a year of living in close proximity to several farms, and half a year of llama ownership, I'd grown quite accustomed to the pungent smell of manure. Mother, on the other hand . . .

If it smelled this much right now, after hours of heavy rain, what would it be like by party time if the weatherman was right and the rain gave way this afternoon to partly cloudy and unseasonably warm for May?

Dad popped back in. His expression was a curious mix of apprehension and stubbornness.

"Apparently your father got up in the middle of the night, went off to fetch a truckload of . . . organic fertilizer, and spread it all over our flower beds."

"You'd be thankful for that manure if you really cared about how our rose bushes were doing," Dad said. "How do you think I've managed to produce such spectacular blooms for you to show? Regular applications of manure, that's how."

"I have no problem with regular applications of manure," Mother said. "I understand the necessity. I do my best to endure the unappealing side effects. But why did you have to do your latest application now? Why couldn't you have waited till after the show?"

"And more important, after the party she's giving this evening," I added.

"But the party's for the garden club and the other competitors," Dad said, sounding bewildered. "I thought the whole idea was to show off our rose beds."

"Along with the house," I added.

"Well, of course," Dad said hastily. "The wonderful décor in the house, and the wonderful condition of the rose beds."

"But the rose beds won't be in wonderful condition," Mother wailed. "They'll reek!"

"They're supposed to reek," Dad said. "Not all the time, of course, but I'm sure everyone in the garden club has smelled manure before. They'll love the manure. They'll probably be jealous that we've got such a good, steady supply of it."

"No one will be able to smell the hors d'oeuvres," Mother said. "All those cunning little rose-shaped crab croquettes will go to waste."

"I'm sure the smell will die down by seven," I said.

"I'm sure it won't," Mother said. "So we'll be relocating the party to your house."

"Our house is a disorganized mess," I said. "I've been too busy with the rose show to clean for the last couple of weeks."

"I'll send over a crew to clean."

"And it will take hours to call everyone who's invited."

"We'll put signs out at the head of the driveway; they'll only need to drive a few miles farther," Mother said. "I'm sure it will all go fine."

"Just one little thing," Dad said. "I already put manure on Meg's and Michael's yard."

"Oh, no!" Mother exclaimed.

"Last night," Dad said. "So the smell will have had more time to fade."

"Not enough time," Mother said. "This is a crisis."

She looked expectantly at me. Something about the word crisis always made my family look my way. I racked my brain for a solution to the problem, and my stomach, already queasy from the stress of Mother and Dad's quarrel, clenched into a tighter knot.

"I have an idea," I said finally. "I could ask Mrs. Winkleson if we could have the party at her house."

Mother grimaced. Mrs. Winkleson was not popular with her fellow rosarians. And clearly Mother loathed the idea of allowing Mrs. Winkleson to steal part of the party's thunder. But under the circumstances. . . .

"I suppose that would work," she said with a sigh. "Ask her as soon as possible. And be thinking of a backup plan in case she says no."

Yes, I'd definitely be thinking of a backup plan. If I was misjudging Mrs. Winkleson, and she really was upset over her missing dog, she would be in no mood for hosting a party. Even if she wasn't upset, the dognapping would give her the perfect excuse to turn down my request. I'd have to do a good sales job.

"Will do," I said aloud. "In fact, I'm going over there right now."

"Once you've confirmed that Mrs. Winkleson is agreeable, tell your father to make some signs and post them, so people headed for the party will know where to go," Mother said. She swept out into the kitchen without looking at Dad.

"Tell your mother to make her own damned signs," Dad said, in a rare burst of irritation. "I'm going to fetch some more manure. The grass could use some, too."

He stomped out the front door.

"Oh, dear," Rose Noire said. She flitted after Mother. My grandfather stumped out onto the porch as if to follow Dad. Rob went to the window and peered out.

"There goes Dad in the truck," he announced. "Probably going over to whatever farm he's getting the manure from."

"Probably the Shiffley Dairy Farm," I said.

I remembered, suddenly, that the way to the Shiffley Dairy ran past Mrs. Winkleson's gate. Had Dad seen anything during his early morning manure run? Police activity at 4 A.M.? Suspicious activity even earlier?

For that matter, was Dad's unfortunate manure trip inspired by a sudden desire to fertilize the roses, or had he been up all night again, listening to his newly acquired police radio, and using manure as an excuse to drive by Mrs. Winkleman's farm and snoop?

Mother's head reappeared.

"And don't forget to ask around about who . . . borrowed my secateurs," she commanded.

"I will, I will," I said. Mother vanished again.

"What are secateurs?" Rob asked

"Fancy name for garden shears," I said. "She means those wrought iron ones I made for her."

"Somebody pinched them?"

"We're saying borrowed for now."

"So you're supposed to find them?"

"Yes," I said. "Not that I have a clue how to do it. If one of the other exhibitors has them, she won't be stupid enough to bring them to the show. They'd only be on Mrs. Winkleson's farm if Mrs. Winkleson stole them, and she doesn't exactly welcome people snooping. In the two months I've been working with her on show preparations, I haven't yet seen her rose garden. If I don't even know where she hides that, what chance do I have of finding a pair of purloined secateurs? What's more—"

The front door flew open again. Rob and I both flinched, expecting more fireworks, and then relaxed when Caroline Willner entered, her diminutive frame clad in a khaki shirt, cargo pants, hiking boots, and a canvas vest with about a million pockets, all filled with useful equipment or interesting bits of junk. Dr. Blake, who trailed in after her, was similarly dressed. Of course, he always wore much the same outfit, whether he was embarking on a jungle safari or appearing on the Larry King show to blast some environmental menace. But Caroline normally dressed more—well, normally. If she, too, was in safari gear, they definitely had some project in mind.

"Hello, dearie," she said. "Did Monty ask if we could go over to this rose show with you?"

"The rose show's not till tomorrow," I said. "Today's the setup. But you're welcome to come along for either one or both. Just promise me one thing: don't get into any trouble."

"What the blazes do you expect us to do, burgle the joint?" my grandfather exclaimed.

"You'll have to be discreet about whatever you're doing," I said. "Mrs. Winkleson's dog was stolen last night or this morning."

"Oh, the poor woman!" Caroline exclaimed. "What kind of dog?"

"A pedigreed Maltese."

"Silly kind of dog to have in the country," my grandfather said. "Probably just slipped outside and got eaten by a fox."

"A literate fox?" I said. "One that left a ransom note?"

He growled slightly.

"Now, Monty," Caroline said. "Just because you disapprove of the poor dog's breed doesn't mean her welfare isn't important. I hope the police are taking this seriously."

"I'm sure they are," I said. "After all, if it's a purebred dog, this could be grand larceny. There will probably be police swarming all over the farm."

I hoped I was exaggerating. Just how big a police response did a dognapping get, anyway? Both Caroline and my grandfather blinked in surprise.

"I was thinking of Mrs. Winkleson's emotional loss, not her financial one," Caroline said finally. "But don't worry, dearie. We'll behave."

I looked at my ninety-something grandfather and his eighty-something co-conspirator and sighed.

"Let's go," I said.

Chapter 5

Caroline chattered for the entire length of the drive to Mrs. Winkleson's farm, telling us about a wounded tiger that had just taken up residence at the Willner Wildlife Sanctuary. Fascinating stuff, but it completely derailed my plan to ask a few leading questions, so I could anticipate what sort of trouble my two geriatric delinquents might be planning to get into. But I knew I'd get a chance sooner or later, so I just concentrated on not letting the steady rhythm of my windshield wipers put me to sleep.

I kept turning over in my brain the two difficult tasks Mother and Dad had assigned to me. Find out who had used the doe urine on Matilda. Find Mother's missing secateurs. Three difficult tasks if you included bringing about a speedy end to Mother and Dad's quarrel. And then there was the dognapping. I had no desire to meddle in Chief Burke's investigation, but I probably couldn't say the same for Dad, who devoured mystery books by the hundreds and reveled at the idea of getting involved in a real investigation. And if the dognapping threatened to derail the rose show, it could suddenly become problem number one.

I let Caroline's and Dr. Blake's animal talk flow over me as I puzzled over all these problems, making plans and then discarding them as useless.

We were within sight of Mrs. Winkleson's gate when my grandfather finally changed the topic.

"So, how much farther are we going?" he asked.

"Funny you should ask," I said. "There's the entrance now."

I pointed to where two large pillars of white-painted brick loomed up, flanking an asphalt driveway in considerably better repair than the road that led to it. The black wrought-iron gate was shut and probably locked.

Since the farm was surrounded not by an impenetrable wall topped with razor wire but a neatly painted white board fence, I couldn't see the logic of the locked gate. Any burglar—or dognapper—with half a brain could just hop over the fence. All the gate did was inconvenience people like me who had legitimate business with Mrs. Winkleson.

The pillar on the left bore a small black-and-white sign that read "No solicitors." Dr. Blake snorted aloud as he read the larger black-and-white sign on the other pillar.

"Raven Hill?" he said. "I suppose she might have ravens on the grounds. Of course, they usually prefer a more wooded area to nest. But hill? Flat as a pancake as far as I can see."

He was exaggerating a little. The land around us was gently rolling, but certainly none of the slight elevations deserved to be called hills.

"There are plenty of woods on the farm," I said, as I pulled up to the intercom box. "And Raven Flats wouldn't sound nearly as elegant. Besides, I don't think the raven part is really about the birds. It's about the color. She has adopted a monochromatic color scheme. Everything on the farm is black or white or gray."

I rolled down my window and pushed the call button.

"Sounds pretentious to me," Dr. Blake boomed.

"Shhh!" I said, putting my hand over the intercom grille in what was probably a fruitless attempt to mute his voice.

"Well, it is," he muttered.

The intercom's speaker crackled.

"Yes?" said a tinny voice. The transmission was so bad I couldn't tell if it was Mrs. Winkleson or one of her long-suffering staff.

"Meg Langslow coming to help get ready for the rose show," I shouted into the intercom. "And to see Mrs. Winkleson."

"Is she deaf as well as colorblind?" my grandfather asked loudly. If he'd been in the front seat beside me, I could at least have kicked his ankle. I settled for glaring.

"Come on up to the house," the voice said. I heard a buzzing noise, and the gate began to swing open.

"Thanks," I shouted back. I rolled up the window and grabbed a couple of tissues to mop at the now sopping wet left shoulder of my black shirt. Mistake; now I had a sopping wet shoulder with bits of pink tissue stuck to it. I sat tapping my fingers on the steering wheel as the gate inched open.

"I'll need to speak with her about leaving the damned gate open," I said.

"Odd, isn't it, locking your gate in a place like this," Caroline said. "I imagine plenty of people around here don't even bother locking their doors, much less barricade themselves in gated compounds."

"And obviously it didn't stop her dognappers," Dr. Blake said. "So why bother?"

"Well, I know why she does it," I said. "To keep her nephews out. The first time I came out here to start planning the show, about two months ago, one of them showed up. They had a shouting match over the intercom, and she wouldn't even open the gate to him. Apparently they're too citified to take off over the fields to get to her house."

"Oh, dear," Caroline said. "So sad when families don't get along."

"They're nephews by marriage," I said. "And I think she resents them showing up to inspect their future inheritance."

"They'd better watch out or she'll disinherit them," Dr. Blake put in. "It'd probably serve them right, the greedy bastards."

"Ah, but she can't disinherit them," I said. "According to the local grapevine, she only has life occupancy. When she goes, the nephews split the farm and whatever's left of their uncle's fortune. Which is probably a lot smaller than it used to be before she turned the farmhouse into a palazzo."

"Are you sure?" Caroline asked.

"About the palazzo? Wait till you see it," I said. "And about the fortune getting smaller, I have no idea, though it stands to reason, given everything she's been doing to the house."

"I meant about her nephews getting Raven Hill after she's gone," Caroline said.

"I haven't looked it up, but I expect someone on the grapevine has," I said. "Wills are a matter of public record, you know."

"Under the circumstances, I think I can understand her caution about the gate," Dr. Blake said.

"Yes, but she can't keep the place locked up like a fortress this weekend," I said. "It's bad enough for her to buzz Garden

Club members in one by one for meetings. At least it encourages car pooling. But today we've got a dozen people coming over to do setup and hundreds expected tomorrow for the show."

"Hundreds?" my grandfather echoed.

I glanced up at the sky and sighed.

"Well, dozens, anyway," I said. "Just the exhibitors would be two dozen, and some of them will bring friends and family, and we're bound to get a few spectators. But she'll probably balk at leaving the gates open after the dognapping."

"We'll reassure her," Caroline said. "With Chief Burke on the case, I'm sure it will turn out well."

I hoped she was right. But the thought of the poor missing dog darkened my mood.

Inside the gate, the driveway curved gently to the left though a charming line of cherry trees, still shedding a few last blossoms, while white daffodils, and other white flowers bloomed lushly on either side. They were all a little the worse for the past week of rain and wind, but it still looked nice. Normally I could enjoy the beauty of the drive, but today, all I could think of was how expensive it all was. She had a large squad of full-time gardeners, and probably a full-time painter to keep the fences white. We passed a place where a spring storm had knocked over a cherry tree. The gap in the line had been filled with a full-grown tree. I didn't want to think what that cost. But if I were a dognapper looking for someone who could afford to pay a hefty ransom, Mrs. Winkleson would be high on my list.

Through the cherry trees we could see a small lake where a

pair of black swans were swimming majestically, while to the right the landscape was dotted here and there with black-and-white cows.

And, in one meadow, a pair of uniformed officers were combing the ground, stopping every once in a while to call out something. When we came close, the nearest one waved at me.

"Mimi!" he called out. "Here, Mimi!"

He appeared to be holding a bag of treats. The other officer was squeezing a squeaky toy. He might have been overdoing it with the toy, and wearing it out. Instead of a cheerful squeak it seemed to be emitting an unfortunate noise, halfway between a mournful wail and an asthmatic wheeze.

"That must be the dog's name," Caroline said. "Mimi. Such a pretty name."

I nodded. I was scanning the surrounding landscape for something small, white, and furry.

We came to a fork in the road, and I turned left, toward the house. We were holding the rose show down in the barns, which were a considerable distance from the house, the better to insulate Mrs. Winkleson from the less decorative aspects of her menagerie. But I had to talk to Mrs. Winkleson first.

The road to the house ran around the edge of the lake, and the two swans sailed along, keeping pace with the car, as if escorting us.

"Nice farm," my grandfather said.

"Estate," I said. "At least if you happen to say anything to Mrs. Winkleson about it."

He snorted.

"Lovely," Caroline said. "But a little bland and monochromatic for my taste."

"Apparently not monochromatic enough for Mrs. Winkleson," I said. "Too much green. She grudgingly acknowledges the necessity for some leaves to produce the white flowers, but that doesn't mean she has to like it."

"What a dingbat," Dr. Blake pronounced.

"Yes, and isn't it lovely how nature conspires to ruin Mrs. Winkleson's color scheme?" Caroline said, smiling as she gazed out the window. "The lush green grass, the glorious blue sky."

"Blue?" my grandfather said. "Looks gray to me."

"Today, maybe," Caroline said. "But other days it must be blue enough to annoy her. The grass, the sky, the—oh, look at those peculiar cows." She was pointing to the pasture on our right.

Yes, the cows were unusual. They were uniformly a deep brownish black, except for the wide white band around their middles, which made them look more than a little like walking Oreo cookies.

"Another reason Mrs. Winkleson's nephews are peeved, from what I've heard," I said. "She's spending thousands of what could eventually be their dollars buying designer livestock. The cattle are called Belted Galloways—Belties for short."

"Old Scottish breed," my grandfather said. "Excellent for grazing on rough land—they can thrive on coarse vegetation that other breeds won't even eat. High quality beef."

"I think they're charming," Caroline said.

"Lot of people do these days," my grandfather said. "What do you bet these are just for show instead of for food?"

"What a lot of calves she's got," Caroline said. "They almost outnumber the cows."

"Actually," Dr. Blake said, frowning, "those don't appear to be calves."

"You're right," Caroline said. "She's acquired matching goats. This is a new development."

Chapter 6

"What do you mean, a new development?" I asked. "The innocent tourist act wasn't very believable to start with. Why not drop it and tell me what you're really up to?"

Caroline and Dr. Blake exchanged a look and then Caroline sighed.

"As I suppose you guessed, we're actually not here out of idle curiosity," she said. "Clarence Rutledge is concerned about whether she's treating her animals properly."

"So, this is actually a covert animal welfare mission," I said, with a sigh. "And you're using me as cover to help you infiltrate enemy territory."

"Precisely," my grandfather said.

"Does this have anything to do with the missing dog?" I asked.

"Missing dog?" my grandfather said.

"Missing as in stolen, you old fool. The dognapping Meg told us about. Not specifically," Caroline added to me. "We're not ignoring her safety, of course, but the chief is on that case, and there's the welfare of all the other animals to think about."

I would have liked to ask what reason Clarence had to worry about Mrs. Winkleson's animals, but we were approaching the front of the house. Mrs. Winkleson was standing at the top of her sweeping white marble front steps in a neat black-and-white checked suit and an oversized black hat.

I parked, as I usually did, slightly to the side, where a stretch of white brick wall would screen my car from the front steps. Of course she'd probably already seen its bright blue color during my drive up from the gate, but I figured out of sight, out of mind. A single police car, presumably belonging to the two officers doing the search, was the lot's only other occupant.

Of course, there was nothing I could do about the umbrellas. Caroline's was hot pink, and my grandfather's bright blue and emblazoned with the logo of the Blake Foundation. Lacking an umbrella, I settled for pulling up the hood of my slicker.

We strolled around to the front of the house and waved to our hostess. I noticed that a black-clad butler was holding a black umbrella over her and getting soaked himself, poor man.

Like most of Mrs. Winkleson's staff, the butler was exceedingly short—so short he almost had to stand on tiptoe to let the umbrella clear her hat. I suspected that she only hired short people because she didn't like being towered over. She couldn't have been more than five feet tall, but held herself so rigidly upright that she gave the impression of greater height until you found yourself standing beside her and had to fight the urge to lean down when talking to her.

"Ms. Langslow," she called down, with a slight nod. I suspected that the nod was calculated to convey the precise amount of respect due to someone in my social position. Mother would no doubt have known whether to bristle with resentment or beam in satisfaction. Being largely oblivious to such social niceties, I just smiled.

"May we come in and sit down for a moment?" I called up. "I have something to ask you." Sitting down, I'd have a better chance of talking her into hosting the party. At five-ten, I annoyed her, and since my grandfather loomed well over six feet, he'd probably send her into a rage if he stood up too long.

Mrs. Winkleson nodded, and turned to go back into her house.

Caroline and Dr, Blake were standing there, umbrellas in hand, eyeing the marble steps.

"You two can start exploring if you like," I said. "Or wait here in the car. I'm just going to ask her about hosting the garden club buffet."

"No, let's beard the lioness in her den," Dr. Blake said, offering Caroline his arm.

"More like a zebress, don't you think?" Caroline said. "And we can offer her our sympathies about poor little Minnie."

"Mimi," I corrected.

I knew better than to offer to help them with the steps. Both of them were too independent for their own good. But I fell into step behind them, where I would have at least a fighting chance of catching them if they slipped and fell on the rain-slick steps.

At the top of the marble steps—seventeen of them—a broad marble terrace ran across the front of a white-pillared portico. If you focused just on the portico, the house bore a striking resemblance to the way Monticello would look if you painted all the red brick parts white. If you looked at it from farther away, you noticed that the elegant neoclassic portico was stuck onto a disproportionately large white cell-block of a house, making the poor thing look rather like a graceful little tugboat trying to guide an oil tanker into port. I felt so sorry for the poor little portico that I always tried not to look at it until I reached the terrace.

Mrs. Winkleson was waiting at the top of the steps. I'd never actually seen her go up or down them, and was more than half convinced she had an elevator hidden somewhere in the house that no one but she was allowed to use.

"Mrs. Winkleson, this is Caroline Willner and my grandfather, Dr. Montgomery Blake," I said.

Mrs. Winkleson turned her gaze from me to them, as if waiting for them to perform. Luckily my grandfather was slightly winded from the climb and only nodded at her, rather than attempting the Vulcan Death Grip, as Michael and I had nicknamed his excessively firm handshake. Caroline leaped into the breach.

"What a lovely estate!" she exclaimed. "And it was so gracious of you to agree to hold the flower show here!"

"Thank you," Mrs. Winkleson said. Her tone was rather stiff, but for Mrs. Winkleson, this was relatively gracious, so I could tell Caroline's enthusiasm had charmed her.

"Let's go in," Mrs. Winkleson said, and turned on her heel to lead the way.

I stepped aside to let the others go in first and turned to look down toward the barns where we'd be holding the flower show. My heart sped up slightly when I saw that there was a police car parked by the barns, with a uniformed county deputy getting out of it. Was this just part of the search, or were the barns becoming a key part of the dognapping investigation? If that happened, there was no telling how much damage it would do to my plans for the show.

Then the deputy tripped over his own feet and I realized it was only Sammy Wendell, who had volunteered to help out with the setup for the rose show. I wasn't sure whether to be relieved that he was still available to volunteer or concerned that the chief hadn't cancelled all leave to mount an all-out investigation into the disappearance of Mrs. Winkleson's dog.

Sammy walked over to a large pickup truck whose bed was piled high with folding cafeteria tables. My cousin Horace, wearing the battered gorilla suit that might as well have been his uniform, was letting down the truck's tailgate, and Sammy ambled over to help him unload.

No other cars or volunteers visible, but most of them would be in the way anyway if they arrived before the tables were set up. Sammy and Horace could handle that. I turned back to follow Mrs. Winkleson inside.

As usual, I mentally kicked myself for not remembering to bring a sweater, though I was never sure whether the chill I felt on entering Mrs. Winkleson's house was entirely due to her overuse of air conditioning. The stark black and white décor and her own chilly personality probably contributed just as much.

"What a lovely house," Caroline exclaimed. Knowing her, I could tell she was just barely restraining herself from adding something like, "Too bad the way you've decorated it looks like a cross between a funeral parlor and a museum."

"Pawn to king four," my grandfather muttered, looking down at the marble floor, which was laid out in large black and white squares and did rather look like an oversized chess board.

Around us, the walls and woodwork were all painted stark white. A white-painted chandelier hung from the ceiling, decorated with a few strands of jet beads. In four little alcoves, recessed spotlights highlighted large, elegant vases made of black pottery or glass. At one side of the foyer, an enormous black-painted Victorian hall stand was festooned with a variety of black hats, black gloves, black umbrellas, black coats, and one lone white silk scarf.

"You may put your wraps there," Mrs. Winkleson said, waving at the hall stand. I reluctantly shed my parka, and hung it on one of the lower hooks. Dr. Blake deposited his umbrella there, and Caroline was following suit when one of the gloomy black garments fell on her—a voluminous cloak. It took both my efforts and my grandfather's to extricate her from its massive folds, while Mrs. Winkleson looked on disapprovingly. Or maybe she disapproved of my sturdy hiking boots. If that was it, tough luck. They were the only sensible shoes for dealing with the amount of mud I'd be encountering at her farm, and I'd wiped them carefully before coming inside.

Then again, was she frowning from disapproval or worry? Maybe she was thinking of her missing dog.

Strange, though, that I'd never seen any sign of a dog on my previous visits. No water bowls or chew toys; not even a leash hanging on the hall stand. Then again, I couldn't imagine Mrs. Winkleson taking any chances that a dog might shed, pee, or chew on the furniture in any of her immaculate public rooms. She probably had a dog-proofed room somewhere for the Maltese. Maybe even a canine suite. The place was big enough.

It suddenly came to me how one of the maids had come to

find the ransom note at four in the morning. By that hour, they were already up cleaning.

"This way," Mrs. Winkleson said, when we'd finally rescued Caroline from the rain cape. We followed her into her living room—half an acre of black leather, white brocade, black marble tile, white carpeting and black lacquer furniture. Dr. Blake chose a black leather armchair that I knew from experience was a lot less comfortable than it looked, while Caroline and I both perched on the edge of a white brocade couch. Mrs. Winkleson took a chair across the room, a mere fifteen feet from us. For her, that was almost intimate.

Out in the foyer, I saw a tiny, black-uniformed maid scuttle out and begin mopping up the water our wraps and umbrellas had shed. Mrs. Winkleson spotted her, and glanced at her watch, as if timing how long it had taken the maid to arrive. I hoped for her sake—for all our sakes—that she'd been fast enough. I'd seen her give a maid a ten-minute tongue-lashing for breaking a teacup, and had only just barely kept my mouth shut, partly because I didn't dare do anything that would make her cancel the rose show, and partly because I was afraid if I offended her she'd take it out on the maid. But I wasn't sure I could hold my temper any longer if she put on a repeat performance.

"The garden club would like to ask you another favor," I said, launching directly into the business of the day. "They were going to hold their cocktail reception at my parents' farm, but there's a problem."

"What sort of a problem?"

I was hoping she wouldn't ask that. I wasn't sure she'd understand Mother's squeamishness about the manure smell, and

I certainly didn't want the whole world to know that my parents weren't speaking to each other because of it.

"An odor problem," I said. "It's . . . um . . . well, have you ever had a septic field go bad?"

Her face wrinkled into an expression of disgust. Caroline and Dr. Blake looked at me with amusement.

"I won't go into the details," I said. After all, if I quit now, I hadn't actually told a lie.

"Thank you," Mrs. Winkleson murmured.

"But there's no way we can have the party there, and we thought—what a great opportunity to let the exhibitors see a little more of your fabulous estate. And of course it won't cost you anything—the catering's all being paid for by the garden club, and they'll do a thorough cleanup after the party's over. In fact, the whole garden club will do whatever's necessary to ensure that the cocktail party is absolutely no trouble at all to you."

She frowned.

"Of course, everyone would completely understand if you didn't feel up to it under the circumstances," Caroline put in. "I'm sure you must be worried sick about your poor puppy."

"Then again, it might be comforting to have a distraction at such a difficult time," I said, looking pointedly at Caroline, in the hopes that she'd get the message—if she couldn't help me convince Mrs. Winkleson, at least she could refrain from undermining my efforts.

Mrs. Winkleson's face took on the prunelike look that signaled she was engaged in serious thought. Dr. Blake was scowling in disbelief, but Caroline and I kept our faces fixed in expressions of eager pleading. I found I was holding my breath.

"Well . . . yes," she said at last. "I suppose that would be acceptable."

"That's great," I said, standing up to make my exit while the going was good.

"As long as everyone wears black and white to the festivity," Mrs. Winkleson went on.

I should have guessed.

"I know I've agreed to relax my standards for the show itself," she went on. "One cannot expect proper behavior from the masses. But members of the garden club and cultured rosarians—well, I'm sure they will understand."

I was opening my mouth to protest when Caroline chimed in.

"Of course," she said. "Very suitable for an evening event. We'll go start spreading the word. I'm sure everyone will be very grateful. Won't they, Meg?"

"You can't imagine," I said.

"So gracious of you under the circumstances," Caroline said. "So what is the news about your poor puppy?"

"It was a purebred Maltese," Mrs. Winkleson said. "You can't imagine how expensive it was."

"I'm sure Chief Burke will find him—er, her," I said.

"I'm not," Mrs. Winkleson said, with a snort.

"You must be so worried about her," Caroline said. "Was there really a ransom note?"

"They didn't ask for ransom," Mrs. Winkleson said. "Just made vague threats. 'Don't tell the police, keep your mouth shut or else.' "

"Smart of you to ignore that and tell them anyway," I said.

"I can't very well file an insurance claim without a police report, now can I?" Mrs. Winkleson said.

Conversation came to an abrupt halt with that. No doubt Dr. Blake and Caroline were thinking much the same thing I was— that perhaps Mrs. Winkleson's dog was better off with the dognappers.

"When was she taken?" Caroline finally asked.

"Probably sometime yesterday," Mrs. Winkleson said. "Could have been a day or two earlier. The maid who feeds it swears it was there yesterday morning, but she could be lying to save her job."

In other words, Mrs. Winkleson hadn't seen the dog for days.

"We should be off," my grandfather said finally.

As we shuffled out of the living room, I realized that I'd made no headway at all in my search to discover the truth about Matilda's fate and the whereabouts of the secateurs. I hadn't even really satisfied my curiosity about the dognapping. I reminded myself how unlikely it was that I'd learn anything from Mrs. Winkleson herself. But now that I was established for the whole day as a welcome guest—not many of those at Raven Hill, I'd bet—who knows what I could accomplish if I approached the staff properly. Behind Mrs. Winkleson's back. I patted my tote, where the little amber bottle and the spare secateurs clinked reassuringly.

For that matter, maybe I could have a word with Sammy. Could I find a way to ask if the police had spotted any secateurs or amber bottles?

Mrs. Winkleson ushered us into the hall where we ceremoniously retrieved our raincoats and our gaudily colored umbrellas.

"By the way," I said, as Dr. Blake was helping Caroline into her rain parka. "I'd love a tour of your rose gardens someday."

"My rose gardens?" From the look on her face and the way her whole body had stiffened, you'd have thought I'd asked for the combination to her safe, or maybe a sneak peek at her underwear drawer.

"Not today, of course," I hastened to add. "I know you have far too much to do between the show and your missing dog. But Dad's such a utilitarian gardener—never cares what the rose beds look like as long as they're producing nice blooms. Someday I'd really like to see what other people's rose beds look like."

"I'm afraid you'd find mine very utilitarian as well," she said, with a slight and not very convincing smile. "But perhaps after the show is over we could arrange something."

"Great," I said. "Thanks again. Oh, by the way, I know you don't want to keep the gate open unattended, so I'll post someone with a volunteer list down at the gate to check people in. I'll let you know when that's in place so you can leave the gate open. I don't want you and your staff to have to let every single one of our crew in."

"Fine," she said. I silently congratulated myself for slipping that last request in when she was in the genial mood she always fell into when saying good-bye to someone.

She stood at the top of the steps until we reached the pavement below and then turned on her heel, without any word of farewell, and strode back toward the house. I was never quite sure whether she was trying, in her odd way, to be gracious, or just making sure we left without making a detour into whatever part of the house she kept the valuables in.

Beside me, Caroline and my grandfather both exhaled rather loudly, as if they'd been holding their breaths. To my surprise, I realized I'd been holding mine.

Just then I heard a shriek from the top of the steps. I turned and started running up the steps, to see what was the matter. Then I heard Mrs. Winkleson's voice.

"You stupid girl! That floor was just waxed! Now look what you've done!"

Her voice went on and on, an endless, repetitive, abusive tirade. In the background, I could hear another woman's voice, softer, sobbing something in an unfamiliar language—though I didn't have to speak the language to tell that she was apologizing.

I paused, not sure if going to interfere would help or hurt. Then I heard a male voice. Mrs. Winkleson's butler. He seemed to be calming her down. I turned and went back down the steps.

Confronting Mrs. Winkleson now was a bad idea. When the rose show was over, though, I was going to give her a piece of my mind.

If I could keep from strangling her first.

Chapter 7

"Thank God that's done with," my grandfather grumbled when I caught up with him and Caroline. "That was like being trapped in a black-and-white B movie."

"Made you want to break out the finger paints, didn't it?" Caroline said.

Perhaps their hearing wasn't keen enough to catch her browbeating her maid.

"Very suitable for an evening event," I said, echoing Caroline's words. "Do you really think we can get everyone coming to the party to wear black and white? For that matter, do you think it's even possible to reach everyone to tell them?"

"Does it really matter?" she said. "You can spread the word if you like—frankly, I wouldn't even bother. What's she going to do if someone shows up breaking the dress code—kick them out?"

"She'll try," I said.

"And your mother and the other ladies of the garden club will handle it."

"She'll be furious," I said. "She'll never let us use her farm again."

"Us?" my grandfather said. "You planning on organizing this silly shindig next year?"

"Hell, no."

"Then it's not your problem." He shrugged. "Let whoever does it next year deal with it. You'll be gone; they can blame you."

"Sometimes I like the way you think," I said. "So where do you two want to go?"

"Wherever the animals are," Caroline said. "You drive. I'll call your mother and tell her the good news."

Just then we rounded the brick wall that shielded my car from the front steps and I stopped short in dismay.

"Oops." I pointed to my car. "Slight hitch in the proceedings."

One of the black swans was perched on the hood, giving its feathers a leisurely preen, looking like an overripe, mutant hood ornament. It was coal black except for some minor splashes of white around the wings and the enormous bright red beak. Another crack in the perfection of Mrs. Winkleson's color scheme.

"What a magnificent creature!" Caroline exclaimed.

"Not a native species," my grandfather said.

"True, but you have to admit it's beautiful."

"Very aggressive, swans," Dr. Blake went on. "They tend to drive other species out of their territory."

"Yes," I said. "And we're another species, and right now it thinks my car is part of its territory."

"Can't you shoo it away?" Caroline asked.

"Not a good idea," I said. "They don't like being shooed, and

I've heard they can break bones with those wings. One of Mrs. Winkleson's maids tried shooing one a couple of weeks ago and ended up in the hospital."

"Poor thing!" Caroline said.

"Not to mention the fact that Mrs. Winkleson fired her for annoying the swan. She's very protective of the swans. Which reminds me—there are two of them. The other isn't sneaking up behind us, is it?"

We all whirled about, looking in various directions until we spotted the other swan. After pausing and widening at the front steps, the driveway continued down toward the lake and a small dock where a black rowboat was tied up. The dock ended in an ornate gazebo made of intricate white wooden fretwork. The second swan was standing in the gazebo, staring out over the lake as if contemplating whether to swim or row across.

"Ah, there's the gazebo," Dr. Blake said.

"Yes," I said. "Were you looking for the gazebo for some reason?"

"No, but a place like this has to have a gazebo, doesn't it? Silly, useless things."

"Let's hope the other swan doesn't agree with you," Caroline said. "It's safe enough down there."

But our agitation appeared to have annoyed the nearer swan. It stirred slightly, and half rose.

"Damn," I said. "It might be getting ready to attack. You two start walking that way as fast as you can. I'll see if I can create a diversion."

"I can help with the diversion," my grandfather said.

"Someone has to protect Caroline," I said.

"Besides, you old fool, Meg might be able to outrun the creature," Caroline said. "I know I can't, and I doubt you can either."

Grumbling, he gave Caroline his arm and the two of them turned to walk down the long road to the barns.

Just then a pickup came rattling up the drive.

"Hang on," I said. "Help has arrived!"

The pickup pulled to a stop beside Dr. Blake and Caroline and the driver got out—a lanky figure in black jeans, a white shirt, and a gray tweed jacket. I strolled over to join them.

"Morning, Mr. Darby," I said. "Mr. Adam Darby is Mrs. Winkleson's farm manager. This is Caroline Willner of the Willner Wildlife Sanctuary, and my grandfather, Dr. Montgomery Blake."

"Pleased to meet you," my grandfather said, subjecting poor Mr. Darby to his punishingly firm handshake. "We've been admiring your setup here. Very impressive."

"Thank you," Mr. Darby said. As usual, his long face wore an expression of anxiety and gloom, and his shoulders were hunched as if expecting bad news to arrive at any second. But he did brighten slightly at my grandfather's words—though probably only someone who'd met him before could tell.

"We seem to have a slight problem," I said, indicating my swan-infested car.

"Oh, dear. This isn't good." Mr. Darby looked even more lugubrious than usual. He just stood there staring blankly at the swan instead of picking up on my subtle plea for help. Perhaps subtlety wasn't his forte.

"What do you do when the swans are somewhere you don't want them?" I asked.

"We give them a wide berth," he said. "No telling what it

would do if you tried to chase it off. I'll give you a ride down to the barns. You can rescue your car later when the swan's gone."

"Thank you so much."

Mr. Darby managed to squeeze Caroline and Dr. Blake into the pickup, but I had to make do with the truck bed. He'd been hauling something dirty in it. The truck bed was half covered with mud. Still, better than walking down half a mile of equally muddy road.

As we drove down, I saw the two police officers. They were still slowly and methodically combing the same field they'd been in when we arrived. At this rate, it was going to take them several days to search the whole farm.

On impulse, I pulled out my cell phone and called Chief Burke.

"It's about the dognapping," I said, after we'd exchanged hellos. "I see you only have two officers searching the fields—"

"And that's already two more than I can spare," he said. "I can't pull any more officers away from their other responsibilities on the very small chance that the poor dog is wandering the farm instead of locked up in a cage somewhere."

"I think two officers is an impressive number, considering the small size of our police force," I said. "But could you use some volunteers?"

Silence on the other end. The fact that he hadn't immediately rejected my idea was a good sign.

"I have all these volunteers coming to set up the rose show. Quite possibly more than I need," I said. "How about if I put the surplus at your disposal to augment the search?"

Another silence. But only a short one this time.

"Thank you," the chief said. "Warn them that there's only a small chance of actually finding the dog out there, and if they're still willing, have them report to Sergeant Shiffley. He's one of the two officers conducting the search."

"Will do," I said.

Okay, it wasn't much, but I felt I'd made some small contribution to rescuing poor Mimi the Maltese. And possibly a contribution to my own sanity. If any really annoying volunteers showed up, I could send them out to help Epp Shiffley.

Mr. Darby brought his pickup to a stop near Horace's truck in a small courtyard surrounded on three sides by barns. Sammy and Horace, carrying a folding cafeteria table, disappeared into the one on the left.

Apparently Caroline and my grandfather used the drive to cajole Mr. Darby into promising them a tour of the farm. They were thanking him profusely as he helped them out of the cab.

"We'll just wait right here till you have the time to take us around," Caroline said.

"Thanks for the ride," I said, as I scraped some of the mud off my jeans. At least I assumed it was only mud. Surely he didn't take the horses or cows riding in the pickup.

I must have glanced toward one of the barns at the thought.

"You did get the word not to use the horse barn?" Mr. Darby asked me, suddenly looking anxious.

"Don't worry, Mr. Darby," I said. "We only need the two barns. And I'm sorry if using those is inconveniencing you."

"No problem," he said. "Just let me know if you need anything." With that, he climbed back into the pickup and drove back toward the house.

"Well, that went well," Caroline said, as she waved good-bye. "He seems eager to show us around."

"You don't think he might be a little too eager?" my grandfather asked. "As if perhaps there's something he's hoping we'll find? Something he dares not report himself?"

If he asked me, I'd have said Mr. Darby was not the overeager one.

"Just don't tick her off until after the show," I said.

"Even if we find an imminent danger to the animals!" My grandfather drew himself up to his full six foot whatever and his eyes flashed. I'd have been more startled if I hadn't seen him do the same thing so often, on cue, in just about every episode of his "Animals at Risk" shows on the *Animal Planet* channel. I almost looked around to spot the hidden film crew.

"If you find animals in danger, then of course you should do something," I said. "I suggest anonymous phone calls to the police, the local branch of the Humane Society, and that investigative reporter at the college newspaper. Because remember, if she finds out you reported her and kicks me and the rose show out, you lose your easy access for snooping around."

"Good point, Monty," Caroline said. "We'll be discreet."

For some reason, I didn't find that very reassuring.

Chapter 8

The rain suddenly changed from drizzle to downpour, so I sprinted the rest of the way to the nearest barn, hauled the door open, and we all dashed in.

"This is the cow barn," I said. "Now also known as the show barn. It's where we'll be putting the roses once they're ready to be judged. The barn directly across is for goats and sheep. We'll be using that for the exhibitors to prepare their roses and relax while the judges are at work."

"What about the one in the middle?" Dr. Blake asked.

"Horse barn, and apparently it's all right to kick the cows, goats, and sheep out into the rain for a couple of days, but not the horses. So that's off limits."

"Off limits, eh." Dr. Blake's eyes glinted, and I could tell he was busily crafting a clever way to sneak into the horse barn.

"Off limits for rose show use," I said. "I'm sure Mr. Darby will be happy to include it on your tour if you ask."

"Meg, shall I call your mother and tell her the news about the party?" Caroline asked.

"Yes, thanks," I said. I was rummaging through my tote bag, looking for my notebook-that-tells-me-when-to-breathe, and was happy not to have to add another task to it.

Mother was, of course, delighted with our news, and promised to do what she could to enforce the dress code.

"Ridiculous," my grandfather pronounced. I noticed, though, that he waited until after Caroline had hung up and Mother couldn't hear him. I began going over my to-do list for the day while the two of them strolled around examining the interior of the barn, every inch of it painted stark, glaring white.

"Now, now," Caroline said. "It takes all kinds, and if I ever need a donor to help sponsor my zebras, I know where I can look. But why a rose show, anyway? Why not a show that celebrates flowers in general?"

"Why limit it to flowers?" my grandfather asked. "Plants with visible, showy flowers are a distinct minority in the plant kingdom. Why discriminate against all those useful or interesting plants that don't happen to make pretty garden specimens?"

"You'll get no argument from me," I said, looking up from my notebook. "The Caerphilly Garden Club's planning a general garden show next month, if you're interested, but even so, I don't think the categories will be all that broad."

"Still the focus is on plants' utility to humans, rather than their place in the ecosystem," Dr. Blake said. He was lifting up the lids of feed bins and poking into their contents.

"Yes, which means that they probably won't even have a Most Vigorous Weed category, which Michael and I could win hands down with the crabgrass we're growing in our lawn. And you can bet they won't have a Noxious Fungi class for the mold that's probably growing on the leftovers in the back of my refrigerator these last few weeks, when I've been too busy with the rose show to clean."

"Still, I imagine the general show will be much more interesting than the rose show," Caroline said, as she methodically looked inside the doors of a long row of storage cabinets. "More varied. I might look into exhibiting myself. I have a few rather nice plants in my butterfly garden."

"Hmph," Dr. Blake snorted.

"If it makes you feel any better," I added, "half the garden club are protesting the rose show."

"The half who don't grow roses?" Caroline asked.

"Right," I said. "And they're all particularly sore at me."

"For organizing the rose show?"

"For not also organizing the garden show," I said. "Two of the non-rose growers volunteered to handle it, and by all accounts, it's a disaster. There's some talk that they might have to cancel it."

"Gardeners are resourceful," Caroline said. "I'm sure they'll pull it off somehow."

"Probably by getting Meg to organize it," my grandfather said. He had entered a stall and was scuffling through the hay. I felt reassured. He might dislike toy dogs, but he was doing his bit to search for poor Mimi.

Just then we heard a vehicle outside. I strolled over to peer out the barn door.

"Mr. Darby back already?" Caroline said.

"Not yet." Michael's truck lurched into view, with Rob at the wheel. The truck bed was filled with plastic totes and tarp-covered boxes. "It's Rob with another load of stuff," I said. The rain had subsided to a drizzle, so I went out to help him.

Rob waved as he stepped down from the cab. On his heels,

a small black and white furball plummeted down from the cab, landing squarely in a mud puddle, sending dirty brown water everywhere.

The furball—now more of a mud ball—got up, shook himself vigorously, sending more muddy water in all directions, and then trotted to the end of his leash and began sniffing everything with keen interest.

"Why in the world did you bring Spike?" I asked. I had deliberately left the Small Evil One at home where he couldn't possibly start fights with animals ten to twenty times his size.

"He needed the exercise," Rob said. "And besides, he fits the color scheme."

"There's been a dognapping here, in case you didn't hear," I said.

"Yeah, but that's for ransom, right? Everyone knows you wouldn't pay ransom for Spike even if you could afford it."

"They haven't asked for ransom yet," I said. "And what if they come back and think Spike also belongs to Mrs. Winkleson? As you say, he fits the color scheme."

"I'll keep an eye on him," Rob said. "And after all—oh, damn. Can you take him for a while? I need to make myself scarce."

"You only just got here," I said. "What's the problem?"

"Here she comes." I turned to see where he was pointing and saw that Mrs. Winkleson was headed our way. The long, flowing black rain cape she was wearing gave her approach a strangely ominous feel, as if Dracula were bearing down on us.

"I don't want her to recognize me," Rob said.

"And why should she?" I asked.

"Remember that big stink she made when someone painted some of her cows red?"

I sighed and held out my hand for the leash.

"Why don't you help Horace and Sammy with the tables?" I suggested. "She'll assume you're the hired help and never even look at you."

"Great idea!" He scurried over to the truck and hid behind some of the tables.

"And when the tables are all in, take the stuff in the truck to that barn," I said, pointing to the left.

I saw a hand pop over the top of a table, giving me the thumbs up sign.

I didn't want to be saddled with Spike, but if Rob was willing to help with real manual labor, I didn't want to give him an excuse to skip out. Sooner or later I could find someone to take Spike home. Meanwhile, I took the end of Spike's leash and stuck my hand through the loop, so I could still hold my clipboard and wield the pen if necessary.

I flipped over to my schedule for the day. The rest of the volunteers were supposed to arrive at noon to begin arranging all the stuff that would occupy the tables Horace and Sammy were setting up. All I had to do for now—

"Ms. Langslow."

I looked up to see Mrs. Winkleson. Frowning.

Chapter 9

"Hello!" I said, stepping between her and the truck. "As you see, everything's going well."

"Yes, yes," she said. She didn't seem to be looking at the tables being unloaded or at those unloading them. She was staring down at Spike.

"How interesting," she said. "Where did you get it?"

She appeared to be pointing at the new harness we'd bought for the Small Evil One. It was rather an elegant harness, in black leather and shiny chrome, totally in keeping with the farm's décor. More to the purpose it did a reasonably good job of keeping Spike from choking himself whenever he saw a squirrel and his killing instincts went on overdrive. Maybe Mimi, in spite of her winsome name, was as much of a terror on squirrels as Spike and needed the same firm restraint. Probably a good thing that Mrs. Winkleson was thinking positively and focusing on Mimi's return.

"At Giving Paws," I said. "You know, the pet shop on Main Street in Caerphilly."

"I didn't know they sold dogs there," she said.

"I'm sorry," I said. "I thought you meant the harness. The dog we got from Michael's mother."

"Hmm," she said. She walked around to inspect Spike from another angle. Following some form of obscure, contrary canine logic, Spike reacted to her attention by sitting down, lifting one leg, and vigorously grooming his bottom.

"Very interesting," Mrs. Winkleson said. To each her own; I usually tried to look away when Spike did that. "What kind is it?"

"No idea," I said. "He's a pound puppy. Probably a mix."

"How much will you take for it?" she said.

"I beg your pardon?"

"I want to buy it," she said. "How much?"

"I'm sorry," I said. "He's not for sale."

I never thought I'd hear those words coming out of my mouth. Although adopting Spike had never been my idea or Michael's, I was still hoping that some soft-hearted relative, like my brother or Rose Noire, would decide to adopt him.

But surrendering him to the care of a besotted animal-lover was one thing, and allowing him to be used as a fashion accessory quite another.

"Nonsense," Mrs. Winkleson said. "Everything has a price. And money's no object."

"He's a member of the family," I said. "Do you really think I'd sell you a member of my family?"

"If the price was right—"

"Spike's not for sale," I said. "Though come to think of it, if you're interested, I could give you a really good deal on my brother. Or a brace of cousins. Or even—"

"*Design in America* is coming over Sunday to do a feature on the rose show and a spread on my house," she said. "I need a dog to add a touch of warmth. And as you know, mine's gone."

Gone? Was she giving up on her dog that easily? And as for adding a touch of warmth, she could bring in the entire population of the local animal shelter and it wouldn't be enough to overcome the chilly perfection of her house. But that was probably not something I should say. At least not until the rose show was over.

"Well, then you don't need a dog permanently," I said. "Especially not a dog like Spike, who's so fond of chewing up furniture and peeing on rugs. But if the chief doesn't find your dog by Sunday, perhaps we could arrange for you to borrow Spike for the photo shoot. I'll ask my husband if he approves."

"You do that," she said, and strode off. We watched in silence as she slid open the door to the horse barn, slipped inside, and closed it behind her.

"Don't let her have him," Caroline said.

"Have him, no," I said. "If she wants to rent him, that's another matter. I'll set a high fee. We can use the money. Why doesn't she just go down to the animal shelter and adopt a dog?"

"I don't think she'd have much luck," Caroline said. "They've heard about her down there."

"Heard about her? What's she done?"

She and Dr. Blake looked at each other.

Something I'd barely noticed earlier suddenly clicked.

"Come on, spill," I said. "You already knew something about Mrs. Winkleson's dog, didn't you? In the car, you called it 'she,' and I hadn't mentioned the dog's name or gender yet. Most people would say 'he' or 'it' if they didn't know the gender."

"She's a four-year-old Maltese bitch," Caroline said. "Mimi's short for Princess Marija Sofija of Mellieha."

"Silly name for a silly little lap dog," my grandfather muttered. His taste in dogs ran more to Irish wolfhounds.

"And then she bred Mimi to the most expensive AKC champion Maltese she could find."

" 'Money's no object,' " I quoted. "It didn't work out?"

"Mimi went AWOL one night a few days before her rendezvous with her champion," Caroline said. "Until the puppies arrived, it never occurred to Mrs. Winkleson to wonder what happened during Mimi's night on the town. Apparently the pups' dad had remarkably diverse ancestry."

"Had to have been several fathers," my grandfather put in. "No way a single dog could have sired that litter."

"It's unlikely, but possible," Caroline said. "If—"

"Why don't the two of you have your genetics discussion later?" I said. "Get back to Mrs. Winkleson. She's clueless about canine behavior, but how does that automatically make her a bad person?"

"Not a single one of the puppies was entirely black, white, or gray," Dr. Blake said. "So when they were three days old, she put them all in a box and dumped them on the receptionist's desk at Clarence Rutledge's veterinary office. Said to put them all to sleep and send her the bill."

"What a—witch," I said.

"You can go ahead and use the b-word as far as I'm concerned, dearie," Caroline said. "Though if you ask me, it's an insult to female dogs. Clarence, of course, was horrified. Tried to talk her out of it, but she was adamant. He fed the puppies with an eyedropper until he could find a mother dog with enough milk to foster them. All doing quite well so far."

"But she's clearly not someone who can be trusted with the welfare of helpless animals," Dr. Blake said.

"Or even animals like Spike, who are quite capable of defending themselves under normal circumstances," I said. "Not that I was even thinking of taking her up on her offer, of course."

"Nonsense," my grandfather said. "Of course you were thinking of it. Cranky little beast like that, I can't blame you. If a real animal lover were asking to take him on, I'd be the first to say do it. But that woman's trouble."

"That's why we wanted you to get us entrée to her farm," Caroline explained.

"To check on whether she was treating Mimi properly," my grandfather put in. "And to investigate the welfare of the rest of her animals."

"While there's nothing we can do about Mimi right now," Caroline said, "we're more worried than ever about the rest."

"Makes you wonder if this is really a dognapping," I said.

My grandfather frowned.

"What are you suggesting?" he asked. "That she did away with her own dog?"

"Somehow I don't see her destroying valuable property," I said. "After all, the puppies were mongrels, but Mimi's pedigreed. Mrs. Winkleson could sell her."

"Could be an insurance scam," Caroline said. "If, God forbid, something happened to the poor dog, I could see Mrs. Winkleson concocting the ransom note as a means to recoup her losses."

"Or maybe this is connected to the mysterious way her animals have been disappearing," Dr. Blake said.

I waited to hear the details, but he just stood with his eye flashing and his leonine head thrown back, as if posing for a photo opportunity.

"Okay, I'll bite," I said finally. "How have the animals been disappearing? Sucked into hovering UFOs while the alien cattle rustlers sculpt crop circles in the pasture? Fading away like the Cheshire cat till there's nothing visible but the cud? Or do you suspect that they've fallen victims to wolves imported by some mad zoologist who shares your dream of reintroducing large predators to the Virginia countryside?"

"Nothing that picturesque," Caroline said. "But Clarence says that he can't account for all the animals born on the farm. He keeps records, you know. And he says that the unwanted ones—the ones that aren't pure black and white or have imperfect markings—just disappear."

"Does he think she's euthanizing them?"

"Not really," Caroline said. "Unlike mixed breed dogs, farm animals have a certain monetary value, even if she doesn't want them. He suspects she's selling them as soon as they're weaned. But where, and to whom? Mrs. Winkleson says she has her farm manager deal with unwanted animals, the manager is evasive and claims Mrs. Winkleson doesn't involve him in the sales, and Clarence can't track down any actual buyers."

Caroline and my grandfather both shook their heads grimly. I didn't want to ask what they thought was happening to the imperfect animals. Were foals and kid goats in much demand as test animals? Or did they suspect the animals were being sold for meat? I wasn't a vegetarian, and I didn't think either of them was, either, but perhaps, like me, they drew the line at eating lamb or veal, or for that matter, any animal to which they'd been introduced.

If only they'd told me about Mimi and her puppies and the disappearing animals to begin with. For something like this, I'd gladly have helped, and might have been able to help more intelligently if I'd had time to think about it, and maybe do a little research.

"Okay, poke around," I said. "Try to stay clear of Mrs. Winkleson. I'd suggest you join the organized search for Mimi—"

"Too confining," Dr. Blake said. "We need to be able to range freely."

"Then if anyone questions you, say you were afraid the organized search would be too strenuous for you, but you still wanted to do your bit."

My grandfather frowned at that, but I knew he could put on a convincing frail act when he wanted to.

"Smart thinking, dearie," Caroline said.

"While you're at it, keep an eye out for my lost secateurs."

"Your what?" Dr. Blake asked. From his expression, I suspected that he not only had no idea what secateurs were but suspected I was referring to some kind of undergarment.

"It's a la-di-dah word for pruning shears," Caroline explained.

"Yes, and these are special handmade Victorian-style wrought-iron secateurs," I said. "Here, they look like this."

I pulled my duplicate pair out of the tote. They weren't exactly normal secateurs, but I didn't know what else to call them. Mother had requested a set that were unusually long, to make it easier to reach deep into the heart of a rose bush while minimizing the chance of getting scratched by thorns. The thin, foot-long, wickedly sharp steel blades flowed gracefully into the equally attenuated wrought-iron handles, making the whole thing look rather like a cross between pruning shears and a mechanical egret.

"Very nice," Caroline said. "Your work?"

"Mother commissioned them," I said. "Luckily I'd already started making a few extras for other people, because hers disappeared at the last garden club meeting."

"That horrible harpy probably nabbed them," Dr. Blake said.

"I wouldn't put it past her," Caroline agreed. "Keep your eye on that puppy of yours."

"Mrs. Winkleson is definitely one of the prime suspects," I said. "That's why I was asking to see her garden. So if you see a pair of secateurs like this, grab them."

Caroline and my grandfather studied the secateurs with keen interest for a few moments, and then I put them back in the shoulder slung tote in which I was carrying all the gear I might need for the day's crises.

Just then another truck rattled up. Mr. Darby, the evasive farm manager, returned to fulfill his promise.

Chapter 10

Caroline and Dr. Blake greeted Mr. Darby with enthusiasm, and he looked almost cheerful himself as he lifted a black-painted bucket out of the bed of the truck.

"What's in that barn, anyway?" Caroline asked, pointing to the middle barn—the one he'd made such a point of telling us was off limits.

"The horses," Mr. Darby said.

"Oh, horses!" Caroline exclaimed. "Such noble animals."

Even a stranger could tell the difference in Mr. Darby's expression now.

"We have twelve black Frisians," he said. "Magnificent animals. Would you like to see them?"

"Oh, could we?" Caroline asked. "That would be a wonderful start for our tour!"

Mr. Darby nodded, and we followed him to the center barn. Like the other two, its exterior was painted a flat, medium gray with glossy black woodwork. It might be sophisticated, but it wasn't the most cheerful color scheme in the world. Mr. Darby began pointing out something about the structure of the barns that he thought we'd find interesting.

"Meg?"

I turned to see Rob scuttling out of the goat barn.

"She's in there," he said, pointing behind him. "Ordering Sammy and Horace around. I should probably leave before she sees me. I wouldn't have volunteered if I'd known she would be hanging around all the time."

"You and me both. Look, why don't you serve as gatekeeper?" I fished around in my tote and pulled out a copy of the volunteer list. "Given what happened to her dog, Mrs. Winkleson is even less willing than usual to leave her gate open. So go down there right now. Call up to the house and tell whoever answers—it won't be her, obviously—that you're on duty and they can leave the gates open. If anyone on this list wants to come in, let them. Anyone else shows up, call me to ask if it's okay."

He hesitated.

"It's about as far from Mrs. Winkleson as you can get," I added. "She never condescends to go down to the gate. Why would she, when she has an intercom?"

"Okay." He took the list and hurried over to his car. Well, it was a quarter of a mile, and he did need someplace to shelter if the rain got intense.

"And if anyone shows up to help with the search for Mimi, that's okay, but take their names."

"Roger," he called, as he pulled out.

He was already out of sight by the time it occurred to me to ask him to take Spike with him. Ah, well. Since Spike tended to erupt into frantic barking at the sight or smell of another dog, he could be my secret weapon for finding Mimi. If she was out here.

I caught up with Caroline and my grandfather just as Mr.

Darby opened the door to the horse barn wide enough for them to enter. A blast of arctic air greeted us.

"Damn," Mr. Darby said. "She's been in the barns again."

The interior of this barn appeared to be painted completely black. All I could see were a few gleams where various bits of metal reflected the light from the door. Then Mr. Darby flipped the light switch and we could see again.

Half a dozen glossy black horse heads appeared over stall doors, and several of the animals whickered. Mr. Darby set down the bucket he'd been carrying, strode over to a thermostat on the wall, and adjusted the temperature.

"I gather the Frisian is not an arctic breed," I said, shivering slightly.

"Keeps turning the thermostat down to what she likes," Mr. Darby muttered. "She'll give the poor things pneumonia one of these days. Grab a couple of those horse blankets, will you?"

Dr. Blake was scribbling in his notebook. I handed him Spike's leash and went to fetch the horse blankets—thick, wool blankets in a subdued black and gray plaid.

"I gather they're stabled here for safety, with so many strange people coming and going," Dr. Blake said.

Mr. Darby was slipping inside the first stall.

"Actually, it's more because of the weather today," he said. "They catch cold easily."

"Let's hope tomorrow's a sunny day, then," Caroline said. "So the rose show attendees can see the horses running free in their pasture."

"No chance of that," Mr. Darby said. "She has me keep them

indoors when it's sunny, too. The sun could bleach out their coats. Hand me a blanket, would you?"

"Is that bad for the horses?" I asked, as I dutifully passed a horse blanket over the top of the stall door. "Like sunburn for a human?"

"Horses could care less," he said. "Bad for her color scheme, though. They don't bleach out to gray. They turn a sort of rusty red. She hates that."

"Don't you ever let them outside?" Dr. Blake asked. I could hear a note of outrage creeping into his voice, and shot him a warning look. We wouldn't gain anything by accusing and antagonizing Mr. Darby.

"At night," Mr. Darby said. "All night, if they like, as long as the weather's not bad. It's quite a sight to see them galloping up and down the pasture under a full moon."

He finished fastening the blanket around the first horse, handed it a carrot from his pocket, and left the stall. I followed him to the next stall and handed over another horse blanket when asked. My grandfather was strolling down the line of stalls, peering into each one with an intentness that might have annoyed Mr. Darby if he'd noticed. Fortunately he was too busy blanketing the horses against the artificial winter Mrs. Winkleson had created. Spike scampered along at Dr. Blake's heels, being rather better behaved than usual. Perhaps he was just entranced by all the fascinating new smells the barn had to offer. I was about to warn Dr. Blake not to let Spike roll in any manure, but then I realized that unless Spike got into a stall immediately after one of the horses had produced some, he probably wasn't going to have the chance. The barn was cleaner than most of my house. Did Mr. Darby do it all, or did he have an army of stable boys hidden out of sight somewhere?

In spite of the presence of the horses, the barn seemed more of a show place than a place where animals really lived and breathed. Maybe it was the absence of the usual clutter of bridles, combs, buckets, pitchforks, horse medicines, and other equine paraphernalia. All those things were probably here, hidden behind the pristine, glossy-black doors of the cabinets built into the walls at intervals, but I was too busy to grab one of the black wrought-iron cabinet handles and see. Luckily, Caroline was trailing behind, poking into all of them.

"Domestic animals aren't my specialty," Dr. Blake said, as we were finishing up the last horse. "Is this business of keeping them indoors all day typical?"

"Typical?" Mr. Darby said. "No. Silly, but not unheard of. She's not the only horse owner who worries more about frivolities like color than essentials, like proper feed and medical care. But at least she doesn't nickel and dime me on what they need. As long as the horses are still coal black and beautiful, she could care less what she spends on them. I can get the best feed, have Dr. Rutledge out as often as they need him. When we found some jimson weed in their pasture, she let me call a service in to clear it up. She's peculiar as all get-out, but not stingy."

"That's good," my grandfather said. "And you certainly have a first-rate barn."

Mr. Darby nodded.

"If I could just keep her away from the thermostat, I could rest easy about the horses," he said.

Just about the horses? Did that mean there were other animals he didn't rest easy about? I could tell from the look on his face that my grandfather wanted to ask the same question.

"So you have to work hard to keep the horses from getting pneumonia," Dr. Blake said, finally. "Any worries about the other animals?"

Mr. Darby scowled.

"Tell you the truth, I wish to hell I could keep her away from the goats."

"Away from the goats?" I repeated. "What's she doing to them?"

Mr. Darby sighed.

"Long story," he said. "Easier if I show you."

He led the way back to the other end of the barn, retrieved his bucket, and went out into the courtyard again. Caroline strolled along beside him and was peppering him with questions about the horses. I reclaimed Spike from my grandfather and fell into step beside him. We seemed to be going the long way around. Why not just walk through the goat barn, instead of circumnavigating it? But perhaps he was trying to stay out of Horace and Sammy's way. Or, for that matter, away from Mrs. Winkleson.

As we walked, I gave Rob a quick call.

"Everything okay out at the gate?" I asked.

"Everything's great," he said. "Nothing out here but black sheep. I feel right at home. Oh, here comes the first car. Oops, false alarm. It's just the stalker again."

"Stalker?"

"Some guy who came by and slowed down as if he was going to turn in, and then when I stepped out to greet him, he sped up again and went on. I wouldn't have thought anything of it if he didn't just do the same thing on his way back."

"Maybe he's one of my volunteers," I said. "What's he look like?"

"Middle-aged white guy in a blue Lexus. Got a really long nose, like Pinocchio after he's told a few whoppers."

That didn't ring a bell, but I didn't know all the rose growers that well, much less their vehicles.

"Just make sure no one gets in unless they're on the list or cleared with me," I said. "And if the stalker comes by again, try to get the license plate. Remember, there's been a dognapping and—"

"I know, I know. I tried to read the license plate when he came by just now, but it was so caked with mud I couldn't. But if you like, I'll call the chief."

"Do that," I said.

"Roger."

I breathed a little easier.

"This is the way to the goats?" Dr. Blake was asking Mr. Darby. He sounded a little impatient.

"Some of 'em, yes," Mr. Darby said. "Yesterday we moved the rest to another pasture for the weekend, so your flower show could use their barn. Same with the cows. Left a few down here for show and took the rest up where they won't be in anyone's way."

"Is it a problem, them not having the barn for shelter?" Caroline asked.

"There's a shed over there they can use for shelter if the rain gets heavy." He pointed to a weathered gray structure in the distance. "Almost as good as the barn for them," he said.

"Almost," I repeated. "But not quite. Sorry we're inconveniencing you and them. In fact, if now's a bad time, we could look at the goats later." Actually, I was less worried about Mr. Darby's time than about what could be happening back in the barn where my volunteers were supposed to be setting up for the show. Had I left them alone too long? Of course, Sammy and Horace, the only volunteers on hand at the moment, were fairly reliable, but how were they coping with Mrs. Winkleson chivvying them? Then again, now was a better time to help Dr. Blake and Caroline—and make my small contribution to the search for Mimi—than later, when things got busier.

"No problem," Mr. Darby said. "Today's not such a busy day." Was he implying that yesterday, when he'd had to move the cows and goats out of our way, was? Or that tomorrow, with the hordes of people, would be? Or was I just too ready to read reproach into his melancholy tone? And was it just melancholy or was there a little anxiety as well? Was there something about the goats he didn't want us to see? No, he didn't sound defensive or angry. Just sad. After several weeks of talking to him about various rose show-related problems, I wasn't sure if sad was his most common mood or his whole personality.

"So how many goats do you have?" my grandfather asked.

"Twenty-three in this pasture," Mr. Darby said. "And—"

The handle of the bucket clinked just then, and Spike began barking furiously at it.

"Hush," I said. Spike subsided into soft growls. I watched

Spike closely, but he seemed to be focused on the bucket, and not anything else in the vicinity.

"You might want to keep him away from the goats," Mr. Darby said, as we neared the fence. Ahead, I could see a pasture, with half a dozen shaggy black-and-white goats peering expectantly through the fence, as if waiting for dinner.

"He's on a leash," I said. I tightened my grip on the loop, just in case. "And his bark is really worse than his bite. Or were you worried that they might trample him?"

"Not really," Mr. Darby said. "Actually—"

Spike lunged forward as far as the leash would permit and erupted into a frenzy of short, sharp barks. His bark was remarkably deep for an eight-and-a-half-pound furball.

When they heard him, the half dozen goats loitering near the fence turned as if to run. Then all but one keeled over as if an invisible bowling ball had slammed into them. They lay on the ground with their legs held rigid and straight out, looking for all the world like wooden toys knocked over by a careless child. The last goat remained upright, but froze in place. I suspected he was as rigid as the others, but had the good luck or good balance to remain upright.

"Shut up, Spike," I snapped. "Look what you've done."

Chapter 11

Spike actually shut up, as if he was just as startled as I was.

"Myotonic goats!" my grandfather exclaimed. "Fascinating!"

He ambled over to the fence and peered down at the prostrate goats with far greater interest than he'd shown when he'd thought they were mere color-coordinated yuppie farm accessories.

"What's a myotonic goat?" I asked. I was relieved to see that the goats were coming around, shaking their heads and starting to scramble to their feet. The one who had remained standing started walking, stumbling a bit with the first few steps, but quickly returning to a normal gait.

"Also known as Tennessee belted fainting goats," Mr. Darby said. "Or wooden-leg goats."

"Or stiff-legged goats," Caroline put in. "Nervous goats. Sometimes Tennessee scare goats."

"Stiff-legged goats is probably the most accurate term," my grandfather said. Had everybody heard about these goats except me? "They don't lose consciousness, so they're not technically fainting."

"Then what is happening to them?" I asked. The goats seemed

fine, and Mr. Darby didn't seem particularly upset by what Spike had done to them.

"They suffer from an hereditary genetic disorder called myotonia congenita," my grandfather said. "Basically, when startled, their muscles lock up temporarily. If they're not well balanced at the time, they fall over."

"It's not just being startled that does it," Mr. Darby said. "Any sudden stimulus. Heck, if I give 'em an especially good feed, half of them will keel over out of sheer joy."

"Hasn't anyone tried to fix this?" I said. "Identify the goats with this genetic defect and keep them out of the gene pool?"

"On the contrary," Caroline said. "Some breeders have worked hard to keep the trait *in* the gene pool."

"It's not considered a defect," Mr. Darby said. "It's just a feature of the breed."

"A useful feature for sheep herders," my grandfather said. "A lot of them use these goats to protect their sheep."

"Like llamas?" I asked. "But if they faint when startled, how do they scare off predators?"

"Not like llamas," my grandfather said. "They don't scare the predators off. They fall down and get eaten, allowing the more valuable sheep to escape."

"The ultimate scapegoat," Caroline said, shaking her head.

"That's horrible," I said.

"Presumably predators aren't a problem for these goats," Caroline went on. "You don't have many wolves roaming the Virginia countryside."

"More's the pity," said my grandfather. "We need more natural predators to keep the deer population down."

"No wolves," Mr. Darby muttered. "Just her." Meaning, I had no doubt, Mrs. Winkleson.

He leaned over to pour the contents of his bucket into a trough just inside the fence. Five of the goats scampered toward the trough, while one keeled over, possibly startled by the clanking sound the bucket made hitting the trough. From farther off, we could see other black-and-white forms headed our way.

Spike wasn't reacting, just watching the goats. I deduced that it was only goats he could smell, not another dog.

"You don't just let them forage the landscape for their food?" my grandfather asked.

"Most of it," Mr. Darby said. "But I give 'em a little feed once a day with a specially mixed vitamin and mineral supplement. Makes up for any soil deficiencies. It's what Dr. Rutledge recommends."

Dr. Blake nodded, and I could tell by his expression that he wasn't finding anything to disapprove of in Mr. Darby's care of the goats. If Clarence Rutledge was their vet, they were lucky goats indeed. They certainly looked healthy as they jostled and butted each other to get a good share of the feed. Another one keeled over suddenly, for no apparent reason, but kept on chewing for the whole ten or fifteen seconds it took him to come to and reclaim his place at the trough.

Maybe Mr. Darby's lugubrious expression wasn't due to any problems here at Raven Hill. Maybe he was just a natural Eeyore.

"I just wish she wouldn't keep selling off so many of the kids," Mr. Darby said suddenly, as if he'd been trying to hold the words back and finally couldn't. "She inspects every single one born, and if they don't meet her standards, off they go."

"Her standard being that they have to be pure black and white?" I asked.

He nodded.

"Off they go where?" my grandfather asked, snapping to attention again.

"We've got a back pasture that's not technically part of the farm," Mr. Darby said. "If a kid has even a touch of any color but black and white, we take the doe and kid both up to the back pasture, and once the kid's old enough to leave the mother, we sell it. Good market for registered fainting goats these days. Same with the Belties who aren't perfect. If the calves don't have a well-shaped white belt, or if they've got white spots anywhere else or black spots in the belt, off they go to the back pasture till they're old enough to sell."

"At least she waits till they're weaned," Caroline said.

"She wouldn't if Dr. Rutledge hadn't convinced her it's bad for the health of the cows and does to have the natural cycle of motherhood interrupted," Mr. Darby said. "Pretty clever of him."

"So who does she sell them to?" Dr. Blake asked.

"Always a market for fainting goats," Mr. Darby said.

"Have you checked on any of them after they left the farm?"

"She hasn't told me where any of them have gone."

Dr. Blake frowned and looked at me as if to say, "See? Evasive!"

We pondered the fate of less-than-perfect kid goats as we watched the remaining goats scarf up the last of their feed. Mr. Darby wasn't looking at the goats but up at Mrs. Winkleson's house. At the far side of the pasture, I could see a fence and a line of trees separating the goats from the next field, and then, over the trees, the top of the house. It was slightly surreal to see the goats feeding calmly, apparently oblivious to the huge architectural monstrosity looming over them.

"And she's starting to take way too much interest in which ones faint the easiest and which ones don't," Mr. Darby went on, pointing toward the far side of the pasture. "Sneaks out through her garden to the back pasture over there and flaps that damned parasol of hers at them. If they don't all keel over, she starts asking what's wrong with the upright ones."

"That sounds mean," I said.

"It is," my grandfather said. He stuck his notebook in one of the many pockets in his fisherman's vest and leaned against the fence beside Mr. Darby.

"Yes, very mean," Mr. Darby said. "Although at least it doesn't really hurt the goats. If it did—well, not much I could do to stop the old bat, but I wouldn't stay around to see the animals mistreated. I could always resign in protest. Hard as that would be."

He reached over to scratch one of the goats behind the ears and his usually sad face suddenly looked almost cheerful for a few seconds, before it lapsed into its normal lugubrious expression. I found myself wondering how likely it was that he really would resign and leave his beloved goats at the mercy of Mrs. Winkleson.

Maybe he was being evasive about who bought the missing goats because he didn't really want to think about their fate.

"Does Mimi like to chase the goats, too?" I asked.

"Mimi?" Mr. Darby's face was blank. Either he didn't recognize the name or he was a remarkable actor.

"Mrs. Winkleson's dog," I said. "The one who's been dog-napped."

"Oh," he said. "I wouldn't know. The poor thing's a show dog, not a farm dog. She never lets it out of the house. I've hardly ever seen it."

All of which might be true, but I wasn't quite sure I believed his blank reaction to the dog's name. Had he somehow missed the police search party, still shouting "Mimi" at regular intervals as they combed the pastures?

"Ms. Winkleson's pretty much the only one bothering the goats," he said. "But she does it a lot. Before long she's going to start telling me to send off the goats that don't faint enough to suit her. They go to good homes and all but still, it doesn't seem quite right somehow."

How did he know the goats went to good homes if only Mrs. Winkleson knew where they went? I was liking this less and less.

"Well," my grandfather said. "It's not as if—hey!"

One of the goats had reached up and grabbed the notebook from Dr. Blake's hand.

"Sorry about that," Mr. Darby said. He hopped over the fence. Several of the goats, including the notebook thief, keeled over. But even though the goat with the notebook in his mouth was lying on his side with his legs held stiffly in front of him, his jaw was still working, and he did some damage to the notebook before Mr. Darby managed to retrieve it.

"Sorry," he said again. "I should have warned you. Paper's like caviar to them."

"No real harm done," my grandfather said. "Could have been worse. I could have been counting my money."

"They're darling," Caroline cooed. She reached out a hand to pet one of the goats.

"Don't touch their faces," Mr. Darby warned.

"Oh, does that bother them?" Caroline paused with her hand hovering above the forehead of one of the smaller goats.

"Doesn't bother them any, but you might not be so happy," Mr. Darby said. "They just cleared out a big stand of poison ivy in the back of the pasture this morning, and they've probably got the sap all over their faces."

Caroline recoiled from the goats.

"Doesn't poison ivy affect them?" I asked.

"Doesn't seem to," he said. "One of the few things they like as much as paper. And you know what their third favorite food is?"

Dr. Blake and Caroline shook their heads, but I had a suspicion.

"Don't tell me. Roses," I said.

"Got it in one," Mr. Darby said. He chuckled softly.

"Please tell me they don't often get loose," I said.

"Sometimes," he said. "But Mrs. Winkleson has a good, tall fence around her roses, and we'll be keeping a close eye on them tomorrow, what with all the extra roses coming in for the show. No! Naughty goat!"

We all jumped, and several goats fell over, including one who had been sneaking up with his head lowered, as if about to charge and butt Mr. Darby in the rear.

"Bad, bad goat," Mr. Darby said, shaking his finger at the fallen goat. "He's a terror, Algie. Always trying to butt people. One of these days he'll do it to Mrs. Winkleson and get himself sent up to the back pasture."

From the sound of it, he was looking forward to Algie's probable fall from grace. Was Algie's fondness for butting a natural trait or the result of training?

Mr. Darby reached down to scratch Algie's ear fondly before scrambling to the safety of our side of the fence.

I glanced at my watch. Almost eleven.

"Speaking of the show, I should get back to the barns," I said. "The volunteers will be arriving any time now. But if you two want to continue your tour—"

"We'll come with you, dearie," Caroline said. "We're going to help out with the setup, remember? Thank you so much for the tour," she added, turning back to Mr. Darby.

"You're welcome," he said. "Just let me know if you need anything."

He nodded genially to each of us. I noticed he made a point of gripping the bucket tightly in both fists, perhaps for fear that Dr. Blake would attempt another potentially crippling handshake.

"Okay, so something probably needs investigating," I said, when Mr. Darby was out of earshot. "Either he knows something he's not telling, or he's deliberately closing his eyes to avoid learning something he doesn't want to know. And his reaction to Mimi's name was suspicious, too."

"Then you have no objection to our snooping?" Caroline asked.

"Snoop away."

"As long as you're not short of volunteers," Caroline said. "I gather the garden club members will be doing most of the work."

"No," I said. "The garden club members are almost completely useless as a source of volunteers. None of the non-rose growers are coming. They're too peeved about this show going well and too busy trying to rescue theirs. And most of the rose growers are too busy prepping their blooms."

"I thought that started tomorrow?" she asked.

"The final frenzy will be tomorrow, but there's stuff you have to do the day before a show. In fact, if Mother and Dad are typical, stuff you have to start doing nearly a week before the show."

"So who's volunteering, then?" Dr. Blake asked.

"Most of the New Life Baptist Choir, thanks to Minerva Burke," I said. "And most of the county's off-duty law enforcement officers, thanks to Chief Burke. Minerva's taking no chances that the show will fall through. She wants to exhibit her miniature roses. And Rose Noire has drafted most of her lovelorn suitors. And Mother strongarmed some of the family. Aunt Beatrice is coming, and Aunt Patience, and probably Aunt Calliope. So—"

"Aunt Calliope?" My grandfather had pulled out his pocket notebook and was scribbling in it.

"Yes," I said. "I don't think you've met Aunt Calliope before."

"I haven't met half the aunts and uncles you keep mentioning," he said. "How many siblings does your mother have, anyway? I started keeping a list this weekend, and so far various members of your family have referred to at least thirty-seven people as aunt or uncle. Salmon spawning would be hard pressed to keep up with these Hollingsworths."

He was shaking his slightly gnawed notebook as if he'd found compelling evidence of . . . something.

"Well, they're not literally aunts and uncles," I said. "For example, if memory serves, Aunt Calliope is technically my second cousin by marriage, once removed."

"Then why do you call her an aunt?"

"Because she's Mother's generation," I said. "Term of respect. At least in the Hollingsworth family, anyone approximately your age is a cousin. Anyone your parents' age is an aunt or uncle. The generation below you are nieces and nephews."

Dr. Blake considered this notion for a few moments, staring balefully at his notebook.

"Has anyone got such a thing as a Hollingsworth family tree?" he asked finally.

"Not that I know of," I said. "I'll ask around if you like. But I'm not sure anyone's tackled that."

"Someone should," he said. "I'll ask your mother."

"Oh, no!" I said. "Don't ask Mother! The last time someone made her try to draw a family tree, the effort so exhausted her that she spent the rest of the day lying down with a cold compress on her forehead."

"I see," he said. He was wearing the look again, the one that said, more clearly than any words, what he really thought of the family his long-lost son had married into.

"Getting back to your question, I have plenty of volunteers. So many that I expect to divert some of them to helping out with the search for Mimi. So go snoop as much as you like. Just be careful."

"Time's wasting," Caroline said. "Let's get cracking."

"Indeed," Dr. Blake said, offering her his arm.

"Take Spike," I said. "He's not exactly a bloodhound, but he tends to react noisily when other dogs are around."

"Good idea," my grandfather said, taking the offered leash.

"Don't worry, dearie," Caroline said, seeing the expression on my face. "We'll stay out of trouble. If anyone questions what we're doing, we'll say that we realized we were just in your way here and were trying to do our small part with the search till you have time to take us home."

They both assumed genial, mild-mannered expressions that might have fooled someone who didn't know them, and strolled away, until all I could see through the drizzle was the two brightly, colored umbrellas floating along at very different heights.

I wondered if there was any chance they'd keep their word and stay out of trouble, and whether there was any chance they'd find a clue to the whereabouts of the stolen Mimi or the other missing animals.

No time to worry about it now. Several more cars were parked nearby, and I heard loud voices inside the cow barn.

Chapter 12

I was still standing in the doorway, shaking and unfolding my umbrella, when one of the new arrivals dashed up to me. She was a petite, gray-haired woman in a navy blue tracksuit.

"Where is she?" the woman asked. She was scowling, and her voice sounded half anxious and half angry. I didn't remember her name, but I remembered her as one of the rose growers, one of the few who'd agreed to show up and help.

"I assume you mean Mrs. Winkleson?" I asked. People usually did when they used the word "she" in that tone. "She was over in the horse barn a few minutes ago, but she could be anywhere by now."

"Maybe you can answer my question then," the woman went on. "When did it change from whites only? Why didn't someone tell me?"

"I beg your pardon?"

"Why didn't someone tell me that colored roses were allowed after all?"

"Who ever said they weren't?" I asked "They always have been in past shows; why would you think this was different?"

"I got a phone call from Mrs. Winkleson. She told me that the committee had decided to restrict the show to only white roses and competitors for that black rose trophy she created. If I'd known that had been changed—"

"She what?" I exclaimed. Perhaps a little too vehemently. The woman shrank back as if afraid I'd strike her.

"She said it," she stammered. "I'm sure she did. Don't take it out on me!"

"I'm sorry," I said. "I'm sure she did. It's just that I'm so angry that Mrs. Winkleson did this to you. The committee never voted to restrict the show to only black and white roses. Mrs. Winkleson made a motion to restrict it, but the motion was defeated, 47 to 1."

"Well, I did wonder," the woman said. "It seemed so peculiar."

"And Mrs. Winkleson had no right to call you like that," I went on. "If I'd known she was doing it, I'd have called you and everyone else involved to make sure you knew the right story. But I had no idea."

"I almost didn't come because of the white-only policy," the woman said. "Most of my really nice roses are pastels, you see. Pinks and apricots. I finally decided to come anyway because I do have a few white roses. Margaret Merril has been doing quite nicely, and the white Meidilands, and I did have hopes of Frau Karl Druschki till it got so rainy."

I smiled and nodded as if I had some idea what she was talking about. Presumably these were the names of roses. Hanging around with rose growers was as confusing as reading the supermarket tabloids, whose headlines were always reporting the romantic ups and downs of people on a first name basis with everyone in the reading public except me.

"Can't you just bring some of your other roses tomorrow?" I asked.

"I've been focusing all my efforts on the white roses for the last two weeks," she said. "None of the others are anywhere near ready!"

I supposed that made sense. Mother and Dad had been slaving over the roses for the last fortnight. I'd have thought Mother Nature could be trusted now and then to produce some pretty decent roses, but apparently no one in the Caerphilly Rose Society agreed.

"And I gave up on my red roses because none of them are all that dark," she went on. "I'm not into trying to breed new roses like Mrs. Winkleson, and I really don't see what the fuss is about a black rose. Maybe that's silly of me."

"It seems remarkably sensible to me," I said. "I sometimes think the pastels are the prettiest anyway. Look, I need to run, but let me assure you that the committee had no idea Mrs. Winkleson was doing this, and you can rest assured that the committee will be looking very closely into it."

I hoped the looking into didn't happen until after I'd tendered my resignation.

"I suppose when I get home I could see if I have any other blooms that I could possibly enter," the woman said. "For moral support, if nothing else."

"That's the spirit," I said. "And knowing your garden, I'm sure you're being too hard on yourself. I bet you'll find any number of roses you overlooked because you were so focused on the white ones."

Actually, I didn't know her garden at all, and I had no idea if she'd find any good roses—I still couldn't remember her name—but I'd noticed that gardeners rarely objected when you praised their handiwork. She preened as I'd hoped.

"And remember," I added, "Mrs. Winkleson will probably consider every brightly colored rose a thorn in her heart."

A little melodramatic, but the woman liked it.

"Ooh," she said, as a sly smile spread across her face. "You're absolutely right. Even if they aren't quite competition worthy, I'm sure I can find any number of roses to annoy her."

"That's the spirit!" I said. "Fill the barns with a riot of color."

The woman strolled off, looking a lot happier. I saw her stop to talk to the only other person in the barn—another of the rose growers. From the conspiratorial looks on their faces as they whispered together, probably another rose grower being enlisted in the plot to offend Mrs. Winkleson's sensibilities.

"Isn't that just like old Wrinkles?" I heard the other woman say, and the two dissolved into laughter.

The first woman began shaking out tablecloths and covering the folding tables with them.

The other woman opened a nearby box and took out something. One of the programs, fresh from the printers. She flipped through a few pages and I saw her mouth tighten at something she saw. I braced myself. I'd warned the garden club that I needed someone who knew a lot more about rose shows to proof the program. Half a dozen people assured me that they'd be glad to help, and not a one of them had been reachable during the couple of days when the proofing had to be done. I'd done my best, and if I'd missed something, I wasn't going to take the heat for it.

But the woman didn't rush up to complain. She slipped the

program into a tote bag at her feet, then hoisted the tote to her shoulder and walked softly out the back door of the barn, pulling up the hood of her raincoat as she went.

An unsettling thought struck me. What if Mimi's disappearance on the eve of the rose show wasn't a coincidence? Most of the rose growers I'd met were delightful people, if a little obsessive, and would probably be among the first to volunteer to help search for Mimi. But there were a few exhibitors expected whom I didn't yet know, and a few I did know who I'd already decided needed watching. The garden club members had assured me that no matter how competitive these shows were, no one ever tried to cheat or take unfair advantage of another exhibitor. I hoped they were right, but I wasn't going to take any chances.

And Mrs. Winkleson was probably number one on my list of people who needed watching. Was her phone call to the woman in navy merely a manifestation of her eccentricity? Or a deliberate attempt to cripple the competition?

Could Mrs. Winkleson have faked the dognapping to give her some advantage in the rose show? I couldn't think how it would help her. The judges didn't see the names of the exhibitors until after they'd ranked the roses, so it wasn't as if she could benefit from sympathy. And I couldn't imagine the dognapping scaring anyone away from the show.

I filed it away to brood on later. I left my one diligent volunteer arranging the tablecloths and went to check on what was happening in the other barn.

But as I was crossing the courtyard, Sammy and Horace came

scuttling out of the goat barn, looking for all the world like birds fleeing a feeder when you make a sudden move behind the glass. They went to the truck and busied themselves with something that probably didn't need doing. I went over to see what was wrong.

"Good thing you got white tablecloths for those folding tables," Sammy said. "'Course, she's disappointed that they aren't black."

"Mrs. Winkleson is doomed to disappointment in many ways," I said. "How's the setup going?"

"We've got the tables ready, I think," Horace said. "What next?"

"Grab those boxes," I said. "And take them in."

"Into that barn?" Horace asked, pointing at the one they'd just left so hurriedly.

"I'll go ahead of you and run interference," I said. "Oh, Horace, here."

I reached into my tote, fished out the Baggie containing the empty doe urine bottle, and placed it on top of the box he was carrying.

"Um . . . is there something I'm supposed to do with this?" he asked, peering at the Baggie.

"Do forensics on it," I said, as I led the way into the barn. "Dad thinks someone used it to lure deer into their yard to eat the roses."

"Not sure that's a crime," Horace said. "You might get whoever did it on trespassing, I suppose."

"Or poaching," I said. "The land's posted no hunting. Or

was until this morning. They take that pretty seriously around here."

"Why don't you hang onto it for the time being?" Horace handed back the Baggie. "I don't want to risk losing it while I'm running around here."

I was a little disappointed that I couldn't unload the nasty little thing immediately, but I saw his point and tucked it back into my tote.

"By the way, what's up with the dognapping?"

"You know I can't tell you anything about a police investigation," Sammy said.

"I'm not asking for state secrets," I said. "But Rob brought Spike over. Should I worry? Is there any danger of someone coshing Dr. Blake over the head and stealing the Small Evil One?"

Sammy and Horace exchanged glances.

"I wouldn't worry too much," Sammy said. "The chief isn't sure whether the dognappers want ransom or whether they're just out to get at Mrs. Winkleson. But I shouldn't think Spike was in any danger."

"Do you think it's possible that someone did it as a prank, to try to sabotage her participation in the rose show?"

"That would be pretty stupid," Horace said. "Dognapping is a felony in Virginia. Punishable by up to ten years in prison."

"You think many of these rose breeders know that?"

"Probably not," Sammy said. "And we haven't really established that there is a dognapping. There's no evidence besides the note."

"You think she could be faking it?"

Both Horace and Sammy shrugged.

We had reached the door of the barn. Horace and Sammy stopped and looked expectantly at me. I stepped into the barn, ready to confront Mrs. Winkleson. In fact, I was almost looking forward to it.

Chapter 13

"The coast is clear," I called back to Sammy and Horace. I was almost disappointed. The thought of defending Sammy and Horace from Mrs. Winkleson sent adrenaline coursing through my system, which probably meant that I should avoid encountering her until I'd calmed down.

Horace and Sammy came in, set down their boxes, and opened the top flaps to inspect the contents.

"Mine's nothing but vases," Horace said. "Dozens and dozens of clear glass vases."

"Mine too," Sammy said.

"Mine are bigger," Horace remarked, glancing into Sammy's box.

"The competitors use identical vases," I said. "To keep the focus on the flowers rather than the vases. And the garden club supplies the vases. Sammy, you've got the bud vases for miniature roses. Put six of them on each of those tables. Horace, you've got the vases for the regular-sized roses. Put a dozen of them on each table."

They hurried off to follow orders.

I glanced at my watch. Where were all the other volunteers? Apart from Horace, Rob, and Sammy, who had came early to set up the tables, everyone else was supposed to be here by noon, and now, at twelve-fifteen, only two volunteers had appeared, and only one of them was working. This meant not only were my rose show preparations falling behind, but I hadn't been able to steer anyone to help with the dog hunt.

Make that three volunteers present and accounted for. Dad pulled up with his truck. Mother, of course, was not with him. If they were still feuding by the time the show was over tomorrow, I had some serious diplomacy ahead of me. No time to worry about it now.

"Thank goodness you're here," I said. "Most of the volunteers are late. Maybe the rain will keep them from showing at all."

"There are a great many people stuck in the backup at the gate," Dad said, as he stepped down from the cab. "Chief Burke and Minerva were right after me, and he's furious, I can tell."

"There's a backup at the gate? Isn't Rob there to check people in?"

"Yes," he said. "But then he has to call up to the house for every car, and sometimes it seems like forever before he gets an answer. Cars are really stacking up outside the gate."

I closed my eyes and counted to ten. The whole purpose of sending Rob out there to stand in the rain with the volunteer list was to eliminate the need to call up to the house. What was Rob thinking?

Then again, unlikely that Rob was the real problem, unless you counted Rob's unwillingness or inability to argue with Mrs. Winkleson a problem, and I didn't. More like a normal, healthy sense of self-preservation.

"Start unloading those over there," I said, indicating the goat barn. "I'll be back shortly. I need to talk to Mrs. Winkleson."

I strode off toward the house, using the potential shortcut I'd spotted during my tour with Mr. Darby, through the goat pasture, then over the fence into the other field that I had deduced led to Mrs. Winkleson's garden. Of course, I didn't know for sure it was a shortcut. For all I knew, there could be a ten-foot brick wall blocking my planned path. Mad as I was, I didn't think that would slow me down much.

I slowed down a little when I got to the pasture, to reduce the number of goats I startled. I sped up again after vaulting the fence at the far side of their pasture. I could see snowball bushes and more white cherry trees beyond the fence at the other side of this second pasture. I succeeded in startling the occupant of the gardens—probably one of Mrs. Winkleson's staff. I heard a gasp. Through a privet hedge, I fleetingly glimpsed someone in black, moving faster than Mrs. Winkleson seemed capable of. When I finally did run into my imagined brick wall, I also found a stairway beside it, leading conveniently up to the front terrace. I took the steps two at a time and still arrived at the front door only slightly winded. I punched the doorbell a couple of times and waited, fuming.

The door opened, and at first I thought no one was there. Then I glanced down and saw a tiny, frightened maid looking up at me. She was so short that I found myself wondering for a moment if she qualified as a little person.

"Meg Langslow to see Mrs. Winkleson," I said.

She backed away from the door, pointing toward the archway to the living room, and then turned and fled.

It couldn't possibly be what I'd said, and I thought I'd managed to keep my voice calm and civil. Did my face look that stern? Or had Mrs. Winkleson's high-handed treatment of her staff rendered them as easily startled as the fainting goats?

"Ridiculous!" Mrs. Winkleson bellowed. I confess, I jumped myself, before I realized that she wasn't even in the room with me.

"It's not ridiculous, and I won't keep quiet any longer," said another woman's voice.

"If you dare say that in public, I'll sue you for every penny you have! I'll ruin you!"

"Sue away." I didn't recognize the second voice. It was softer than Mrs. Winkleson's, but you could tell she was angry. "Every penny I have wouldn't begin to pay your lawyers' fees. I'm tired of covering this up. And if I went public with it, you'd be the one ruined."

Their voices were coming from the living room. The maid had waved toward it. Should I go in? I was dying to see who Mrs. Winkleson was arguing with, but then again, I'd probably learn more by eavesdropping from here in the hall.

Too late.

"I must insist that you leave my house!" Mrs. Winkleson said. I heard the brisk tapping of her shoes on the marble floors as she headed for the front door.

I didn't particularly want her to know I'd heard the quarrel. I opened the door, ducked outside, and shut it behind me. Then I waited a couple of seconds and rang the bell again.

After a few more seconds, Mrs. Winkleson answered the door.

Chapter 14

"Yes?" Mrs. Winkleson said. She didn't look happy to see me. Of course, Mrs. Winkleson never looked particularly happy to see anyone, but she looked even less happy than usual.

"May I come in?" I was using my most icily polite tone. Rob called this the Mother voice.

She hesitated for a few moments, and glanced back. Then she opened the door.

I stepped in, and looked around to see if whoever she'd been quarreling with was still here. No such luck. I did see the tiny maid pop out of the usual door and stare at me for a few seconds in puzzlement before she disappeared back into the door. A few seconds later the butler popped out to stare in her place.

"So sorry to bother you, but I think there's been a miscommunication," I said.

"Can we discuss this later?" she asked. She seemed uncharacteristically anxious.

"Your staff don't seem to have gotten the message to leave the gate open for the arriving volunteers," I continued. "My brother is standing there with an official list of volunteers, to make sure no unauthorized people come in. But whoever's in charge of the gate keeps shutting it, and he has to call up to the house every time—"

"Fine," she said. "Marston—deal with it."

She strode out through a door on the same side of the foyer as the servants' door, slamming it behind her. I glanced at the butler.

"You're Marston, I assume," I said.

"Technically no, madam," he said. "But that's what she likes to call me."

His rich, deep voice sounded slightly incongruous coming from someone barely five feet tall. He had a faint accent, so faint I couldn't be sure what it was. Hispanic? Slavic? All I could say for sure was that he wasn't from around here.

He walked across the foyer, and I followed him, glancing into the living room as I passed the wide opening. No one there. Apparently whoever Mrs. Winkleson had been arguing with had slipped out before she opened the door to let me in.

Marston opened a door to what I would have assumed was a coat closet. Inside I saw the gleaming components of a very modern security system. A pair of computers occupied most of a shelf spanning the width of the closet. On one of the monitors, I saw a grainy view of the front gate. There were five cars lined up at the gate, and for all I knew there could be others behind them, off camera. A damp human figure, hunched against the steady rain, was standing beside the driver's window of the lead car, talking to its occupant. Then the figure turned around and pushed the intercom button again. Rob, of course.

"Hello?" he said, into the intercom. "Anyone there?"

Marston shook his head and pressed a button on the wall, just inside the closet door. The gate began slowly swinging inward.

"Gee, thanks," Rob said, without enthusiasm.

Marston leaned toward a microphone perched between two keyboards.

"You're welcome, sir," he said. "Please accept my apologies for the inconvenience. The gate will now remain open for as long as you require. Please buzz the house when you wish to have it closed again."

"Hey, that's great!" Rob said. "Wagons ho!"

He gestured to the first car in line.

"May I?" I asked, gesturing to the microphone.

"Of course, madam," he said, stepping aside.

"Rob," I said, into the microphone. "Now that we've got Mrs. Winkleson to leave the gate open, don't blow it. If you need a break, either ask Mr. Marston to shut the gate temporarily or call my cell phone so I can send someone to take over."

Rob broke into a wide grin.

"Will do," he said. "Good going!"

From which I deduced he knew who had pried the gates open.

"If you will permit me, madam." Marston gestured to the microphone. I stepped back to give him room.

"Mr. Langslow," he said, into the microphone. "Should anyone purporting to be one of Mrs. Winkleson's nephews seek entry, please refrain from admitting them."

A short silence.

"Purporting?" Rob said. "You mean, someone's been pretending to be her nephew? Should I ask for ID?"

Marston winced, and looked at me.

"They're not pretending to be nephews," he said, softly. "But Mrs. Winkleson doesn't want them on the premises. They are . . . estranged."

"So I've heard," I said. "Hang on."

I snagged the microphone again.

"You ask for ID on anyone you don't know personally, and if any of them turn out to be Mrs. Winkleson's nephews, keep them out. Their names are . . ."

I looked at Marston.

"Theobald and Reginald Winkleson," the butler said into the microphone.

"Okay," Rob said. "No more Winklesons. Mrs. Winkleson herself is quite enough. I can relate to that."

"Should they become importunate," Marston said, "please notify me and I will deal with them."

Rob frowned, and I could see him silently repeating the word "importunate."

"He means if they won't go on your say-so, call him and he'll kick them out."

"Okay," Rob said. "That works."

I stepped out of the closet and Marston shut the door.

"Nephews by marriage, I assume," I said.

"You assume correctly," Marston said. "And since under the terms of the late Mr. Winkleson's will, they will inherit upon their aunt's demise, their presence tends to agitate her. It really will be best for all concerned if they can be excluded from the property as much as possible."

Not new information, but at least I now knew what I'd heard from the town grapevine was accurate.

"The rose show tomorrow's open to the public," I pointed out.

"If they show up on the morrow, we will admit them along with any other members of the general public, and allow them only so much access as the general public is permitted."

More potential headaches for tomorrow. But if their presence would annoy Mrs. Winkleson, then perhaps I didn't care if Rob failed to identify and exclude the nephews.

"Sounds reasonable," I said aloud. "Anyway, thanks for your help in getting the gate open."

"Thank you, madam," he said. "The constant trips to the console were beginning to interfere with the staff's routine."

"By the way," I said, "was that Mrs. Emberly talking to Mrs. Winkleson just now? Because if it was, I'd really love to catch up with her. I need to talk with her about the show."

"I'm sorry, madam," Marston said. "I'm afraid I don't know."

"Sorry," I said. "I guess that was the kind of nosy question you're not supposed to answer."

Marston's lips twitched slightly, as if suppressing a smile.

"As it happens, I don't actually know who was talking with Mrs. Winkleson just now," he said. "They must have come in through the garden entrance."

Garden entrance. Much more elegant than back door. Perhaps Michael and I should adopt the phrase.

"Ah, well," I said. "Thanks anyway."

"If I see Mrs. Emberly, I'll tell her you were looking for her," he said, as he ushered me outside.

"That would be super," I said. Also astonishing, since I'd made up the name Emberly on the spot.

Outside on the terrace, I scanned the surrounding landscape. No sign of Mrs. Winkleson. The black swan had abandoned my car, so theoretically I could drive it down to the barns. But it wasn't in the way here, and if I drove back, I'd have no chance to snoop.

I stood for a moment scanning the landscape. The two officers had finished with the field they'd been searching and moved on to the field containing the lake. Dr. Blake and Caroline were standing in the gazebo overlooking the lake, talking with someone. Someone Spike didn't particularly like. He was barking furiously.

The third person left the gazebo and I recognized her, or at least her clothing. One of the maids. She was scurrying back to the house.

Dr. Blake and Caroline headed in the other direction. I made a mental note to send someone to check on them. Spike was behaving badly, almost pulling my grandfather's arm out of the socket. And I should have noticed that Caroline's oversized purse was unsuited for a long walk around the farm. She was visibly canting to one side under its weight.

Well, the sooner I got back to the barns, the sooner I could deal with it. I headed back down the brick stairs toward the garden.

Finding my way to the house was easy, partly because I'd been too mad to worry about getting lost, and partly because the great ungainly hulk of it dominated the landscape. Finding my way back to the goat pasture and from there to the barns proved slightly more difficult. The garden was an established one, older by several decades than the house. When Mrs. Winkleson had bought the farm, she'd torn down a quaint little farmhouse to build her mansion, but she'd left most of the garden intact partly because the previous owner had designed it as a moon garden—a garden containing only white flowers that could be seen in the dark, and preferably those that also had a strong fragrance.

But however enchanting the moon garden might be by night, right now it was a soggy, muddy morass filled with a great many trees tall enough to block my view of the barns. I got turned around several times and found myself heading back to the house.

Then I stumbled out of a grove of trees into an open area and saw something that made my jaw drop.

Chapter 15

I was in a small field, surrounded on three sides by woods and on the fourth by a fence that I hoped would turn out to be the goat pasture. In the middle of the field an area about half an acre in size was completely enclosed with a twelve-foot chain-link fence topped with razor wire. Floodlights and speakers were mounted on all four corners and at intervals along the four sides of the enclosure. Other mechanical devices whose purpose I couldn't even guess hung on the fence or were arranged around the perimeter of the fence. The whole thing looked like something you'd find on the grounds of a penitentiary rather than a farm.

"You lost?"

I started, and turned to see Mr. Darby standing behind me.

"Very lost," I said. "I'd appreciate a steer in the direction of the barns. But first, what's that? The cell block where she keeps any brightly colored flora or fauna that invade her farm?"

"You're not far off," he said. "That's where she keeps all her rose beds."

"Is she that afraid people will steal her prize roses?"

"It's not really people she's worried about," Mr. Darby said. "It's the deer and the goats. To goats and deer, roses are like chocolate, caviar, and champagne, all rolled up into one, remember? You should have seen the time she saw one of the goats out here eating all her Black Magic roses. I thought for a moment we'd be eating goat stew that night. She had the contractors out the next day to build all this."

From his tone, I gathered he shared my belief that the rose enclosure was a hideous eyesore.

"I'm going to take a peek inside," I said.

"It's locked," he said.

"I can look through the fence," I said. "Unless that's *verboten*."

"Careful, then." He shrugged, as if disavowing any responsibility for the consequences of my nosiness. "She's not dead keen on human intruders, either. And I don't have a key. She doesn't let anyone else inside, except maybe sometimes one of the garden staff, with her looking over their shoulders every second."

"Still, no harm in just looking in through the fence," I said. I figured if Mrs. Winkleson saw me and objected, I could claim I thought I saw a glimpse of white fur among the plants.

I stuck my face right up against the chain link, the better to see her roses. Even if you could forget about the surrounding fortifications, no one would ever call her rose garden pretty. For one thing, it was a little monotonous. Four long rows of precisely pruned bushes sported uniformly white flowers. I imagine if you got closer, you'd probably see enough subtle variations in size, shape, and texture of the white blossoms to make them interesting, but from where I stood they all blended into one. A rose factory.

The most interesting part of the whole enclosure was in the

far corner, where there was a much smaller collection of roses. Many of them bore deep red or purple blooms, presumably Mrs. Winkleson's potential entrants for the Winkleson prize. And also her breeding stock. Here and there I saw bushes sporting plastic bags over some branches, so I gathered Mrs. Winkleson was trying to develop her own black roses. I knew from Dad's efforts that you used the bags when you were cross-pollinating, to keep stray insects from contaminating the results with unwanted pollen.

I followed the fence around to the corner where the red roses lurked so I could peer in and check Dad's competition.

"She's got some awfully dark roses," I said. A couple of the bushes bore buds that were almost black, and she had plenty of roses in deep velvety reds. Even a few that I'd almost call purple.

"They drive her bonkers, those roses."

"Why?" I asked. "She's got some lovely ones. Very dark ones." Not as dark as some of Dad's I thought. Then again, I didn't know whether his best roses had survived the depredations of the deer.

"Yeah, pretty dark, but the darn things are still a long way from coal black," he said. "You should see her out here sometimes, swearing at the roses, like she thought she could order them to turn black."

"She probably does think that," I said. "But if her roses are anything like Dad's, swearing at them won't do any good."

"More likely to do harm."

"Oh, are you a believer in talking positively to your plants?" I asked. "I have a cousin who swears she can double a plant's growth rate by regularly talking to it in a warm, encouraging fashion."

"That's interesting," Mr. Darby said, though by his expression I suspected interesting was his euphemism for wacko. "What I meant was that sometimes she gets so worked up that she rips a plant or two up, roots and all. White ones that aren't pure white enough. Dark red ones she's bred that aren't turning out as dark as she wants."

"Self-defeating," I said, shaking my head.

"And then the next day she drags one of my gardeners in there to replant it," he said. "Which doesn't always work too well. They're delicate things, roses."

"So I've heard," I said.

A sudden clap of thunder made both of us start, and then we both pulled up the hoods of our rain parkas as the heavens opened. We stood hunched against the downpour for a minute or two. I could see petals falling from some of the roses.

"This isn't doing the roses any good," I said. "But I suppose she's already cut the ones she's planning to exhibit tomorrow."

Mr. Darby shrugged.

"No doubt," he said. "Like I said, she doesn't let anyone else mess with the roses. I'd best be getting on. Got a lot of work to do. When you're finished inspecting the roses, you can head that way to get back to the barns. Over the fence, turn right, and mind the goats.

"Thanks," I said.

He trudged off heading at right angles to the path he'd pointed out for me, and disappeared into the woods.

I gazed through the chain link for a few more minutes. Were

these the bushes that had produced the blooms destined to defeat whatever black roses Dad had left? Or would Dad's blooms triumph over the regimented inhabitants of Mrs. Winkleson's rose prison?

I peered closer, trying to read the tags attached to the bushes. A couple of the ones closest to the fence appeared to say "Black Magic." I couldn't read any of the rest.

I found myself feeling sorry for the poor bushes, stuck out here in the middle of nowhere, blooming unseen and unsmelled, except by Mrs. Winkleson. A sad life.

I was starting to sound like Rose Noire.

I flinched at another sharp clap of thunder, but the rain had started easing off. I turned away and sloshed in the direction Mr. Darby had indicated.

Yes, as I approached the fence, I could see the goats, about two dozen of them. Some were still clustered hopefully around the feeding trough, while the rest were grazing nearby, and a small cluster were horizontal. Perhaps the thunder had startled them. I began climbing over the fence, moving as slowly as possible, to avoid startling them again.

I was halfway over the fence when I heard Spike barking in the distance.

"Blast!" My grandfather's voice. "Come back, you rebellious cur!"

I hopped down and looked around. First, I spotted Dr. Blake, running slowly toward the fence, with Caroline following about ten feet behind. But they were no match for the Small Evil One. With his leash trailing behind him, Spike made a beeline for the goats.

Most of the goats that weren't already lying down toppled over immediately. A few managed to whirl and take a few steps away from Spike before they succumbed. Several of the larger goats just froze in place, much like kids playing a game of Statues.

Spike seemed overjoyed with his victory. To my relief, he didn't try to bite any of the goats. He just pranced among his victims, head high, tail wagging, uttering an occasional sharp bark of triumph.

"What's going on?" Mr. Darby appeared out of the woods at my right and began scrambling over the fence.

"I'm so sorry," I called back to Mr. Darby as I trotted after Spike.

"Not your fault," he said. "Happens all the time. Dogs. Little kids. Herself with that damned umbrella."

I was getting close to Spike, and had to watch my step, lest I trip over one of the recumbent goats.

"Perfect example of a maladaptive mutation." Dr. Blake sounded out of breath, and was leaning heavily on the fence. "In the wild, anything that keeled over at the first appearance of a predator wouldn't live to reproduce."

"It's not their fault," Mr. Darby said, sounding a little peeved. "They were bred that way."

"Precisely my point," my grandfather said. "We humans have taken the goat, one of the most admirably rugged and self-reliant of ruminants, and then deliberately bred it for a trait that's at best inconvenient for the animal and at worst dangerous."

"Well, there's some truth to that," Mr. Darby said.

"Don't let them kick that poor little puppy!" Caroline shouted. "Catch him, quick!"

"I'm trying," I said.

Spike wasn't seriously at risk, since most of the goats were still horizontal. He wasn't eager to be caught either, and the longer he eluded me, the harder catching him would be. I chased, he dodged, and then the goats began getting up, which made it easier for him to use them for cover. Some of them were still a little shaky, others recovering more quickly and bounding toward the fence to greet Mr. Darby, who was reaching into his pocket and feeding bits of carrot to them. My grandfather reached over, took some of the carrots from Mr. Darby's hand, and began feeding the maladapted goats himself.

"It's the same as how we've taken an animal as magnificent as the wolf and turned it into—well, something like that," he went on, pointing with a carrot at Spike, who was sniffing at one of the larger fallen goats. As if spurred by my grandfather's words, Spike suddenly leaped away from the goat and began backing toward the fence, growling. I leaned down and managed to grab the end of his leash.

"Even in captivity, you'd think the extreme version of myotonia would be a handicap," Dr. Blake went on. "The ones that succumb less readily and recover more quickly have a better opportunity to get food."

"I make sure none of 'em starve," Mr. Darby said.

"They look very healthy," Caroline said.

"Yes, of course, but my point is that the myotonia gives them a competitive disadvantage," my grandfather said. "Some of these goats have had half a dozen carrots by now, and that goat over there hasn't had any."

He pointed at the goat Spike had been sniffing. It still lay slightly apart from the rest of the goats, nearer the fence that separated their pasture from the farther one beyond. I took a few steps forward to take a closer look.

"That's because it's not a goat," I said. "It's a person. And I see blood. Call 911."

Chapter 16

I tossed the leash to Dr. Blake and ran toward where the figure was lying. Definitely a human form. Probably a small one, though it was hard to judge size since the figure was lying down, curled on one side, and swathed in a voluminous black garment.

"I'm coming," Caroline shouted. "Remember, I'm a nurse."

I thought I recognized the black garment on the fallen figure as a rain cape, quite possibly the one Mrs. Winkleson had been wearing all morning as she strode around barging into things and ordering people around. I wondered, briefly, if we were panicking over a cloak someone had dropped in the pasture. No, there was a foot sticking out from under the black fabric, with a thick ankle and a familiar-looking sturdy black shoe on the end of it. I plopped to my knees beside the figure and scrambled for her wrist to check for a pulse.

"Emergency!" I could hear Dr. Blake shouting into his cell phone.

What was Mrs. Winkleson doing out here in the pasture? No time to waste figuring it out. She had no pulse. But she was still warm—normal body temperature as far as I would tell. My mind raced to figure out what Dad's instructions would be. Chest compression, probably.

"No pulse," I said over my shoulder to Caroline.

"We should do CPR, then," she said. "Turn her over."

"Dammit, I don't know," my grandfather was saying on his phone. "Looks like a dying nun to me. No, *dying*. D-Y-"

I reached to turn Mrs. Winkleson on her back and realized there was a complication. A pool of blood was spreading out from under her, and she had something sticking out of her back. Caroline knelt down beside me and tugged at the object. It didn't budge.

"My secateurs," I said aloud.

"Hang on, Debbie Anne," my grandfather said to the dispatcher. "Meg's saying something. Who did you say it was, Meg?"

"Pull those out and turn her over," Caroline said. "I can do the chest compression, but I can't budge those."

I gulped, then grabbed the secateurs and pulled, hard. The secateurs came out. I didn't see a lot of blood come out with them. Was that a good sign or bad? I wondered, as I rolled Mrs. Winkleson over on her back. Not good, I decided, from the look on Caroline's face. She started rhythmically pumping on Mrs. Winkleson's chest. I stood up and stepped back to give her room.

"Someone used my secateurs to stab Mrs. Winkleson in the back," I said. I could hear my grandfather repeating my words into the phone.

Mrs. Winkleson's face was covered with blood and mud, and there was an enormous amount of blood on her clothes and the ground—Caroline's hands were red, and the knees of my jeans were soaked. But I didn't see a lot of new blood flowing from the wound. Even in the short time since I'd turned her over, the rain had begun to dilute and wash away the existing blood.

She was facing toward the barns, I noticed.

"They're sending an ambulance," Dr. Blake shouted. "I'm calling your father."

Suddenly I noticed Mrs. Winkleson's hands. Her left hand had fallen back behind her head, as if she were waving to someone, but her right hand, which had flopped out to the side when I turned her, was clutching something white. White and red, actually. A bloodstained piece of paper.

I reached down to secure the paper, but just as my hand touched it, an enormous hairy goat head swooped down and chomped on it with large, yellow teeth.

"Hey! Stop that!" I said, smacking the goat on the nose. The goat turned to flee and keeled over after a few steps. Unfortunately, he continued chewing vigorously, and swallowed just as I reached him.

"What's wrong?" Mr. Darby said, racing over. "Did someone hurt Elton?"

"You mean the goat—he's fine," I said. "But he just ate some evidence."

"What kind of evidence?"

"She was clutching a piece of paper in her hand, and the goat ate it."

"Well, you can't blame Elton for that," Mr. Darby said. "As I told you before, paper's like candy to them."

"Can't you make him cough it up?" I asked. "He can't have digested it yet."

"They're fainting goats, not puking goats," Mr. Darby said, sounding rather cross.

I went back where Caroline was still briskly administering CPR to the victim. I checked Mrs. Winkleson's hand and found she was still holding a corner of the paper. I gently teased it out.

"What does it say?" my grandfather asked.

" 'Or else,' " I read.

"Or else what?"

"Or else, period," I said. "It's just the lower right hand corner of the paper. That's all that's left."

"No signature?"

"No."

"Do you recognize the handwriting?"

"It's typed." I showed him the paper.

"Well, that's not much help," he said. "You shouldn't have let that goat eat the rest of it."

Luckily we were interrupted before I could answer.

"Meg! What's up!"

I turned to see Dad climbing over the fence.

"She's been stabbed," I shouted back. "Caroline's doing CPR."

"Oh, dear!" Dad was over the fence now. He turned back to take his black medical bag from Chief Burke, then trotted toward us while the chief climbed over the fence more slowly, as if he already knew that Dad's medical effort was doomed to failure and his own investigative work about to begin. Or maybe it only seemed that way to me because I'd seen how badly off Dad's latest patient was.

The chief turned to me.

"You found the bo—the victim?"

"Actually, Spike found her," I said.

"I can't very well question him, can I? What happened?"

"Mind if I sit down?" I suddenly realized that my knees were shaking.

I walked over and sat down on one end of the goats' trough. The chief followed me over and took out his notebook. He scribbled furiously as I told him how I'd found Mrs. Winkleson. Then, at his request, I did an instant replay of my entire morning. I turned over the small scrap of paper I'd pried from Mrs. Winkleson's hands and he pulled a pair of gloves out of his pocket and put them on before taking it and peering at it over his glasses.

As we talked, both of us watched the effort to save Mrs. Winkleson—first by Dad and Caroline, and then by the EMTs who arrived with the ambulance.

At least the chief watched. I tried hard not to. I didn't faint at the sight of blood, like my brother—if I did, I'd have become as horizontal as the goats the second I looked at Mrs. Winkleson. I could handle blood, but I had a hard time watching all the technological marvels of modern medicine. I was profoundly grateful they existed, of course, and hoped people like Dad and the EMTs would be around if I ever needed them, but I also hoped if that ever happened I'd be temporarily unconscious and unable to watch.

They were putting her on the stretcher, about to take her away, before the chief showed any sign of being finished with me.

"One more thing," he said, his eyes on the EMTs. "Any

possibility she was already out here when you went through the first time?"

"No," I said. "Because I saw her up at the house, remember? And besides——"

"What is all this commotion? What's going on here?"

Several goats fainted, and everyone else turned and gasped. Mrs. Winkleson was standing at the fence, her hands on her hips, scowling fiercely at us.

Chapter 17

"I thought you said the victim was Mrs. Winkleson," the chief said, frowning at me.

"Victim?" Mrs. Winkleson said. "What do you mean, victim?"

"I thought it was," I said, ignoring her. "Right size and weight, wearing black clothes. And her face was covered with blood and dirt, and I didn't really look at it for long."

"I said what's going on here?" Mrs. Winkleson shrieked.

"We're investigating a mur—an attempted murder," the chief said.

"What? On my estate? Outrageous!"

She stormed over to the gate, unlatched it and strode into the pasture.

"Madam," the chief said. "Please stay outside the fence. This is a crime scene. Madam, I—"

He took a step in her direction, tripped on a horizontal goat, and fell over.

"Watch the goat!" Mr. Darby said.

"Stop that woman!" the chief shouted.

Mr. Darby didn't move. Clearly crossing his employer wasn't something he could do. Or perhaps he was still in shock at the discovery that the victim wasn't Mrs. Winkleson. He'd seemed quite calm when we thought she was Mrs. Winkleson, but since her arrival, he'd been staring at the frail form Caroline and Dad were working on, with his mouth hanging open and a horrified expression on his face.

Mrs. Winkleson kept going. The chief was still trying to disentangle himself from the goat.

I jumped up and ran after her.

"The chief said to stop!" I called.

"I want to know what is going on here!"

She was only ten feet from the victim.

I tackled her. We went down in a muddy heap amid the stiff forms of half a dozen startled goats.

"Arrest her!" Mrs. Winkleson cried. "Assault and battery! Trespassing!"

"I'd be happy to, madam," the chief said, limping up to us. "But then I would have to arrest you for disturbing a crime scene and interfering with a police investigation. Please stand back and let the medical personnel do their job."

She glared at both of us, and then turned and walked back to the fence. She stopped in front of the gate and crossed her arms.

"Algie, no! Bad goat!" Mr. Darby said. Not in a very loud voice, but the goat that had been lowering his head and aiming at Mrs. Winkleson's derriere straightened up and looked around as if to say "Who? Me?"

"You could at least tell me who has managed to get himself killed on my property," Mrs. Winkleson said, apparently unaware of her narrow escape.

"Herself," the chief corrected. "She's not dead yet, and I have no idea who she is."

"We thought it was you," I said. "I thought I recognized your rain cape. But now we don't know who she is."

"Yes we do," Dad said, over his shoulder. "Sandy Sechrest. One of the rose growers exhibiting this weekend. From northern Virginia, I think. Very nice person. Unsound on the use of manure, but she had—has—quite a gift for raising miniature roses."

"Had," the chief repeated. "She's gone, then?"

"Has," Dad corrected. "We're doing what we can."

The chief's lips tightened. He could read the message on Dad's face and in his tone.

"Do you know Mrs. Sechrest?" the chief said, turning to Mrs. Winkleson.

"Of course," Mrs. Winkleson said. "Not well, but I know all the members of the rose club. No idea what she was doing out here the day before the show, though. Unless she was one of Ms. Langslow's volunteers."

I shook my head.

Just then the EMTs picked up the stretcher and began carefully picking their way across the rough ground and between the goats.

"Getting back to what you saw," the chief said, turning back to me. "Now that we know the de—the victim is not Mrs. Winkleson, is there any chance she could have been already lying here when you went by the first time? On your way to the house?"

I thought for a few moments and shook my head.

"No idea," I said. "I was focused on getting to the house and not startling the goats. I don't think I would have noticed if one of them was already lying down. I noticed her right away when I came back from the house, but I mistook her for a cluster of unconscious goats."

"If it makes any difference," Dad said, "I doubt if it could have happened before you went up to the house."

He'd been following the EMTs but paused when he heard the chief's question.

"Are you sure?" I asked. "I don't think I spent more than half an hour on my trip up to the house."

Dad shook his head.

"Still probably too long."

"You can tell that by the body?" the chief asked.

"I can tell that by the blood," Dad said. "There was quite a lot of it when Caroline and I first got here, but by now it's been mostly washed off by the drizzle. And we had quite a frog-strangler there for a few minutes, just before I got the call to come out here. If she'd been attacked before that, there wouldn't have been much blood left for us to see."

"He's right," I said. "I saw that myself, just in the short time I was with her. A whole lot of blood washing away before my eyes."

"What if she was stabbed before the first time Meg came by and continued to bleed the whole time?" the chief asked.

My stomach churned at the thought. If that was how it had happened, my failure to see her the first time would probably end up costing her life.

"No," Dad said. "With those wounds, she'd have bled out in

much less than half an hour. This had to have happened very close to when Meg found her."

Dad's words set my mind more at ease, though apparently it was going to take a while for them to calm my stomach.

The chief studied Dad's face for a few moments, then nodded, as if grudgingly acknowledging a good point.

"Do you need me here?" Dad asked. "If not, I'm going to ride along to the hospital."

"Go," the chief said, waving toward the ambulance. "And keep me posted."

Dad nodded and hurried after the EMTs.

"Did I see your cousin Horace over in the barn?" the chief asked.

I nodded.

"Want me to find him?" I asked. Caerphilly didn't have any CSIs of its own, so the chief usually borrowed Horace on those rare occasions when a case warranted doing forensic work.

The chief nodded, and I was happy to have a reason to leave the goat pasture.

"If you're quite through here—" Mrs. Winkleson began.

"No, madam," the chief said, interrupting her. "My officers and I are nowhere near through here, and I'm afraid I'll have to ask you to go back up to your house. I'll come up later to find out what you can tell me about this sad business."

"Are you ordering me off my own property?"

"No, madam," the chief said. "I'm asking you to stay away from my crime scene. I'm investigating what I expect will soon become a murder, if it hasn't already. The requirements of my investigation take precedence over anything else."

"The nerve!" Mrs. Winkleson exclaimed. From past experience, I could tell she was winding up for a full-scale hissy fit. I turned back to do what I could to head her off.

"How terrible for you, Mrs. Winkleson!" I said. "Knowing that the person who tried to kill you is still at large! But of course, the chief will be doing everything he can to find the perpetrator before he can strike again, and in the meantime, if there's anything anyone can do to help you through this dreadful ordeal, please don't hesitate to ask."

She blinked as she considered this. Then she turned back to the chief.

"You'll be providing me with police protection, of course," she said.

"Alas, madam, we do not have the personnel to do that," the chief said. "With a crime of this magnitude, we'll need to seek whatever help we can get from nearby counties and from the State Bureau of Investigation."

"But I've been receiving threats!" Mrs. Winkleson snapped.

"What kind of threats?" The chief looked up from his notebook with an expression of genuine interest. No doubt, like me, he was thinking about the "or else" typed on the scrap of paper I'd rescued from the goat.

"I don't know," she said. "The usual thing. Stop the rose show or you'll be sorry. Stuff like that. And they took my dog, too. You haven't forgotten that, have you?"

"My officers are even now searching for your missing dog," the chief said. "Why didn't you report these threats when we talked earlier this morning? Did it not occur to you that they might be relevant to your missing dog?"

"I thought they were nonsense until now," she said. "Now I realize they were serious."

"The disappearance of your dog didn't convince you?"

"That, too."

I could see the chief, himself a dog owner, found her cavalier attitude toward Mimi's absence as unsatisfactory as I did.

"It would have been helpful to know about these threats earlier," he said. "We will certainly keep them in mind as our investigation progresses."

"Are you telling me there's nothing you can do to protect me?" Mrs. Winkleson bellowed.

"I can catch whoever did this as soon as possible," the chief snapped. "That's the best thing I can do to help you and everyone else in this county, and I hope I can expect your full cooperation."

They glared at each other for a few moments. Mrs. Winkleson suddenly put on her Lady Bountiful face.

"Of course," she said. "Please let me know if there's anything I can do to help. Or if any of my staff are less than fully cooperative. I'll leave you to your work."

She gave him the same sort of gracious nod I'd seen her give her butler when she was in a good mood, and then sailed off toward the barns.

"Motive's going to be a problem in this one," I said, when she was out of earshot.

"I don't see why," the chief said. "For a few moments there, I wanted to kill her myself."

"That's your problem," I said. "Everyone feels that way. Too many suspects."

"We'll manage," he said. "Could you find your cousin Horace now?"

In other words, mind my own business. I nodded and went back to the barns in search of Horace.

Chapter 18

Horace and Sammy were in the show barn, staring at some of the tables.

"Meg, do we really have to paint all the table legs black?" Sammy asked. "I could go into town and get some paint, but we borrowed them from the New Life Baptist Church, and I think they'd rather get their tables back the same color they started out, and besides—"

"I agree," I said. "No painting the table legs. And if Mrs. Winkleson has a problem with that, tell her to talk to me. Horace, the chief could use your help."

"Something wrong?" he asked.

"Someone tried to knock off Mrs. Winkleson just now," I said. "Unfortunately, they attacked someone else by mistake. The chief could use your forensic talents. Sammy, he could probably use your help, too."

Horace hurried off. Sammy started to follow, then turned back to me.

"Who's the, um, victim?" he asked.

"Mrs. Sechrest. One of the rose growers. Not from around here."

Sammy nodded.

"I suppose I should be ashamed to say that's a relief, but it is," he said. "You said tried. Will she make it?"

"We don't know yet," I said. "Dad didn't look too cheerful."

Sammy shook his head and hurried after Horace.

No one else was in the barn. Were the volunteers all in the other barn, working on the setup there? Out helping with the search for Mimi? Or all up at the goat pasture, staring at the crime scene?

I was determined not to do that myself, so I looked around for something to do. I spotted an open box, presumably what Sammy and Horace had been working on when Mrs. Winkleson blew through and demanded that they paint the table legs black. The label on this box read, helpfully, "labels."

I opened the box up and looked inside. It was full of small black and white plastic labels. I picked up one. Class 130. Okay, the classes were the different categories in which the roses would be entered. I knew that much from proofing the program. I dumped the box's contents on a nearby table and began to sort them. I ended up with labels for classes 101 through 149, and also three sets of alphabetical labels. Where were all those A–Zs supposed to go?

And why was I assuming the show would go on? For all I knew, the chief would declare the whole area a crime scene, and before the afternoon was out I'd have to pack up the little plastic labels again.

"Something wrong?"

I looked up to see one of the rose growers watching me.

"Do you know what to do with these?" I asked, indicating the labels.

"Just how much do you know about rose shows, sugar?" the woman asked.

"Next to nothing," I said. "My mother suckered me into doing this because I have a reputation in the family for being organized. But she promised there would be someone here to help who knew how this whole thing is supposed to run."

"I can help with that. Molly Weston."

Since there were no roses nearby, I assumed that was her name. I shook the hand she held out, and then stood by while she started shuffling the little plastic rectangles.

"Do you have one of the programs?"

I rummaged around until I found the box of programs and handed her one.

"Okay," she said. "This is pretty straightforward. Class 101 is for hybrid teas or grandifloras from a grower with 75 or fewer rose bushes," she said. "And 102 is for growers with 76 and above. Those are the two biggest categories—so big that we need the alphabetical tags underneath. I'd say use the first four tables for 101 and the next four for 102. The next few are fairly small, maybe half a table each, until you get to the miniatures. That's what the third set of alpha tags is for. I'd say another four tables for them. Here—follow me."

She handed me a couple of stacks of plastic tags and I trailed after her, placing the tags on the tables, closer together or farther apart, depending on how popular she thought the categories were apt to be.

We had only done a couple of tables when my cell phone rang. I pulled it out of my pocket. Michael.

"It's my husband," I said. "I should—"

"Go talk to the man," she said, waving me away. "I'll handle this."

I flipped the phone open and strolled outside, where I could have some privacy.

"Hey, beautiful," Michael said. "Do you miss me?"

"You have no idea how much," I said.

"Rose show even worse than you anticipated?"

"About as bad as I anticipated up until an hour ago," I said. "Then it took a nose dive when someone tried to kill Mrs. Winkleson."

"Tried? She's all right, then?"

"She's fine. Unfortunately the attacker probably managed to knock off another one of the rose growers. Dad went with her to the hospital, but it's not looking good."

"Oh, no," he said. "Who?"

"Sandy Sechrest."

"I don't recognize the name," he said.

"That's because she was never anything but polite, helpful, and cooperative in the last few weeks," I said. "It's only the rude, demanding, unhelpful, nasty ones you'd recognize, because they're the ones I come home and bitch to you about."

"Actually, the only name I can think of off the top of my head is Mrs. Winkleson."

"That figures," I said. "There are some others you'd probably recognize if I said the names, but she's been the worst. Did you hear that someone abducted Mrs. Winkleson's dog last night?"

"My God, you have had a morning. Do you think they're related? The murder and the dognapping, I mean?"

"No idea. And unlike Dad, I'm trying to leave the detecting

to Chief Burke. Let's talk about something else. How's the trip going?"

"Could be better," he said. "I don't suppose the attempted murder counts as a crisis for which you need me standing supportively at your side?"

"What's wrong?" I asked. "I thought you felt duty-bound to see your student's play."

"That was when it was a play," he said. "He didn't tell us that during the rehearsal period it had mutated into a musical."

"You're kidding."

"Used to be *Millard Fillmore and the Compromise of 1850: A Tragedy of American History*. Now it's *Millard! The Musical!* With two exclamation points no less."

"Actually, that sounds as if it could be an improvement."

"I doubt it. According to a review we read on the way up, the only halfway hummable tune in the whole show is a ballad about the Wilmot Proviso."

"Oh, dear."

"And since we're all professors, and hate to admit ignorance of anything, even if it's not in our field, now we're all frantically trying to pretend we know what the Wilmot Proviso is and what it has to do with Fillmore. You don't happen to know, do you?"

"Actually, yes," I said. "It was a law that was supposed to outlaw slavery in any territory the U.S. acquired from Mexico. Introduced several times in the 1840s but never passed. Often cited as one of the earliest signs of the split that eventually resulted in the Civil War. Not exactly what I'd call ballad fodder, but you never know."

"I should have called you when the subject first came up."

"I wouldn't know the first thing about it if I hadn't helped one of the nephews with a term paper last semester. Which reminds me: can you bring me—"

"Ms. Langslow?"

I looked up from the phone to find the chief looking expectantly at me. What now?

Chapter 19

"I'll be off the phone in just a moment," I told the chief.

He nodded, smiled, and assumed a visibly patient expression. He did not, however, move out of earshot.

"Bring you what?" Michael asked.

"Some cheesecake," I said. "Remember that deli where we had such good cheesecake? You don't get cheesecake like that down here."

"I don't actually remember where that deli was."

"But there's good cheesecake all over New York," I said. "Maybe you can ask your student for a recommendation."

"Will do," he said. "Talk to you later."

We said our good-byes, and I hung up

"What can I do for you?" I asked the chief.

"One of my officers found Mrs. Sechrest's car behind some bushes along a lane that runs around the other side of the farm," the chief said. "Pretty impossible to get good tracks after all this rain, but it looks as if she hid her car there, snuck in the back way, and was making her way toward the house when she was attacked."

"Why do you suppose she did that?" I said.

He sighed.

"I was hoping you could tell me," he said. "Was she on your list of volunteers?"

"No, but Mother was going to call around to guilt trip a few more people into helping. Maybe she talked Mrs. Sechrest into coming. You could ask her. Mother, I mean. Or Mrs. Sechrest if—when—she regains consciousness."

He nodded.

"Only that's not likely to happen, is it?" I blurted out. "We all keep correcting ourselves, saying 'attacker' instead of 'killer' and sticking attempted in front of murder, and using the present tense when we talk about Mrs. Sechrest, but we're not really expecting her to pull through, are we?"

The chief sighed slightly and tightened his lips.

"Any of your other volunteers come in the back way?" he asked.

Okay, I wasn't really expecting an answer to my question. Or maybe I'd already gotten my answer.

"Not that I know of," I said aloud. "But I'm sure more of them would have if they'd known there was a back entrance. People were getting really tired of waiting for the front gate. It was supposed to have been left open for the volunteers, but Mrs. Winkleson forgot about that, or changed her mind after the dognapping, and at one time we had at least a dozen vehicles stacked up and waiting for up to half an hour."

"I know," he said. "Remember, Minerva and I were trying to get in to help out."

"That's right," I said. "Anyway, maybe she knew the back way and decided to avoid the crowd."

"The back way into the farm, or into the house?"

"Either." I shrugged. "Both. Who knows?"

He frowned and looked down at his notebook.

"Sorry," I said. "I wish I could be more help, but I don't actually know everything about Mrs. Winkleson and her farm. Just what I've learned over the last couple of months while planning the rose show."

"You probably know more about her than anyone, actually," the chief said. "At least anyone who's willing to talk to me."

"What about her staff?"

"Darby claims he doesn't pay attention to anything but the animals," the chief said. "Can't answer the simplest questions about her friends or her habits. He might actually be telling the truth. The man doesn't seem to notice anything that's not on four legs. And the rest of the staff aren't even *that* helpful. Can't get a sensible word out of them. The ones who even speak English, that is."

This was more information than the chief normally shared with civilians, which must mean he was getting incredibly frustrated.

"I wouldn't have expected them to be that loyal," I said aloud.

"Loyal? Hell, they're scared silly. More of her than of me. And none of them are local."

Which meant that he couldn't rely on his officers, all of them local, to tap the Caerphilly grapevine and bring him information witnesses wouldn't share officially.

"If you hear anything, let me know," he said. "Note that I said *if* you hear anything. I'm not asking you to go out and snoop around."

"Okay," I said.

He sighed.

"I don't suppose I can convince you to leave the detecting to us," the chief said. "It's not like finding the victim obligates you to solve the crime."

"I know," I said. "But I am taking it a little personally that she was stabbed with my secateurs."

"Your what?"

"The garden shears that someone used to stab Mrs. Sechrest," I explained. "Secateurs is another name for them."

"Why don't you just call them garden shears, then?" the chief grumbled.

"I do, but the ladies in the garden club think secateurs sounds more elegant," I said.

"So these—blasted things belong to you?" the chief asked.

"Not really. I made them for Mother. She wanted something more elegant and ornamental than the ordinary shears you can find in garden centers."

The chief studied me with a familiar scowl on his face. He got very testy at anything that even hinted of interference with his criminal investigations. I wasn't sure I wanted to find out how he felt about someone who had, however inadvertently, furnished the would-be killer with his weapon.

"So if you made them and gave them to your mother," he said, finally, "what were they doing over here, stuck in Mrs. Sechrest's back?"

"I have no idea," I said. "Mother and I haven't seen them in almost two weeks."

"You lost them?"

"They were stolen," I said. "By someone in the garden club."

"The garden club?"

"It happened the Sunday before last, when the garden club all met here to go over the plans for the show," I said. "I'd only just finished the secateurs, and Mother was so proud of them that she pretended to have stuck them in her tote by mistake. She found an excuse to pull them out and wonder why on earth she'd brought them, so she could show them off. Everybody wanted their own set."

"Nice for your business."

"Yes, though it would have been nicer if Mother had waited to wave them around at the show," I said. "You have no idea what a pain it's been, trying to find the time to make forty-two pairs of shears on top of all the things I have to do to get ready for the show."

"How many have you made so far?" he asked.

"Seventeen."

"Then how can you be sure this is the one your mother lost at the garden club meeting?"

"Had stolen from her at the garden club meeting," I corrected. "I'm pretty certain for two reasons. One is that I still have the rest of them locked up in my forge, except for this pair."

I fished through my bag and pulled out the secateurs I'd brought. The chief flinched, and I saw him reach toward his holster.

Chapter 20

"I surrender!" I said, dropping the secateurs and putting up my hands.

"You startled me," he said. "Blast it all, put your hands down. People are staring."

I put my hands down, then bent to pick up the secateurs, which I gave to the chief, handle first.

"And just what are you doing walking around with an identical duplicate of my murder—attempted murder weapon?" he asked.

"It wasn't any kind of a weapon this morning, when I put it in my tote," I said. "And it's not identical. See this little decorative bit?"

I pointed to a small, stylized twig and leaf that curled inside the handle. The chief leaned over slightly and peered at the secateurs. From his wary posture, you'd have thought he was being asked to inspect a rattlesnake.

"On the first pair I made, the hole inside the handle was smaller, and that little sprig dug into your hands in a really annoying way. Not into Mother's hands, which are very small, but most people would find it uncomfortable. So when I started making them in larger numbers, I rethought the design. Every pair of secateurs I've made since has had a hole about this size. The one I saw stuck in Mrs. Sechrest's back was my original."

"The pair that was stolen from your mother at the garden club meeting."

"Yes."

He scribbled a little in his notebook. I wondered what. Was he writing down what I just told him? Or did he use his notebook to vent things that it wouldn't do to blurt aloud? Had he just scribbled, "Meg Langslow: found victim. Made weapon and seventeen virtually identical copies. Definitely a suspect"? Or something more like. "Blast, but I wish I were back in Baltimore, where people try to kill each other for normal reasons, like drugs and money"?

He saw me looking at his notebook and tilted it a little more toward his chest, as if he thought I was about to try to read upside down.

"Do you know who stole your shears?" he asked.

"Mother suspected the Pruitts and Mrs. Winkleson," I said. The chief nodded, and scribbled. "Of course," I went on, "that could just be because she doesn't particularly like the Pruitts and Mrs. Winkleson." The chief stopped scribbling long enough to glance up at me as if checking to see if I was joking. I shrugged apologetically. He dropped his eyes again and scribbled longer than seemed quite necessary to record what I'd just said.

"Which Pruitts?" he asked.

"I'm not sure," I said. "There are usually three or four of them at garden club meetings, trying to give orders instead of doing any useful work."

"What else is new?" the chief muttered.

"I've got the membership list here," I said, raising my clipboard. "I can't swear every member was there for the meeting, and there might have been a few non-members tagging along, but it would give you some idea. And here's a copy of the volunteer list. It's shorter."

"A lot shorter," he said.

"That's because I only wrote down the people who actually committed to show up and work."

The chief nodded, and scanned the lists.

"Will it inconvenience you if I keep these?" He didn't sound as if a "yes" would change his mind.

"Be my guest," I said. He glanced up in surprise. "Everyone knows I keep the member list with me at rose show meetings, and they're always asking to borrow it and not giving it back, so I've learned to bring a few photocopies. And any volunteers who aren't here already either aren't coming at all or won't be in time to do any useful work, so that list's pretty useless by now."

"Thank you," he said. "But I mean it. Stay out of this."

"I will."

"I'm serious. There's a murderer—attempted murderer—running around loose, and if that person thinks you can point the finger at them—"

"Got it," I said. "Solving the murder—or attempted murder—is your job."

For that matter, I could stop worrying about solving the theft of the secateurs. Odds were the chief would see that as an integral part of solving the larger crime. Even poor Mimi's abduction would probably get a lot more attention because of the possibility that it was connected to the subsequent attempt to murder her owner.

But it was still my job to figure out whether or not someone was sabotaging Dad's black roses, and if so, who.

Not that I was going to say as much to the chief.

My cell phone rang. Rob.

"Meg? I saw the ambulance leave, and Dr. Smoot just came in asking for the chief. I sent him up to the barns. What's going on?"

"Someone tried to kill Mrs. Winkleson and got the wrong person," I said. "Rob says Dr. Smoot's here," I added, to the chief.

"Damn," the chief said. "As if he could do any good out here, with the . . . victim heading off to the hospital. Let me have that a second."

I gathered from the chief's side of the conversation that Dr. Smoot was already out of earshot. The chief began giving Rob instructions about keeping out unnecessary personnel, particularly reporters. I left him to it and went outside to greet Dr. Smoot.

I spotted him already up at the goat pens, leaning on the fence. At least I assumed the figure in the inky black cloak was Dr. Smoot. Mrs. Winkleson would approve if she saw him, but he wasn't dressing in black for her approval. The county's acting medical examiner had developed a taste for the supernatural, and had begun habitually wearing a black cloak with a red satin lining, looking like a refugee from an old-fashioned horror film.

Then again, the last time I'd made assumptions about someone in a black cape I'd been dead wrong. I began strolling toward the figure.

The chief caught up with me halfway and handed me my cell phone.

"Thanks," he said. "Did you call Smoot?"

I shook my head.

"Probably listening to his police radio again," the chief grumbled. "Can't seem to get it through his head that we'll call him if we need him. Been showing up whenever there's a 911 call, scaring people to death with that vampire getup and that old-timey hearse he's taken to driving."

I noticed he kept his voice down so Smoot couldn't hear him.

Dr. Smoot turned to greet us as we neared the fence.

"Now this is what I call a proper crime scene," he announced. "Plenty of room to work in."

Chief Burke closed his eyes, as if counting quickly to ten. He knew, of course, that what Dr. Smoot really liked was the fact that the crime scene was outdoors. Dr. Smoot was a severe claustrophobe, and tended to have panic attacks when asked to examine a body in any indoor space smaller than a ballroom. He was gazing over the flat field toward the distant tree line with great satisfaction.

"Yes, very nice," the chief said. "Unfortunately, you've come all this way for nothing. We don't have a body, at the moment. We just sent the victim off to the hospital. You'll have to catch up with her there. More convenient anyway if you end up having to do a post mortem."

"Oh." Dr. Smoot's face fell. Clearly he wasn't enamored of

the idea of a visit to the county morgue. Of course, the one or two times I'd been there, I'd felt a little claustrophobic myself, but I'd have thought with Dr. Smoot's keen appreciation of all things funereal and supernatural he'd find the morgue a congenial place, even if it did have four walls.

"Well, they'll do what they can for her at the hospital," he said, finally. "No rush. As long as I'm here, I might as well see if I can help out in any way."

Chief Burke didn't look overjoyed at the offer.

"There's still the search for the missing Maltese," I said. "I imagine the chief will have to pull his officers off that to solve the attempted murder, so perhaps you could help out with that."

"Maybe I can take a look at her vampire horses," Dr. Smoot added, with a gleam in his eye.

Chapter 21

"Vampire horses?" the chief echoed. He stared at Dr. Smoot with dismay. More dismay than usual.

"She has a bunch of horses that she doesn't let out in the daytime," I said. "Because she doesn't want the sun to fade their perfect black coats."

"So she says," Dr. Smoot intoned. "But has anyone tested this?"

"Tested it?" the chief repeated.

"What are you planning to do?" I asked. "Wave garlic at them? Sprinkle them with holy water?"

"Just walk them outside in the sun," Dr. Smoot said. "See what happens."

"Not much sun right now," I said, glancing up at the clouds that looked ready to rain again at any moment. "Wouldn't be much of a test."

"It's daylight that does the trick, not actual sunshine," Dr. Smoot said.

"You should probably check with Mrs. Winkleson's farm manager before you bother the horses," I said.

"Right, right. Where are they, anyway?"

I shrugged. The chief stared impassively at him. Dr. Smoot sighed, pulled his cape around him, and strode off.

The chief watched him go with a frown on his face.

"Damn fool thing, showing up at my crime scenes in costume," he muttered.

"Chief?"

We turned to see Horace, wearing his tatty gorilla suit and holding a pitchfork, standing nearby with a stricken look on his face. He looked like one half of a gorilla-themed parody of "American Gothic."

"Oh, not you, Horace," the chief said. "It's Smoot. Gets on my nerves."

"I don't normally wear the suit when I'm on duty," Horace said, "but—"

"And since you're a volunteer and were off-duty when we called on you, you can wear what you like," the chief said. "I appreciate your helping out. Did you need me for something?"

"I can go and change," Horace said.

"Horace," the chief said. "I don't have a problem with you wearing whatever you want to the crime scene, because when you show up, you're a hundred and twenty percent professional. You don't waste my time with all this nonsense about vampire horses. And if I catch Smoot messing around with Mrs. Winkleson's horses instead of doing his job, I just might lock him up in a small closet and misplace the key for a few hours. Now go on and tell me what you came to tell me."

"Actually, I was coming to see Meg," Horace said. "Meg, do you think you could find Mr. Darby and get him to move the rest of those goats out of our crime scene?"

"Are they disturbing evidence?" the chief asked, frowning.

"Mainly they're just disturbing us," Horace said. "Most of

them are okay, but there's one who keeps coming up and trying to butt us whenever we bend over. That's why I'm carrying
this."

He indicated the pitchfork.

"Go back and fend the blasted thing off, then," the chief said.
"Meg, I'd appreciate your help finding Mr. Darby."

I was already flipping the pages of my notebook.

"I've got his phone number," I said. "Cell phone, I think. It's
what I'm supposed to call if I need anything while we're here
for the show."

The chief pulled out his cell phone and dialed the number as
I read it. I watched his face, which grew gradually more impatient. Apparently the phone was ringing on unanswered.

"Mr. Darby," he said finally. "This is Chief Burke. Please call
me when you get a chance."

He hung up and looked at me.

"Next suggestion?" he said.

I pulled out my own cell phone and dialed the house.

The butler answered.

"Hello, Mr. . . . I'm sorry; what is your real name? I can't
very well keep calling you Marston now that I know it's not really your name."

"Thank you," he said. "I have become accustomed to using
the name professionally. But I much appreciate your courtesy.
How may I help you?"

"We need to find Mr. Darby to help us move the goats," I
said. "And he's not answering his cell phone.'

"He's probably in his cottage, madam," Marston said. "It's in
the woods, between the goat pasture and the rose garden."

"Thanks," I said, and hung up.

"His name's not really Marston?" the chief said.

"Mrs. Winkleson named him that," I said. "I think he's Russian, so maybe she can't pronounce his real name. He thinks Mr. Darby is in his cottage. Do you know where that is?"

"No." The chief glanced up from scribbling in his notebook. "Do you?"

I hesitated for a few moments. When it comes to finding my way around, I am an urban creature. Set me down in any city in the world, and I could probably find anything I wanted in half an hour. Fifteen minutes if the natives spoke some variant of English. Give me directions like "in the woods, between the goat pasture and the rose garden" and normally I resign myself to staying lost. But after a day of blundering around Mrs. Winkleson's property, I was beginning to get a rough map of the place in my head.

"I think I could find it if I try," I said finally, hoping I was telling the truth.

"Good," the chief said. "Find him and send him over here. I have some questions for him as well."

I slogged through the muddy goat pasture. Horace and Sammy were over to one side. They'd marked off a large, roughly circular area with yellow crime scene tape and were defending it by waving pitchforks at the encroaching goats. One of the goats left the herd and headed my way. I hadn't yet learned to tell one goat from another, so just in case this was the belligerent Algie, I made a run for the fence and leaped over just in time to miss getting butted.

"Bad goat, Algie," I said, shaking my finger at the goat before turning to look around. I strolled along the edge of the woods, heading away from the fence, and eventually spotted a corner of Mrs. Winkleson's rose garden in the distance. Since I was looking for it, I spotted a path to my left, leading into the woods. If it wasn't the same path Mr. Darby had taken when he left me at the rose garden earlier, it led in about the same direction. I followed it until I arrived at a tiny, dark cottage that appeared to be squatting in a small clearing like a malign toad.

"How unfortunate," I muttered. If you painted the cottage white, with maybe a nice soft accent color for the shutters, it would have looked like something out of a fairy tale and almost too cute for my taste. But since Mrs. Winkleson had painted it dark gray with matte black shutters and had shingled the roof in black, the poor cottage looked like the perfect home for a wicked witch. As I walked toward it, I more than half expected to hear a gleeful cackle and then a cracked crone's voice saying, "Come in, my pretty." Instead, silence.

I knocked with my knuckles before noticing that there was a black wrought-iron knocker on the door, almost invisible against the black paint. After a minute or so I tried again with the iron, and added my voice.

"Mr. Darby!" I called. "It's Meg Langslow. Are you there?"

Chapter 22

I was reaching for the knocker to try again when I finally heard a stirring inside Mr. Darby's cottage. A thud as if something had fallen from a table. A scraping sound, like a chair being moved.

The door finally opened, and Mr. Darby peered out. He looked a little befuddled.

"Wha's up?" he asked. There was a faint odor of bourbon on his breath.

"The goats are interfering with the crime scene," I said. "Can you move them to another pasture?"

He blinked as if it was taking the words a few seconds to reach his brain, and then nodded.

"Of course," he said. "Be right there."

He stepped back into the interior of the cottage, without closing the door, and I seized the chance to step inside and look around. I breathed a sigh of relief to see that Mr. Darby hadn't followed Mrs. Winkleson's decorating rules. Even I might have felt claustrophobic if he had, so tiny was the room. Room rather than apartment. There was a kitchenette at one end and a carelessly made bed at the other. It was overheated for my taste, but it was so small it probably didn't cost much to overheat, especially since the heat appeared to come from a wood stove. He could probably get his firewood for free in the estate's woods.

An open door gave a glimpse of a minuscule bathroom, and a curtain partially concealed a closet only about two feet wide. Every square inch of the walls was covered with shelves, mostly mismatched and battered—probably trash heap rescues—and every square inch of the shelves contained the sort of parapher- nalia you usually saw in a barn. Bits of tack and grooming equip- ment. Veterinary manuals and supplies. A few framed pictures of cows, horses, sheep, or goats. Everything neatly and tidily arranged, but the sheer amount of stuff was overwhelming, as if he'd tried to squeeze the entire contents of a half-acre feed and tack store into his cottage. Okay, the mystery of the over-tidy barns was solved.

And I saw no signs of canine occupation.

"Anything I can do to help?" I said, trying to pretend there was a reason for me to hang around. A reason other than snoop- ing. I reached for the door knob as if about to close the door.

"No, they'll pretty much follow me if I bring some special feed," he said. He snagged a bucket from a hook and grabbed a scoop from a burlap bag on the floor. He filled the bucket halfway from the bag—the special feed, I assumed—and then began stumbling toward the door.

I preceded him out. As I hoped, he simply pulled the door shut, without checking to make sure it was locked, so he didn't notice that while he was filling the feed bag, I'd surreptitiously twisted the button on the inside of the doorknob to the unlocked position.

Instead of taking the path, he dived into the woods. Taking

another, less visible path, I realized. I glanced at my watch and followed.

A mere two minutes later, we arrived at the edge of the goat pasture.

"I'll leave you to it, then," I said, pausing still inside the woods. He didn't seem to notice. He stumbled forward, shaking the bucket slightly, and I could see goats converging on him from all over the field.

I took the barely visible path back to the cottage.

It would have taken him five minutes at the most to walk from the rose garden to where I'd found Mrs. Sechrest's body. Not a lot of time, but still enough to get there and commit the deed. The short time frame actually made it more plausible that he wouldn't notice he was killing the wrong woman, as long as Mrs. Sechrest had her back to him. I closed my eyes and tried to picture the body. Yes, she had been facing toward the barns, and away from the direction Mr. Darby would have been coming from.

If he'd gone to the pasture to kill her. He could have been just going back to his cottage to take a break. Maybe to sneak a drink. I couldn't remember him smelling of bourbon before, though, and suspected that he'd achieved his current tipsy state in an effort to cope with the shock of the attempted murder.

Interesting that he hadn't seemed all that shocked until the true identity of the body was revealed.

I reached his cottage, glanced around to make sure no one was in the little clearing around it, and slipped inside.

Fifteen minutes' careful search revealed nothing at all suspicious. From the look of it, Mr. Darby had no interests other than animals, mainly farm animals. I saw no signs that he was a dog owner or lover. Even his TV was tuned to the *Animal Planet* channel, and the only light reading in sight was a complete set of James Herriot's *All Creatures Great and Small* series.

A framed diploma informed me that Mr. Darby had a B.S. in Agriculture from Caerphilly College. Behind it was another framed diploma from Clay County High School. So Mr. Darby was relatively local, Clay County being Caerphilly's more rural next-door neighbor.

He had a few anti-hunting pamphlets in the mix, which would make it hard for him to explain away any little bottles of doe urine I might have found. But I didn't find any, or, for that matter, anything that seemed to indicate he was plotting revenge on Mrs. Winkleson. Of course, my search was a little hampered by the fact that I couldn't really pick things up or dig too deeply into anything. I didn't want to leave any trace of my hurried search—or for that matter, any fingerprints, in case Chief Burke eventually decided that Mr. Darby was suspicious enough to warrant Horace's attention.

I stood by the wood stove for a few moments. I wasn't looking forward to going back out in the drizzle, especially since I'd become used to the temperature in Mr. Darby's overheated cocoon. And—

I suddenly caught a hint of a familiar smell. The sharp, metallic smell of blood. Was it coming from the stove? Or somewhere else in the room? Or—

After a few minutes of sniffing the air like a hyperactive beagle, I realized that the smell was coming from my own jeans. The rain had washed away most of the blood, except, I suppose, in the cuffs. When I stood by the stove, the heat brought the smell out more strongly.

I wasn't going to find anything incriminating or useful here in Mr. Darby's cottage. I decided to return to the barns by way of the house. I had a change of clothes in the trunk of my car. I made sure everything looked untouched, clicked the door knob button back to the locked position, and shut the door carefully behind me.

I only made two wrong turns on my way up to the house, and the swan had not returned to haunt my car. I grabbed my black pants and shirt from the trunk and trotted up the steps to ring the doorbell.

Marston answered and made no objection to my using the powder room off the foyer to change out of my bloodstained clothes.

"If you'd like us to launder the soiled garment, I would be happy to arrange that," he said.

"Thanks," I said. "Tempting, but I don't want to put you to any trouble."

I shed my jeans and T-shirt and looked to see if there was any blood on the underwear or skin beneath. I couldn't see any, but then the light in the powder room wasn't the greatest. Considering that this was where any guests would go if they wanted to check their hair and makeup, I'd have installed something brighter than a 25-watt bulb. But Mrs. Winkleson might not have many guests to worry about.

I'd also have gone for a different interpretation of the black and white color scheme. The black sink and toilet were a little hard to spot against the black tiles, black walls, and black ceiling.

Even the mirror was black tinted glass that made me look like one of the undead.

It occurred to me that since the hand towels were also black, I didn't need to worry about leaving stains on them. I grabbed one, drew a basin full of water, snagged the soap—where in the world had she found black soap?—and gave myself a quick scrub, just in case there was blood that I couldn't see for the dim light.

As far as I could tell, I was bloodstain-free and looking reasonably presentable in my party gear. Of course, by party time my nice clothes would probably be damp and mud-spattered. The other party guests, the ones who hadn't spent part of the day finding a blood-soaked stabbing victim, would have to overlook that.

I didn't see a laundry hamper, so I placed the towels I'd used on the floor beside the sink, neatly folded. Knowing Mrs. Winkleson's staff, I had no doubt that they'd be replaced with fresh ones within minutes of my departure.

I drove my car back to the barns and parked it near Horace's truck. When I strolled into the goat barn, I found four volunteers there gathered around a box. They looked up when they saw me enter.

"Thank goodness you're back!" one of them said. "We have a crisis!"

Chapter 23

A crisis? On top of a real or attempted murder? I braced myself as three of the volunteers surrounded me, waving copies of the show program.

"There's a horrible typo in the program!" one of them shrieked.

"We'll have to throw them away!" the second added,

"We should burn them!" the third exclaimed.

Molly Weston, the fourth volunteer, strolled up in a more leisurely fashion. She was the only one who didn't look panic-stricken.

"There's no time to print a new program," she said, shrugging. "These will have to do."

"There's no need to throw away the whole program over a single typo," I said. If there was only a single typo, I was going to award myself some kind of medal, since I'd done most of the proofing all by myself, despite many calls for help. "If it's something that would confuse people, we can always run off some error sheets."

"We can't possibly use it," one of them said. She held out her program, one finger pointing dramatically to a spot on the page. I read the entry in question: "Category 127: The Winkleson

Trophy for the darkest rose grown or hybridized by the exhibitor. Trophy donated by Mrs. Philomena Wrinkleson."

Oops. Old Wrinkles wasn't going to like that.

A pity that instead of my suggestion of a one-page, black-and-white photocopied program they'd opted for a much longer, saddle-stitched booklet with a four-color picture of a rose on the cover. It was beautiful, but there was no way to do a reprint by tomorrow.

"She'll be furious," one of the volunteers said.

"She'll have to deal with it," Molly said. "We got the name right on the first line, so it's obviously just a silly typo."

Or was it? I dug into my tote bag and found the two-inch-thick folder in which I kept all the paperwork about the show. I leafed through the papers until I found my copy of the printer's proof. I'd kept a copy because I'd found and corrected two typos, and meant to demand a discount from the Caerphilly Quick Print Shop if the corrections hadn't been made.

I checked. My corrections had been made. Then I flipped the proof to the page with the offending entry.

"Just as I thought," I said. "That typo was not there when I proofed the program earlier this week."

The three agitated volunteers crowded around to inspect the proof.

"Then how could it possibly have gone so wrong?" one wailed.

"Clearly, someone at the print shop doesn't like Mrs. Winkleson," Molly said. "Nothing we can do about it now."

This viewpoint visibly upset the three other volunteers.

"Actually, I can think of something that would help," I said. "Hand me one of those."

I pulled a black felt tip pen out of my tote bag and carefully made a small black spot that completely covered the R and I in Wrinkleson, along with a little bit of the W and the N.

"There," I said. "R's a pretty narrow letter. You might not even guess that there are two letters covered instead of one. Looks like what would happen if you had a dirty spot on the printing plate."

The volunteers inspected my work and cheered up significantly.

"Of course, someone would have to make little fake ink blots on all the programs we pass out," Molly said. "Just doesn't seem that important to me."

"Or me," I said. "But if anyone wants to work on it . . ."

The three volunteers eagerly accepted black felt tip pens from my tote and hauled the box off into a corner.

"Silly things," Molly said to me, in an undertone. "But everything else is in pretty good shape. I'm going home to change for the cocktail party."

"Already?" I said. But when I glanced at my watch, I realized it was five o'clock. Where had the day gone? Well, at least it was so late that my party clothes wouldn't get too messed up after all.

"You need anything, just holler," Molly said. "See you at the party."

I took a quick tour through both barns. They looked ready for tomorrow. In the show barn, row after row of tables covered with spotless white tablecloths stood ready to receive the entries. The little black and white plastic category tags were all in place along the front edges of the tables. At the far end of the room was the table where the winners would be displayed. A few of the trophies were already on display there, mainly ones that had no great material value. The rest of the trophies, including all the silver cups, gold medals, Waterford bowls, and other objects that a thief might find of interest, were still locked up at my house. I checked my notebook to make sure "load trophies" was on my action list for the morning.

In the other barn the tables were covered with white plastic tablecloths, and each already held a dozen large and half a dozen small glass vases. At the far end, several tables held more regimented rows of vases, along with a supply of tags, black pens, and other paraphernalia that the exhibitors might need while prepping their roses.

In one corner was a table that I hoped wouldn't still be there in the morning. At it, the three volunteers sat, laboriously blotting out the offending extra R from Mrs. Winkleson's name. I paused by their table.

They had one program—possibly the one on which I'd demonstrated the ink blot technique—propped up in front of them and were referring to it constantly. How hard can it be to fake an ink blot? But I suppose they wanted to make sure the ink blots were sufficiently identical to be plausible. It looked as if they'd completed about thirty programs, and a nearby trashcan contained the crumpled or torn up remains of at least that many. At this rate, they'd be here all night.

"When you're ready to leave, could you call Mr. Darby to lock up behind you?" I said. I pulled a piece of torn-up program out of the trash can and wrote his cell phone number on it.

"Of course," one of them said. "In fact, we were going to

knock off very soon, put in a token appearance at the party, and take the rest of these home to finish tonight."

"Great," I said. I think I even managed to sound as if I meant it. Someone had abducted a harmless animal, someone—possibly the same someone—had killed an equally harmless woman, and they were worried about a silly typo.

Time for me to go home and collapse. Or time for me to spruce up a bit and make my own token appearance at the party. I was leaning toward the former. But maybe I'd feel better by the time I drove up to the house. And then—

My cell phone rang.

"Meg?" It was Horace. "Um . . . we could use some help over here."

Chapter 24

"What kind of help?" I asked. And where are you."

"We're in the goat pa—I mean at the crime scene," Horace said. "It's kind of hard to explain."

"What's wrong?" I asked. "Didn't Mr. Darby remove the goats?"

"Yes, thanks. But you know those giant mutant black swans Mrs. Winkleson has on her pond?"

"They're not giant mutant swans. That's the size swans usually are," I said. "Just keep your distance from them."

"That's what I told Dr. Smoot," Horace said. "But one of them just showed up here at our crime scene and he tried to shoo it away."

"Bad idea."

"Yeah, we noticed. Is there something we can do to make them go away?"

"Is Mr. Darby still around?"

"No, he left with the goats."

Just then I saw Mr. Darby stumble by the open door of the barn.

"Hang on," I said. "Mr. Darby!"

He waved, and strolled inside. I put my phone on speaker.

"I took care of the goats," he said. "I'm heading back to——"

"We have another small problem," I said. "Now it's the swans menacing the crime scene. How can we make them go away?"

"I don't know," he said. "I've never tried. Evil monsters, those swans. The only thing to do is wait until they go away on their own. I told you that when one of them was sitting on your car, remember?"

"Did you get that, Horace?" I asked.

"Yes, but we can't just wait for it to leave. It knocked Dr. Smoot down, and it's still standing on top of him. He thinks his arm is broken. Dr. Smoot, that is."

I looked back at Mr. Darby, who shook his head hopelessly.

I closed my eyes and took a deep breath.

"Meg?"

"Snopes.com will love hearing about this," I said, as I opened my eyes. "I understand there's some debate over whether a swan actually can break a human arm."

"This won't help," Horace said. "It did knock him down, but the broken arm is probably from the fall. But even a much smaller bird could put an eye out with its beak. I'm not going near it."

"Good point," I said. "Stand by. You know that gate going into the pasture?" I said, turning to Mr. Darby. "Is it big enough to drive a vehicle through?"

He nodded.

"Come with me."

I dashed outside and found that, as usual, Horace had left his keys in his truck. I started it and waited impatiently until Mr. Darby ambled over and got up into the passenger seat.

"When we get there, you open the gate."

He nodded and I put the truck into gear, lurching down a muddy dirt road. When we got to the gate, Mr. Darby stepped out to open it. When he'd closed it after me, he stayed on the outside and leaned against the fence instead of getting back in the cab. I tried not to take that as a vote of no confidence in my rescue plan.

The truck lurched violently as I steered toward the end of the field where I could see Horace and Sammy, waving pitchforks at a black swan. The swan was sitting on a black lump—presumably Dr. Smoot in his cape—and paid no attention to them, apart from occasionally rising slightly to flap its enormous wings.

As I drew near, Horace got careless with the pitchfork and the bird swatted it aside as if it were a toothpick.

When I was about ten feet from the swan, I rolled the window down a few inches.

"Stand by to rescue Dr. Smoot," I said. "I'm going to try to push the swan away."

"But you'll run over Dr. Smoot!" Horace exclaimed.

"Tell Smoot to lie as flat as possible," I said. "Your truck's probably got enough ground clearance to miss him."

"Probably?" came a voice from under the swan.

I began easing the truck forward. The swan didn't like it. When I was five feet away, it stood up and began flapping its wings furiously. I kept inching forward as slowly as I could. Another foot, and the swan fluttered up into the air and landed on the truck's windshield.

"Grab Smoot!" I shouted, as I shifted into reverse and began backing up as fast as I could without dislodging the swan. After all, I didn't want to hurt it—just get it away from Dr. Smoot.

I couldn't see if anyone was following my orders. The entire windshield was filled with swan. I had no idea if a swan could break the glass with its beak or wings, and I wasn't eager to find out. Luckily the swan wasn't, either. It just continued to stand on the hood, flapping its wings and uttering menacing cries.

"If you'd just stay on the lake where you belong, we wouldn't have to upset you like this," I told the swan.

I was getting close to the fence. I turned as I reached it, and cruised along the fence line until I could see where the others were. Then I slowed down to an almost imperceptible crawl. The swan was getting calmer, and I was almost getting used to driving backwards, using the rearview mirror instead of the windshield.

I saw Sammy vaulting over the fence. Off on a useful errand, I hoped.

"Just drive it on into the field," Mr. Darby was calling after him. He and Horace were hovering over Dr. Smoot. Sammy was fetching transportation. Good.

"They did it," Dr. Smoot said. "The swans!"

"Yes, we know," Horace said, in his most soothing tones. "But don't worry, we'll get you to the hospital in no time."

"You don't understand," Dr. Smoot said. He sat up, looking very pale but determined. "One of them must be the murderer!"

"Attempted murderer," Horace said, automatically. He and Mr. Darby looked at each other and then back at Dr. Smoot.

"Just how do you figure that?" Horace asked.

"Perhaps they're not really swans," Dr. Smoot said. "Perhaps they're possessed."

"They're possessed all right," Mr. Darby put in. "But they haven't killed anyone yet, that I know of."

"That you know of," Dr. Smoot said. "Just wait. You'll see."

"How could they possibly have stabbed someone in the back with a pair of shears?" Horace asked. "It's not as if they have prehensile wings."

"Maybe they attacked someone who was holding the shears and they fell down on the point," Dr. Smoot suggested.

"Doesn't seem likely from what I saw of the wound," Horace said.

"You're not a doctor!" Dr. Smoot snapped. "Wait till my autopsy! I'll show you!"

"We don't know for sure there will be an autopsy," I pointed out.

"Right," Horace said. From the look on his face, I could tell Horace was having the same thought I was. How wise was it to entrust any autopsy to a medical examiner with a preconceived notion of how the murder had been committed, and by whom? Not to mention a grudge against his prime suspect?

"We'll keep that possibility in mind," Horace said. I could tell from his tone that he was humoring Dr. Smoot. Dr. Smoot could probably tell, too.

"I'm sure they're responsible!" he exclaimed. "Just look at how bloodthirsty they are!"

"They're just being very territorial because it's mating season," Mr. Darby said.

"Mating season?" Horace echoed. "You mean there are apt to be more of them soon? What a horrible thought."

Just then Sammy appeared, driving Dr. Smoot's vintage

Pierce-Arrow hearse. Sammy and Horace helped the patient into the back compartment. It would have creeped me out, but Dr. Smoot was smiling happily in spite of his pain. The hearse was a new toy, and he was very proud of it. As Sammy drove slowly off, Horace and Mr. Darby turned their attention to me. I was still cruising gently backwards around the perimeter of the goat pasture. The swan had settled down and was now merely sitting on the hood with its head lifted up as if it enjoyed the breeze.

"Um . . . Meg?" Horace called. "Do you have any idea how you're going to get that swan off my truck?"

I was more interested in getting myself out of the truck without injury, but I hadn't yet come up with any bright ideas for achieving either goal.

The truck shuddered as I hit some obstacle too low to be seen in the rearview mirror, and I could hear a clanging noise that I assumed was part of the truck getting knocked off.

"You know, you don't have to drive backwards," Horace said. "You could turn it around and drive forwards. You'd be a little less likely to run into things."

"No, I'd be more likely to run into things," I said. "I can't see a thing out the windshield except vast expanses of swan."

"You could open the window and lean out," Mr. Darby suggested.

I pressed the button to lower the driver's side window an inch or so. The swan instantly scrabbled at the opening, but fortunately his beak was a little too large to get in. After several minutes of trying, he gave up, but continued to stare at the window as if daring me to open it wider.

"Bad idea," I said. "Any other suggestions?"

"Flap the windshield wipers," Horace suggested. "Give him a little hint."

"Good idea," Mr. Darby said.

I turned the wipers on at the lowest speed. The swan reacted with instant fury, ripping the driver's side wiper off instantly. I flipped the wipers off again.

"Also a bad idea," I called back. "Sorry."

The swan scrabbled at the passenger side wiper for a bit until he figured how to remove that one and fling it aside as well. Then he sat down on the hood and looked from side to side as we lurched along.

"He looks calmer," Mr. Darby said.

Calm wasn't the word I'd have used. To me, he looked as if he'd found slaying the windshield wipers highly therapeutic, and was patiently awaiting the opportunity to wreak more havoc on any other target that presented itself. I didn't fancy being a target.

I continued cruising slowly backwards around the pasture and had almost reached the gate before another idea struck me.

"Let's take your truck closer to the lake," I said. "That's where the swan belongs. Horace, why don't you go on ahead and warn me if I'm about to hit anything."

"Okay," Horace said. He didn't sound too happy.

"Mr. Darby," I said. "Do you have any idea what sort of food would attract the swan?"

"I'm sorry," he said. "I really haven't had much time to learn about the swans. She's only had them a few years."

A few years? I'd have bet anything that he would learn all

about any new mammal arriving on the farm within a few days. Clearly birds weren't quite his thing.

"That's all right," I said. "See if you can find Dr. Blake and Caroline. They should be able to help."

"Right," he said, striding off.

"And can you check to see that the volunteers have gone, and if they have, lock the barn doors?" I called after him.

"Right."

With Horace marching in front of me to clear the way, I made my way slowly down the road toward the house. Unfortunately, people were starting to arrive for the party, and they began stacking up behind me. Since we could only move at the pace Horace could manage, walking backwards in his gorilla suit, we were at the head of a considerable parade by the time we passed the bottom of the marble steps leading to the house. I drove on past the steps, followed the road down to the shore of the lake, and parked near the dock.

"I'll go up to the house and see what Dr. Blake suggests," Horace said.

"Thanks," I called back. I settled down to wait. Maybe my grandfather would have some plan for coaxing the swan off the truck. Or maybe the swan would eventually get tired and go for a swim.

I settled down to wait it out. At least I had a great excuse for skipping the cocktail party. I closed my eyes and was just dropping off to sleep when my cell phone rang.

It was Michael.

Chapter 25

"Hello, beautiful," he said. "How are you? And how are the rose show preparations going?"

"The preparations are done, at least what could be done today," I said. "Which is a good thing, because right now I'm being held hostage by a swan."

A pause.

"A real swan? Or is this one of your cousin Horace's friends?"

"A real swan. Dr. Smoot thinks it's the murderer, but the rest of us aren't buying it. It's just mating season."

"The swan is holding you hostage because it's mating season? I'm liking this less and less."

"Don't worry, they're not after *me*, they're just defending their territory. And actually, this is the most peace and quiet I've had all afternoon."

I gave him the Cliff Notes version of my day. As we talked, the swan grew quiet. Maybe a little too quiet. The last thing I wanted was for the silly thing to go to sleep on the hood of Horace's truck. And where was Horace with the rescue party anyway?

"So how much longer are you going to sit around watching the swan?" Michael asked.

"That depends on how much longer the swan stays," I said. "I'm in no hurry. If I escape in time to get to the cocktail party, I'll have to be polite to Mrs. Winkleson, and I'm not sure I can."

"You'd think the shock of having someone try to kill her would slow her down a bit," he said. "On top of the shock of having her dog abducted."

"Not her. She seems more outraged than terrified by the attempted murder, and the dog hardly registers on her emotional barometer. I think I'm more upset about it than she is. Which reminds me. While you're there could you bring me—"

"What? Sorry," Michael said. "I've got to sign off. Curtain's going up."

"Now? It's only six. I thought Broadway shows started at eight."

"Yeah, but this is way, way off Broadway, and apparently they have to start it this early to get us out by midnight. I'll call you when it's over."

With that, he hung up. I settled back into my seat and contemplated the swan. Even though it was still a couple of hours till sunset, the swan had tucked its head under its wing and appeared to be going to sleep.

I watched it for another fifteen minutes. No movement.

I pulled the keys out of the ignition and gently cracked open the door.

No reaction from the swan.

I eased the door open, slid down from the truck, and pushed the door almost closed. I figured actually closing it wasn't essential. Even if the dozen or so police officers on the premises didn't deter potential thieves, the swan would be standing sentry.

I backed carefully away from the truck. In fact, I backed until I rounded a corner and was out of sight. Then I turned around and walked briskly the rest of the way to the house, looking over my shoulder anxiously every minute or two.

I found myself wondering whether the swans' aggressiveness could have anything to do with Mimi's disappearance. If the dog had gotten loose and ventured into the swans' territory . . .

I decided not to think about that possibility. At least not until I could ask someone knowledgeable, like Dad, or Dr. Blake, whether swans had been known to attack small mammals.

When I got to the marble steps, I saw Dr. Smoot's vintage hearse parked there. Puzzling. Why not just take him to the hospital in that? And an ambulance had joined it. The back doors of the ambulance were open, and the two EMTs were sitting inside, nibbling hors d'oeuvres from white porcelain plates.

"What's going on?" I asked. "Didn't Dr. Smoot go to the hospital?"

"Nope," one EMT said. "They called us, and when we got here, he wanted to wait until your father could look at the arm before he went."

"Isn't Dad still at the hospital with Mrs. Sechrest?"

The EMT shrugged.

"Dr. Smoot seemed to think he was here, or would be before too long," the other EMT said. "You ask me, he's just putting it off as long as possible."

"Doctors make the worst patients," the first EMT said.

"Is it possible that his arm isn't broken after all?" I asked.

"Oh, no, it's broken all right," the first EMT said.

"But he gave himself a painkiller, so he's in no hurry," the second said.

"Doctors get the best meds," said the first EMT.

"He's up at the party," the second EMT added,

Wonderful. After all my efforts to evict the swan so Horace could rush Dr. Smoot and his broken arm to the hospital, the idiot was up here at the house. Probably eating hors d'oeuvres and swilling champagne, stupid as that was on top of painkillers.

A tiny maid carrying a tray was carefully descending the marble stairs.

"Would you like some crab croquettes?" she asked us. "Or melon balls wrapped in Black Forest ham?"

The EMTs refilled their plates. I started up the stairs.

"If you see Smoot, remind him that we're only going to stick around as long as we don't get any other calls," the first EMT said. "If we have to leave, he's on his own for a ride to the hospital."

"Right," I called over my shoulder.

"And could you send the guy with the champagne down here again?" the second EMT asked.

Chapter 26

Marston actually smiled as he bowed me into the foyer. I hung my umbrella and rain parka on one of the folding racks they'd set up to supplement the wrought-iron coat stand, and strolled into the living room

The cocktail party was in full swing. It was reasonably well attended, though it took a few moments for me to realize that. Mother and Dad's farmhouse would have been full to overflowing, but a mere hundred or so people hardly made a dent in the space available in Mrs. Winkleson's cavernous living room, although they did tend to cluster together in the center, as if for warmth. To my relief, almost all of them were dressed in black, gray, or white. Mostly black. I wondered how much of this was in deference to Mrs. Winkleson's dictates and how much was due to the murder. Or attempted murder. I still didn't know. I'd been too busy all afternoon to check on the status of the victim.

"Champagne?"

A tuxedoed waiter held out a tray full of sparkling champagne flutes. He didn't look old enough to drive, much less serve drinks, but then lately more and more of the college students looked that way to me, and the garden club was using a catering service that mostly hired students.

"Thanks," I said, taking a glass. "How's the party going?"

"Oh, fine," he said. "Now, anyway."

"Was it not going fine before?"

He looked around as if in search of an exit, and then swallowed hard.

"You know the lady who owns the house?" he asked.

"All too well," I said. "What's she done now?"

"She kind of had it out with my boss earlier."

I winced.

"It's okay," he said. "It was before most of the guests arrived, and one of the other ladies broke it up. That lady."

He gestured with his head at Mother. She was dressed in an elegant black silk dress with a pouf of white chiffon on one shoulder, and a pair of high-heeled black shoes so simple and understated that I didn't even want to imagine their price.

"What were they arguing about?" I asked.

The waiter shrugged.

"No idea, but if I'm ever in trouble, I want her on my side," he said, looking approvingly at Mother.

Just then Mother looked up, and saw us. She smiled, waved, and said a few words to the people she was with, then turned and headed our way. Standing still, she had been a vision of monochromatic glamour, but as soon as she took a step, a little pleat in her skirt opened to reveal a flash of scarlet satin from waist to hem. I hoped I was around when Mrs. Winkleson noticed the red, especially if she tried to give Mother a hard time about it. Since I didn't remember ever seeing that dress before, I wondered if Mother had had it made specially to annoy Mrs. Winkleson. I wouldn't put it past her. Mother enjoyed guerilla warfare with fashion and decorating.

"Hello, dear." She gave me a quick kiss on the cheek. "Everything going well?" she asked the waiter.

"Fine, thanks to you, ma'am," he said, and slipped away.

"I gather Mrs. Winkleson has been terrorizing the caterers?" I said,

"I'm astonished that no one has tried to murder that woman before," Mother said, frowning. "And I don't think I will ever forgive the murderer for botching things up so badly and mistaking Mrs. Sechrest for Mrs. Winkleson. Such a lovely woman. Quiet. Well-mannered."

"Murderer?" I repeated. "She didn't make it, then?"

Mother shook her head.

"Be kind to your father, dear. You know how hard he takes it when he loses a patient."

"Even one who was probably already dead before she became his patient," I said. "I know. Where is he?"

Mother pointed. Dad was standing with three other garden club members, but he didn't really look as if he cared about the conversation.

"Look," I said. "I know the whole thing with the manure was exasperating, but—"

"Don't worry, dear," she said. "In the face of something like what happened today, such small, petty quarrels seem very silly, don't they?"

I nodded, and sipped my champagne, feeling an enormous sense of relief wash over me.

"Besides," she went on, "he promised never to mulch the roses again without checking with me first." She beamed in Dad's direction.

"Where are Caroline and my grandfather, anyway?" I asked, as I looked around. "I was hoping they'd help rescue me from the swan."

"From the what?"

"Long story," I said. "They don't seem to be here."

"They *said* they were both tired and going home to rest." Mother's emphasis on the word "said" might have been unnoticeable to someone else, but I could tell she was skeptical. "They said to tell you that Spike was fine and they were taking him home with them."

"So where do you think they really went?"

She shrugged.

"Following a lead, I gather, from something I wasn't supposed to overhear. I have no idea what."

"A lead?" I echoed. "They're taking an interest in the murder? That's odd. I'd have bet you could slaughter any number of humans without unsettling them, as long as you didn't alarm any animals in the process."

"No doubt," Mother said. "But in spite of everything they've seen today, they're still convinced that there's some animal welfare issue here at Mrs. Winkleson's, and they're off following their lead. It may not have anything to do with the murder, if that makes you feel better."

"Not appreciably," I said. "But thanks."

"Dr. Rutledge is driving them," she said.

"Then it's definitely animal welfare, not the murder," I said, with a sigh. Our local vet was probably as passionate about animal welfare as Caroline and my grandfather. "Maybe he'll keep them out of trouble."

"I'm sure he will."

I wasn't so sure, but I kept my doubts to myself.

Mother spotted some new arrivals and went to greet them. I strolled over to talk to Dad, who detached himself from the other guests when he saw me.

"She didn't make it," he said.

"Mother told me," I said. "I'm sorry."

"She never really had a chance. So what are your thoughts on the case?"

"That we should be staying out of Chief Burke's hair so he can solve it," I said. "At least until after we get this rose show over with," I added, seeing his disappointed look.

"Poor Sandy," he said, with a sigh. "The miniature rose categories will be pretty sparse without her."

"But not the entries for the Winkleson Trophy," I said. Not that I cared, but maybe I could distract him. "Who else is entering? Besides you and Mrs. Winkleson, of course."

"We won't really know till tomorrow," he said. "Most of the rose club members have been saying they don't have anything worth entering. But of course, everyone's going to say that before the show, about nearly every category. You don't want to jinx things."

"Don't you pretty much know who else is hybridizing?" I asked.

"Yes, but the way she worded the trophy language, it's an odd category. The seedling class is for roses hybridized or found by the exhibitor, and in most shows, every other class requires that you enter only roses that are of ARS approved varieties. The Winkleson Trophy is for the darkest rose grown *or* hybridized by the exhibitor. Very unusual. Not ARS approved."

"Why word it that way, then?"

"I don't know," he said. "Molly Weston's theory was that Mrs. Winkleson was hedging her bets. Making sure she could enter a commercially available rose if her own hybridizing efforts didn't pan out."

"She's probably right," I said. "So that means even if Matilda is darker than any of the other new hybrids, you could all be beaten out by someone who has a particularly good specimen of, say, Black Magic."

"Precisely," Dad said. Then he frowned. "Have you heard someone talking about their Black Magic roses? That's one of the darkest around, you know. I've been using some of them for my breeding stock."

"Mrs. Winkleson has some in her rose beds," I said.

"You've seen her rose beds?" Dad asked eagerly. "She hasn't let anyone from the garden club see them."

"Apparently she's a little paranoid," I said. "She's got them locked behind a twelve-foot chain link fence with razor wire on top."

"Oh, my."

"Keeps the deer and goats from eating them."

"I can understand that," Dad said. "I may have to move my roses farther from the house so I can put up a fence tall enough to keep the deer out."

"You can't just fence them in where they are?"

"Your mother isn't keen on the idea. Not very aesthetic. Though now that they've attacked my last Matilda bush, she might feel differently."

"Did the deer definitely kill the bush?" I asked. "Or just eat all the flowers you could possibly have exhibited tomorrow?"

"They may not have killed it outright," he said. "But they did so much damage that it's going to be touch and go whether it survives. And it's the only Matilda bush I have left. The deer got the other two last fall, back when I was still calling her hybrid number L2005-0013. Ripped them out, roots and all, and ate every bit."

He shook his head sadly.

"Mrs. Winkleson isn't taking any chances on that happening to her roses," I said. "I wouldn't bet on your odds of getting her to let you inside, but you could probably learn more than I could peering through the fence. I can see taking stern measures to keep out the deer and goats, but why would she be so protective of her rose garden that she'd take such extreme measures to keep everybody out?"

"Maybe she's growing them indoors," Dad suggested.

"Is that a problem?"

"It is if she's exhibiting them in a show," he said. "Against the rules. You can only enter roses grown outdoors. And if she's growing her entries in a greenhouse, she wouldn't want anyone in her garden to see what is and isn't there."

"True," I said. "But I haven't seen any signs of a greenhouse. Just rows and rows of roses. Are there any other rules she could be breaking?"

Dad thought about it for a moment.

"Hard to say," he said, finally. "Can you show me where her rose garden is?"

"Now? I doubt if I can find it in the dark."

"Tomorrow, then."

"It might work better if you got Mr. Darby to show you," I said. "I was lost when I found it. I keep getting lost whenever I try to go somewhere on this place, and I'm not a hundred percent sure I could find my way back."

We both looked around and spotted Mr. Darby. I was relieved to see that he looked less disheveled than he had earlier. He was standing toward one side of the room near the bar, sipping a glass of water and eyeing the crab croquettes on his plate with distrust. A meat and potatoes man, no doubt.

"You know him better than I do," Dad said.

"I'll ask him."

"Be careful," Dad said. He looked around as if making sure there was no one near enough to overhear him. "Caroline and your grandfather are very suspicious of Mr. Darby."

"They think he killed Mrs. Sechrest? Thinking he was killing Mrs. Winkleson, perhaps?"

"Well, no," he said. "But they're still mighty concerned about whether there's some kind of animal neglect or abuse going on."

"By Mr. Darby?" I shook my head. "If it was just Mrs.

Winkleson here, I'd worry about the animals, big time. To her they're just decorative accessories. But at least she's hired Mr. Darby and given him free rein, and he seems quite concerned about them."

"Yes—seems," Dad said. "Pop and Caroline wonder if he's really that concerned, or if he's just pretending because he recognized them. Maybe he suspected they were conducting an investigation into the animals' welfare."

"He seems genuine to me," I said. Of course, I was no expert. And wasn't it Clarence Rutledge, the animals' vet, who first suggested Dr. Blake's investigation?

"Talk to him," Dad said.

I nodded and strolled across the room toward our suspect, snagging a second glass of champagne as I went. Mr. Darby looked almost pleased to see me.

Chapter 27

"Evening," Mr. Darby said. "Do you know how much longer this shindig's going to last?"

No hint of bourbon on his breath any longer, and he wasn't slurring. I breathed a sigh of relief.

"The party's only supposed to last until eight," I said. "The rose exhibitors want to make an early night of it. Most of them will be up before dawn, getting their roses ready. In fact, I only see about half of them here, so maybe a lot of them are planning to work all night and have already started."

"Nice to have a reason to stay home," he said. He'd made an effort to dress up for the party, in a slightly more formal version of the clothes I'd seen him in earlier: clean black jeans, a clean white shirt, and a black corduroy jacket. But he was visibly marking time until he could escape. He reminded me of a wild animal who'd found his way into a crowd of humans.

It occurred to me that he was one of the most likely suspects in Mrs. Sechrest's murder. He had motive—against Mrs. Winkleson, of course—and he'd had enough time after he left me to commit the murder and get clear before I found the body, and he certainly had the strength to commit the stabbing. He could well have had access to the shears if Mrs. Winkleson was the one who'd swiped them.

But instead of feeling suspicious, I felt sorry for him.

"Any chance that you could show my dad where Mrs. Winkleson's rose beds are tomorrow? I know you can't let him in or anything, but he seems to think maybe he could learn something useful just from looking at them."

"If you like," he said, sounding dubious.

"And does she have any greenhouses?" I asked. "Dad's thinking of having a greenhouse built over at the farm, and he's very keen to look at what other people have done."

"No greenhouses," Mr. Darby said, with a shudder. "Thank goodness you asked me instead of her. I hate it when she gets some new idea that's going to cause a lot of fuss and bother for everyone."

Meaning him and the animals, I suspected.

"I know what you mean," I said aloud. "If I ever find out who gave Dad the idea of building a greenhouse, I'll give them a piece of my mind."

He smiled slightly, then took a sip of his water and looked around nervously.

"Hey, if you like, I could think of some urgent job that has to be done to keep the rose show on track," I said. "Something that would give you an excuse to leave the party early."

"Thanks," he said, with a faint smile. "I'll stick it out, for a while anyway. But there is something you could do for me. If you would."

"Happy to try," I said.

"There's something I should have told Chief Burke. But I didn't dare."

"Why not?"

"I couldn't possibly, in front of Mrs. Winkleson," he said. "I'd lose my job. In fact, I'd still lose my job if I told him now and she found out. But you could tell him, and pretend you overheard it from one of the other rose growers or something. Keep my name out of it."

"Tell him what?" I wasn't going to promise anything until I heard what his hot information was.

He glanced left and right as if to make sure no one was within earshot. I stifled an exasperated sigh. Any savvy eavesdropper in the room would recognize the gesture immediately and begin creeping closer to overhear.

"She knew Sandy Sechrest a lot better than she's letting on," he said, almost too softly to be heard. "Most of the time she wouldn't let anyone near the roses, except a couple of the garden staff who don't speak much English. But the last three or four months, when she needed some kind of help with the roses, she'd call Mrs. Sechrest."

I pondered this.

"So what does this have to do with the murder? Do you think the killer really meant to kill Mrs. Sechrest?"

"No," he said, frowning. "Why would anyone want to kill her? Mrs. Winkleson, now . . ."

"Yes, no shortage of suspects there. But I still don't get the relevance."

"She lied. About how well she knew Mrs. Sechrest. And you

know why? Because she didn't want to admit that she doesn't know diddly about roses. For months, Mrs. Sechrest was over here every few days, and she'd pretty much move in the last few days before a rose show."

"Mrs. Sechrest was doing all the real work?"

He nodded.

"It's probably what killed her, you know?" he said. "She was over here so often that she'd figured out it kept Mrs. Winkleson happier if she wore black. After the first couple of times, she never showed up in anything but black. Maybe if she'd said the hell with what the old harpy wants and worn pink, she'd still be alive. Wearing black, and being almost as short as Mrs. Winkleson. That's what got her killed, right? But of course, Mrs. Winkleson wouldn't want anyone to know that her stupid rule cost someone her life. It's all her fault!"

Myself, I'd give the person who actually wielded the secateurs a little of the blame, but I didn't feel the need to bring that up.

"I guess that would be why Mrs. Sechrest came in the back way," I said aloud. "So none of the other exhibitors would see her and suspect she was helping Mrs. Winkleson."

"Maybe," he said. "Then again, she lives over by Clayville. The back way turns in off the Clayville Road, so it saves her a good ten miles each way. I use the back way myself sometimes, when I go to visit family."

"So she might use it even if she wasn't trying to sneak in?"

He nodded.

I wondered, briefly, if Mrs. Sechrest's knowledge of the back entrance made her a suspect in the dognapping. Of course, she probably wasn't the only one who knew.

"You should tell the chief all this," I said.

His face froze.

"But I'll see if I can come up with a way to get the information to him without involving you."

"Thanks," he said. "Maybe I'll take you up on that offer to give me an excuse to leave. Oh, by the way, I have something for you."

He dug into his pocket and pulled out a ring with two large keys on it.

"This one's for the cow barn, and this one's for the goat and sheep barn," he said. They looked identical, but I didn't complain. It wouldn't seriously delay me if I had to try both keys to open the first barn.

"I'll probably be there to let you in, of course, but just in case."

"Thanks," I said, as I attached the ring to my own keys.

"Which reminds me, I should check the barns. Make sure they're all secure."

"I would appreciate it if you did," I said.

He smiled briefly, and began slipping along the edge of the room toward the hallway.

"Where is that nice Mr. Darby going?" Mother asked, appearing at my elbow.

"To make sure the barns are secure," I said.

"Very sweet of him. Here, dear." She handed me a plate of assorted hors d'oeuvres. "You look starved."

"Thanks," I said. "But I don't want any crab croquettes. You know I can't eat crab."

"Give them to your father, then."

"And are there shrimps in the egg rolls?"

"I didn't interrogate the waiters, dear," she said. "Just try it."

She sailed off. I looked at the plate with suspicion. Was it too much to ask of my own mother, after more than thirty years of knowing me, that she not try to feed me seafood? She had the curious idea that my allergy to shellfish was either psychosomatic or something I should have outgrown by now.

I put the crab croquettes on an empty plate on a side table. I was teasing apart a little pastry to see if I could trust the contents when I overheard a scrap of conversation that caught my attention.

". . . of course it's very peculiar that it was Sandy who got killed," the first woman was saying. "If it was Louise, now. That I could understand."

Chapter 28

I pretended to be studying my hors d'oeuvre more intently than it deserved and angled a little closer to the guests I was eavesdropping on.

"Haven't you heard? Louise and Mrs. Winkleson had a falling out," the other woman said.

"No! When?"

"Sometime last year. Didn't you notice how subdued she was at the last show? Didn't once use the words 'as dear Philomena says.'"

The two giggled slightly, and then glanced around to see if anyone had noticed their breach of the party's funereal decorum.

"So apparently Sandy has become the new acolyte," the first woman went on.

"But why Sandy?" the second woman asked. "I mean, don't get me wrong, she's a lovely person, but . . . well, hardly the go-getter Louise is."

"Ah, but she knows something about hybridizing," the first woman said. "I expect 'dear Philomena' finally figured out that Louise didn't know any more about hybridizing than she did."

"Ah," the other woman echoed. "Then you think Mrs. Winkleson's whole black rose project—"

"Owes a lot more to Sandy than Mrs. Winkleson."

"But what's in it for Sandy?"

"Money, I imagine. She's retired, you know, living on a fixed income, in that dilapidated old house, but lately she's found enough money to fix the place up rather nicely. New furnace, new roof, new siding . . ."

"Well, if she had to put up with old Wrinkles, she earned it," the second woman said. "Did the old bat call to tell you the show was only for white and black roses?"

"Yes," the first woman said. "Not that I believed her, of course."

My temper flared. I needed to have a talk with Mrs. Winkleson about those phone calls she'd been making. Okay, maybe needed was the wrong word. Confronting her was probably a very bad idea. But it would certainly be satisfying.

"Ooh, look," one of the women exclaimed. "There's Louise."

I tried not to be obvious as I turned to see where she was pointing. And I managed not to shout "aha!" when I saw that Louise was one of the two rose growers who'd come so early to help out. Not the one who'd been so angry to learn that multi-colored roses were permitted after all, but the other one. The one I'd first heard using the nickname "old Wrinkles" for Mrs. Winkleson. The one who'd quietly left the barn. Where had she gone? And how long was that before I found Mrs. Sechrest's body, and had I seen Louise at all between then and now? I didn't think so.

Did Louise have anger management issues? Had she sneaked out of the show barns intent on revenging herself on Mrs. Winkleson, only to learn that she'd killed the wrong person?

Then again, if Louise was the killer, was Sandy the wrong person or the right one? The patron who'd rejected her or the new acolyte who'd taken her place? Who could say which one Louise would hate the most?

Okay, this overheard conversation gave a source other than Mr. Darby for the information that Sandy Sechrest had been a frequent visitor to Raven Hill. I looked around to see if Chief Burke was nearby.

I didn't see him. But I did see Sammy slipping out of the living room into the hall. I followed him.

No one was in the hall, not even Sammy. But just as I was turning to go back into the living room, the doorbell rang. Marston and the miniature maids had enough to do, I decided. I opened the door.

Standing outside was a stout, middle-aged man, soberly dressed in a dark-gray pinstriped suit, starched white shirt, and a black and gray striped rep tie. Okay, he knew the dress code. His face was narrow and almost completely chinless, which made his long, ski-jump nose even more startling. He looked at me with surprise, peered over my shoulder as if hoping to see someone else, and then fixed his eyes back on me with a frown.

"May I help you?" I said.

"What's going on here?" he demanded.

"It's a cocktail party," I said. "Were you on the invitation list, Mr. . . . ?"

I pulled my clipboard out of my tote and brandished it, smiling helpfully, as if ready to verify his welcome if he'd only produce a name that matched one on my list.

"Cocktail party!" he exclaimed. "Who authorized that?"

"Mrs. Winkleson," I said. "I gather you're not here for the party, then. Can you tell me why you are here?"

"I'm here to see about the arrangements," he said.

"Arrangements?" I echoed.

"And to assume possession of the house," he said. "I am Theobald Winkleson, nephew to the late Mrs. Philomena Winkleson. Her heir."

One of her heirs would be more accurate, if Marston was correct. "How nice for you," I said aloud. "But as it happens, she isn't the late Mrs. Winkleson. She's very much alive."

"Alive!" he exclaimed. "That can't be."

"I saw her five minutes ago in the living room," I said. "Sipping a Black Russian."

"But we heard—"

"Just what did you hear?" came Chief Burke's voice from over my shoulder.

"That Aunt Philomena had been horribly murdered," Theobald said. "As soon as I heard, I came right away. I drove all the way from Warrenton."

"You'll no doubt be relieved to know that your aunt is fine," the chief said. "A little shaken up, to be sure, at having one of her guests murdered right here on the farm, but physically she's fine. I'm sure she'll be grateful that you rushed to be at her side in her time of trouble."

From the expression on Theobald's face, I suspected he wasn't expecting a warm and affectionate welcome from his aunt. Nor had he expressed relief at hearing she was still alive.

"Perhaps Meg could let your aunt know that you've safely arrived," the chief said. "I'd like to talk to you for a few minutes."

Theobald drew himself up and appeared to be trying to regain his composure.

"Talk to me? Who the devil are you?" he asked.

"I'm sorry," I said. "This is Chief Burke, who's investigating the unfortunate murder that took place here this afternoon."

Theobald turned pale. The chief gestured toward the little side parlor that I assumed he was using as his headquarters, and after a few moments of hesitation, Theobald obediently stumbled toward the door.

"Don't worry about telling Mrs. Winkleson her nephew's here," the chief said, as he turned to follow Theobald. "I'll take care of that in due time."

"So you can see her reaction," I said, nodding. "Roger."

He frowned, and closed the parlor door behind him.

I was staring at the closed door, pondering this new arrival, when a voice at my shoulder startled me.

"So who is that guy, anyway? And do you think he did it?"

Chapter 29

Rob was standing in the doorway. Apparently he'd arrived at the house too late to hear who the newest arrival was, but in time to see the chief escorting him off for questioning.

"Is someone else minding the gate?" I asked him, as he shed his raincoat.

"One of the deputies," he said. "Chief's orders. Okay, if you're not going to tell me who it is, I'll make a guess. He's a reporter, right?"

"No, he's Mrs. Winkleson's nephew," I said.

"Probably tried to knock her off to inherit, then," Rob said, nodding with satisfaction as he snagged a glass of champagne from a passing waiter.

"He's hoping to inherit all right, but he only just got here," I said. "Apparently as soon as he heard the news of the murder, he drove down here from Warrenton, no doubt salivating all the way. He took the news of her non-death hard."

"He didn't just get here," Rob said. "He was hanging about earlier."

"How much earlier?"

Rob took a meditative sip of his drink before answering.

"Just after I took over at the gate. Remember I told you

about this guy who cruised by, slowed down, and then drove on past?"

"The stalker," I said. "I remember."

"That's why I thought he was a reporter, nosing around. I figured maybe he heard something on the police radio and showed up to snoop. I even called Sammy and Horace to warn them, like you said, in case the guy was just going to drive out of sight and sneak in over the fence."

"You're positive it's the same guy?"

"Yeah," he said. "Who could forget that nose?"

"But you didn't let him in?" I asked.

"If I'd let him in, I'd know who he was, because I'd have asked him. The deputy must have let him in after—wait a minute. I just drove up from the gate. If he came to the gate after the chief replaced me, how'd he beat me here?"

I strode over to the door of the chief's interrogation room and knocked.

After a few moments, the chief peeked out.

"I'm busy," he said.

"I know," I said, sticking my toe in the door so he couldn't shut it. "But Rob just told me something you might like to hear as soon as possible."

The chief stepped out into the foyer and Rob began stammering out his story. I hoped the chief realized that the air of guilt Rob always wore when talking to law enforcement was a relic of his wayward past, and not a sign of present guilt.

I heard a small commotion in the living room, so I left them to it and went to see what was happening.

Everything was just as I'd left it, except that Mrs. Winkleson was supervising as Marston and two black-clad male staff wheeled in a new tchotchke and were putting it up for display in a previously empty niche, complete with a pedestal and several spotlights. Or could you still call something a tchotchke if it was more than a yard tall and probably cost several thousand dollars?

The item in question was a swan made entirely of black glass. Beautifully made, I had to admit that. I knew the glassmaker who'd made it. In fact, I'd recommended him to Mrs. Winkleson some months ago, though I had no idea back then why she'd asked for the recommendation. Now, of course, I realized that she had been intent on commissioning a special objet d'art to serve as the Winkleson trophy.

I'd have found the glass swan completely unobjectionable—almost appealing—if not for its size. At six or eight inches tall, it would have been delicate and charming. But at three and a half feet its sheer bulk made it a little overwhelming in spite of the glassmaker's skill. The two burly servants were visibly straining to hoist the thing into its place of honor in the niche. Unless my memory was worse than usual, the niche was a new feature in the room, specially built to contain the glass swan.

All the other rose exhibitors were busily pretending to be oblivious of the trophy, while stealing covetous glances at it when they thought no one was looking.

From the proprietary gleam in Mrs. Winkleson's eye as she gazed on the glass swan, she obviously expected it to leave her living room for only a brief stay in the show barn before returning in triumph to that specially built niche.

I began making my way through the crowd toward her. I

knew, not just from the conversation I'd overheard at the party, but also from snippets of conversation down at the barns, that several other rose growers had also gotten calls from her claiming that the rose show was going to be for white and black roses only. Mother had been so incensed when she heard of Mrs. Winkleson's attempt to subvert the show that she'd recruited two visiting cousins to call all the potential exhibitors to warn them, so odds were Mrs. Winkleson's scheme wouldn't cause too much heartache. But still, someone should confront her about it. I intended to be that someone.

Unfortunately, by the time I reached the trophy niche, she was gone.

The chief reappeared. After a few minutes, I saw Theobald, the nephew, stick his head into the room. He frowned, looked at his watch, and then his head disappeared back into the foyer. Either he was leaving or he'd decided to wait for his aunt in a more private part of the house.

I returned to my previous occupation of floating through the room, greeting the other guests, and mentally assessing each one's potential for wielding the fatal secateurs.

I saw Dr. Smoot sitting in one of the uncomfortable black leather chairs. He was sporting a sling made out of black material and nursing a champagne flute. Not a good idea if he was on pain meds and expecting to undergo some kind of medical treatment for the arm before the night was out. But not my problem. Dad was standing at his side, and they were arguing quietly.

Dr. Smoot appeared to be yielding to Dad's persuasion. He drained the last of his champagne, and then stood up, with some assistance from Dad.

"I won't have it!" bellowed a voice. Mrs. Winkleson. I glanced over to see two garden club ladies hovering nearby. Trying to placate her, I assumed, from their deferential manner. She flicked her hand at them in dismissal, a gesture that reminded me of a bull shooing flies from his rump with his tail while pawing the ground and preparing to charge the matador. I looked around to see who had triggered her bovine ire. Probably the mild-mannered rose grower who'd had the bad luck to show up wearing a candy-pink suit.

Mrs. Winkleson was, of course, fully in compliance with her own dress code, wearing a black brocade suit with a white rose as a corsage, and a lot of sparkly jet jewelry. In one hand she held a plate with a couple of crab puffs on it, and in the other an old-fashioned glass containing her usual black Russian. As I watched, she glanced down at her plate with an expression of slight annoyance on her face. Perhaps she regretted not demanding that the caterers dye the crab puffs black. Or perhaps she wished she had a hand free to smite the lady in pink.

I strolled over toward her. The lady in pink was clearly shrinking from confrontation, and I was in the mood for it.

"Mrs. Winkleson," I said.

She turned around and frowned at me. The lady in pink glanced at me and began backing away from us. Was it my tone of voice? The look on my face? The look on Mrs. Winkleson's?

"I can see you two have a lot to talk about," the lady in pink said. "Oh, look! More crab puffs!" She scuttled away.

"What is it?" Mrs. Winkleson asked.

"I found out you were calling some of the exhibitors and telling them that the show was for black and white roses only."

"Well, it should have been," she said. "And it would have been if a few more of the committee had been sensible enough to vote with me."

"A few more? The vote was forty-seven to one," I said. "You were the only person who wanted to restrict the show to black and white."

"Lower your tone!" she said. "How dare you raise your voice to me!"

My temper flared at that. I hadn't raised my voice. I'd been careful to keep my tone conversational. She, on the other hand, was practically shouting. Conversations around the room had died down abruptly, and people had begun turning around to watch our clash.

"I haven't raised my voice," I said, still at my normal volume. "I'd be happy to show you what a raised voice sounds like, though, if you don't stop shouting at me."

"How dare you! You have no right to—"

"How dare I? How dare you try to sabotage the other competitors by calling them up and lying to them—"

"I wasn't lying—"

"Telling them that the rose show was restricted to only black and white roses when either that hadn't yet been voted on or, worse, had already been voted down by the committee? I call that lying, and I think some of the competitors affected would be within their rights to file a protest in any category where they weren't able to exhibit a rose because of your calls!"

"It's my house," she said. "And my barns—"

"But it's not your rose show," I said. Okay, by now I was raising my voice. Quite a lot. From hanging around with Michael,

I'd picked up a few things he tried to teach his drama students, like pointers about speaking from the diaphragm to project my voice without straining or sounding shrill. Everyone in the room was unabashedly staring, and if I tried a little harder, people in the next county would be able to hear. Mrs. Winkleson flinched. Clearly she wasn't used to people responding in kind when she shouted at them. She looked as if she wanted to back away, but she stood her ground and bit savagely into a crab puff instead.

"You knew when you agreed to let the garden club hold the show here that people would be bringing flowers that didn't fit your silly black and white color scheme," I said. "If you couldn't live with that, you should have told the garden club to find some other venue."

"I still could," she said, through the remnants of the crab puff. She raised her glass and took a healthy slug of its contents to wash the hors d'oeuvre down. "And what's more—"

Her eyes suddenly bugged out, and she dropped her plate and glass to clutch at her throat.

"What's wrong?" I asked.

"Does she need the Heimlich maneuver?" someone asked.

"Ois!" Mrs. Winkleson gasped, just before she fell to the floor and began writhing in agony.

"What does she mean, 'Ois'?" someone asked.

"She means poison," I said. "Dad!"

Chapter 30

I turned around to find Dad, but he was already falling onto his knees beside Mrs. Winkleson.

"Call an ambulance," he said.

"We have one already," I said. "For Dr. Smoot. Rob! Go fetch the EMTs! Last time I looked they were out front, stuffing themselves on hors d'oeuvres."

Rob, who had turned a delicate shade of green while watching Mrs. Winkleson's collapse, hurried out.

"And my bag," Dad called. "It's in my car."

"I'll get it," Mother said.

"Let me help," Dr. Smoot said. He threw aside his black cape and joined Dad. I wasn't sure how much help he could be with only one working arm, but he got points for trying.

Mrs. Winkleson vomited. People began backing away, widening the circle that had formed around her. Chief Burke stepped out of the crowd, notebook already in hand.

"What happened?" he asked.

"Poisoning's my guess," Dad said.

"Is Horace here?" Chief Burke asked.

"Right here, chief." Horace appeared at the chief's side, already pulling on gloves. Like Dad and his medical bag, Horace was seldom without the tools of his trade as a crime scene technician.

"Bag her glass," the chief said, pointing to Mrs. Winkleson's fallen old fashioned glass. "And the food, too."

"Can do, chief," Horace said.

I backed away to let the experts do their job. Both sets. Dad and Dr. Smoot were soon joined by the two EMTs, one of them hastily stuffing a last crab croquette into his mouth. Chief Burke, assisted by Horace and Sammy, bagged the food, glass, and plate Mrs. Winkleson had dropped and cordoned off the bar. A few people protested about the bar closing until they heard the sound of Mrs. Winkleson vomiting again, and then one by one people began peering at their glasses and sidling over to tables and sideboards to put them down.

"Looks like she ate quite a few of those crab puffs," Horace remarked. Since the only way he could have known that was if the crab puffs were once again visible, I deduced he was bagging the vomit for evidence. Better him than me.

Chief Burke came over to me.

"Can you stop the food service?" he asked. "And stay in the kitchen to keep the caterers and staff there till I can get some more officers here to help process the scene?"

"Roger," I said. I gathered I wasn't quite the prime suspect. I looked around for help.

"No thank you, dear," Mother was saying to one of the waiters. "They were lovely, but I think I've had enough."

"Yes," I said, strolling over to them. "I think everyone's had enough crab puffs for now. Chief Burke wants them and all the wait staff in the kitchen. Can you help?"

"Of course, dear," she said. She sailed off to gather the rest of the waiters. It wasn't hard to spot them. People were beginning to back away from the hors d'oeuvre trays as if they were radioactive. I led the puzzled waiter toward the kitchen. Our path went by the fallen Mrs. Winkleson, and I caught bits of the conversation between Dad, Dr. Smoot, and the EMTs.

"—the telltale bitter almond scent," Dr. Smoot was saying.

"I don't have the gene to smell it," one of the EMTs said. "But if you have—"

"Yes, definitely," Dad said. "Margaret, you weren't serving crab almondine, were you?"

"No, dear," Mother said. "If you smell almonds, don't blame my poor crab croquettes."

"It's very strong," Dr. Smoot said.

"I'll take your word for it. Oxygen, then?"

"Stat."

"Cyanide," I said, nodding.

"What's that?" the waiter asked.

"She was probably poisoned with cyanide," I explained. "It smells like almonds. I gather they suspect the hors d'oeuvres."

The waiter looked askance at his tray, and held it a little farther from his body.

I held the kitchen door open for him, and then stepped into the room myself. I blinked in surprise for a moment. The room was about the size of my high school auditorium, and looked about the way the auditorium had looked when decorated for a Halloween dance. Of course Mrs. Winkleson would continue her color scheme into the kitchen, but since it permitted white as well as black, why on earth had she felt it necessary to have black painted walls, black tile floors, black cabinets with black granite tops, and gleaming black appliances? I more than half expected to see Grandma Addams stirring a bubbling cauldron in the corner while Morticia looked on approvingly.

But now was not the time to gape at the latest evidence of Mrs. Winkleson's lunacy.

"Everyone stop what you're doing, and take a seat," I said, projecting from the diaphragm again. "Police orders."

"What do you mean, stop what we're doing?" A woman in a Caerphilly Catering uniform strode over and planted herself in my path, hands on hips. "If we don't keep the hors d'oeuvres moving—"

"There's been a poisoning," I said.

"Oh, my." Her mouth dropped open and she pressed her hands to either side of it, in a fair imitation of Edvard Munch's *The Scream*.

Silence fell over the whole room—at least until someone at the far end of the kitchen dropped a tray full of champagne glasses. The noise seemed to snap the head caterer out of her shock.

"You're not accusing us of doing it," she said. "I won't stand for—"

"Don't worry," Mother said, appearing in the doorway. "I'm sure no one here has any such idea."

"And I know Chief Burke wants to do everything by the book to make sure no one who's innocent falls under suspicion," I said. "So everyone please stop doing whatever you're doing and wait until he gets here."

Marston appeared in the doorway with a folding chair under each arm.

"Splendid," Mother said. "Just put them there in the middle of the floor, away from the food preparation areas."

"Of course, madam."

Marston was followed by the pair of male servants I'd seen hauling the glass swan to its display niche, each carrying a pair of folding chairs. They set their chairs in a row in the huge open area in the middle of the kitchen. A couple of the waiters plopped down there. Marston and his staff continued to haul in folding chairs from some unseen stash and set them up in rows, and the caterers and household staff took seats as each batch of chairs arrived. Then the guests began streaming in from the living room. Marston and his crew continued to fetch chairs until we were all seated, facing the door to the foyer, like the audience waiting for a play to begin in a somewhat unconventional theater.

Marston and the two manservants took seats in the front row. I joined them. Mother stood looking over the group with a look of distress on her face. Everybody looked anxious, uncomfortable, or downright scared. This was not supposed to happen at parties for which Mother was responsible.

"Now then," she said, in her most cheerful tone. "Who's up for charades?"

It was going to be a long night.

I slipped out to have a word with the chief. He was standing in the archway, watching whatever was going on in the living room.

"We'll get to you as soon as we can," he said. "We're short staffed."

"No problem," I said. "I just wanted to suggest, since you're short staffed, that maybe I could make myself useful. Make you a list of all the witnesses sitting around in the kitchen, get their names and addresses."

"And interrogate them a little while you're at it?"

"In front of all the other witnesses?" I said. "That would be pretty stupid."

He thought about it for a moment.

"Do it, then," he said.

"One other suggestion," I said. "The rose growers all have to get up before dawn to prep their roses, as I'm sure Minerva would remind you if she were here. Maybe if you interviewed them first?"

He frowned.

"I'm sure the fact that so many of the rose growers are prominent citizens with a tendency to whine at the town council when offended carries no weight with you. But keep in mind, the caterers will get paid overtime for the time they spend waiting."

"Mrs. Winkleson's staff ought to as well," he said. "Though I doubt if they know that. Good idea; I'll get rid of the rose growers first. Right now, why don't you bring me up to speed on what you've been doing in the last few hours."

Chapter 31

Bringing the chief up to speed on my last few hours took a while. I made sure he knew about Dr. Smoot's run-in with the swan and my fear that the acting medical examiner might be less than impartial when it came to determining the manner and means of death. And I shared the various bits of information I'd overhead during the party, including what Mr. Darby had revealed about Sandy Sechrest's frequent presence on the farm in the weeks leading up to the rose show. Though I didn't reveal Mr. Darby as the source; I just lumped the information in with everything else I'd heard while eavesdropping.

"Thank you," he said at last. "You can leave if you like."

"After I get you that list of witnesses," I said. "After all, this wretched rose show is my responsibility. I don't feel comfortable leaving until I'm sure things are going well."

Back in the kitchen, Mother had found eight volunteers willing to play charades. Or maybe some of them were draftees. One of them, the lady in pink, was sashaying up and down, clutching an invisible garment around her. Her teammate was Rob—definitely a draftee. Rob loathed charades, no doubt because he was strangely inept at them.

"Model?" Rob said. "Catwalk? Designer?"

The pink lady stopped in front of Rob and stroked the wrist of her invisible sleeve.

"Furry," I murmured.

"Cufflink?" Rob guessed. "Wristwatch?"

The pink lady stroked the whole sleeve.

"Carpal tunnel syndrome?"

I took out my notebook and began making my list of witnesses.

I deliberately started at the far back corner, where Theobald Winkleson was sitting. I couldn't ask him any of the questions I was really curious about, like where he had gone after the chief had questioned him and why he was here in the first place, but I got a chance to study him at close range and form a highly unfavorable opinion. He hardly bothered to meet my eyes, so busy was he inventorying the contents of the kitchen, tightening his lips and narrowing his eyes whenever he spotted anything particularly extravagant or outrageous.

By the time I finished with Theobald, Rob's time to guess the pink lady's charade was almost up.

"The sound and the furry," he was saying, over and over again. "The sound and the furry. The sound and the furry."

"Time!" Mother called at last.

"Fury, you . . . you . . . oh!" exclaimed the lady in pink, doing a very authentic interpretation of the word, now that her time was up. "The Sound and the *Fury*!"

"Oh, of course," Rob said. "Sorry."

Another charades team took the floor. I went on with my name and address gathering.

As I suspected, the catering staff consisted mainly of starving grad students. Most of Mrs. Winkleson's household staff did not speak English well—if at all—and I was only able to get their information thanks to translating help from Marston, who apparently spoke Spanish, French, and some form of pigeon Chinese in addition to his native Russian. His real name was Vladislav Konstantinovich Rozhdestvensky, which probably explained why Mrs. Winkleson preferred to call him Marston.

I finished my list and tried to think of something else to keep me busy, lest Mother recruit me to replace Rob on charade duty, but in the nick of time the chief sent Horace in to begin processing the kitchen and Sammy to move us out into the already processed living room. Chief Burke began interviewing witnesses, and apparently he decided my suggestion was a wise one. He started with the rose growers, while the rest of us were told to stay in the living room and wait our turns.

To my relief, Mother did not suggest resuming the game of charades. Instead, she and Marston put their heads together, and then, after they had a short conference with the chief, Marston brought back vacuums, dust racks, and other cleaning supplies and the maids began cleaning the room.

Fine by me. I was relieved that the noise of the vacuums discouraged general conversation.

The caterers pitched in, gathering their dishes and equipment.

"If anyone would like a doggie bag, we'd be happy to pack one," the catering supervisor said. Curiously, no one was particularly interested, not even in leftover crab croquettes, so her staff begged some black plastic garbage bags from Marston and began disposing of the suspect victuals.

A few guests pitched in to help with the cleanup effort, but most arranged themselves on the uncomfortable chairs and sofas and waited.

Three of the rose growers approached me.

"Do you think she's going to make it?" one of them asked.

Did I look like a doctor? Or a fortune teller?

"I think she has a good chance," I said aloud. "Dad seemed quite optimistic when they left."

"Oh," one woman said. They all looked at each other and sighed.

"I suppose we should keep working on the programs, then," a second woman said. "You'll let us know if you hear anything to the contrary?"

The three of them pulled up chairs next to a small gilt table at one side of the room, pulled stacks of programs and black pens out of their purses and tote bags, and resumed inking blots to cover up the printer's error. After a while they filched an unopened bottle of champagne from the bar, and by the time they'd finished it, they seemed to be enjoying their task a great deal more, though I doubted we'd be able to use much of their handiwork.

"Meg?" It was my cousin Rose Noire, resplendent in a dress that looked like several hundred black chiffon scarves thrown randomly over her body and then sprayed with silver glitter. "I have a question. Do you think it would be okay for me to substitute for Mrs. Sechrest?"

She held her head high, like Sidney Carton on his way to the guillotine.

"Substitute for her how?" I asked.

"I understand she had all her miniature roses ready to bring over for the show," Rose Noire said. "I could groom them. Your mother and a couple of other exhibitors are willing to coach me. Then we could enter them in the show in her name. So she could compete one last time in the shows she loved. And it would be sort of a . . . a 'take that!' to the murderer."

Not Sidney Carton. More like Joan of Arc on her way to the bonfire.

"It's fine with me," I said. "But I have no idea if it's against the ARS rules. Why don't you ask one of the more knowledgeable rose growers? Try her."

I pointed out Molly Weston, and Rose Noire sailed over to confer with her, leaving a small trail of glitter in her wake.

I gathered from Molly's expression that she also thought it a very good idea for Rose Noire to fill in for Mrs. Sechrest. I left them to it.

I found myself keeping an eye on Theobald. He was roaming around the room, inspecting the décor and finding it no more to his liking than the kitchen was, if his frowns and grimaces were anything to go by. I could see his point. However perfectly adapted the house was to Mrs. Winkleson's tastes, if I were one of her heirs, I'd be less than enchanted at the thought of inheriting such a white elephant. Or should that be black elephant? Auctioning off the furniture would be possible, though I doubted it would bring in anything near what she'd spent on it, but the house itself, with its black marble floors and fireplaces and black-painted woodwork, was going to be a huge liability. They'd need to spend thousands of dollars to make the décor more normal before they could hope to put it on the market.

Of course, if Theobald turned out to be the one who'd killed Mrs. Sechrest and fed his aunt the cyanide, selling the house would probably become brother Reginald's problem.

I watched as Theobald turned over a silver tureen to see what was marked on the bottom. I decided I could live with the idea of Theobald as a murderer.

Chapter 32

The chief was being relatively quick with his witness interviews. By nine, all of the rose growers were on their way home, except for Mother.

"Oh, don't worry about me," she said, whenever the chief asked if she'd like to go next. "I have to stay here anyway, to help Meg with the cleanup. I'm sure there are others who would appreciate getting out sooner."

The chief didn't press, so I assumed he didn't consider her a prime suspect. And once Horace had finished work on the kitchen and the chief gave his approval, it was a lot easier to have her around to charm and cajole the catering staff and Mrs. Winkleson's maids into working harder and more cheerfully than they would have for me.

Actually, the maids didn't need much cajoling. One of them burst into tears the first time Mother uttered the word "please."

The caterers were relatively enthusiastic, too. But as I looked out over the dozen assorted people busily tidying, mopping, and scrubbing the huge kitchen, I had to wonder if any of them had an ulterior motive for working so hard. If I'd done the poisoning, maybe I'd welcome a chance to help eradicate any trace evidence that might incriminate me. Assuming Horace hadn't already found it, of course. My money was on Horace.

I found a moment to speak privately with Mother.

"You seem to be getting along very well with Mrs. Winkleson's staff," I said to Mother. "Any chance you could ask them if they've seen this thing before?"

I held up the Baggie containing the doe urine bottle. Mother wrinkled her nose slightly.

"Of course, dear," she said. In spite of her obvious distaste, she took the Baggie, checked to see that the top was securely zipped, and then tucked it into her tiny black purse.

"And give it to Horace when you're finished," I added. "He's going to analyze it."

Mother nodded. She looked tired and a little sad.

"I'm sorry I didn't find the secateurs in time to keep them from being used as a murder weapon," I said. "If it's any consolation, the chief will probably be finding out who stole them in the course of his investigation."

"Mrs. Winkleson stole them," Mother said. "I'm almost positive. I realized it when I saw her tonight. Remember when you were arguing with her?"

"How could I forget it?" I said. "For a few minutes, I thought I'd killed her. Not intentionally, of course, but by making her so mad she had a heart attack or a stroke or something."

"It was nice of you to be concerned," Mother said. "Though if losing her temper was apt to be fatal, the world would have killed her off long before tonight. I think she was enjoying herself."

"I hope so," I said. "If she doesn't make it, I'll never be able to forget that I was the one yelling at her in her last conscious moments."

"Anyway, watching her argue with you jogged my memory. She was standing there, clutching her drink, and she had a look of such . . . such . . . truculent glee. It was the same look she had when she was holding my secateurs at the garden club meeting. I realize that now. I suspect she was holding them, and waiting for her chance to pocket them, and thinking about how much I'd mind when I discovered they were gone. I don't remember seeing anyone holding them after that. She took them. Then the killer found them here, on her property, and tried to use them on *her*."

"You could be right," I said. "And if the killer's someone who knows about the secateurs, he or she might have thought it was a neat trick, using them to kill her. Killed with a weapon she'd stolen herself."

"A pity," Mother said, and then she pursed her lips together as if stopping herself from saying something she shouldn't.

"That the killer got the wrong person?" I suggested.

"That the killer got anyone at all is more like it," Mother said. "And that they used your ironwork as a weapon."

"I'll make you another pair just like them," I said. "Not like the ones I'm making to sell to the garden club. With the delicate handles to fit your hands."

"Thank you, dear," Mother said.

From time to time over the next several hours, I saw her talking in a corner to one or another of the maids. The amber bottle would appear, and the maids would study it and shake their heads. Then Mother would talk some more, and the maids would smile and nod happily. I overheard enough of one conversation to know that she was enlisting the maids not only to keep their eyes out for more doe urine bottles but to search actively for them. From the looks on the maids' faces, I felt confident that if any other little amber bottles were or had been concealed in the Winkleson mansion, we'd hear about it eventually. I only hoped none of them had any idea where they could find more little bottles to plant them on their unloved employer.

I found myself wishing I dared ask Mother to query the staff about the dognapping while she was at it. Poor little Mimi's fate had been rather forgotten in the wake of the two attempts on Mrs. Winkleson's life. But I had the feeling the chief would not take it well if I tried to interfere with his investigation of the dognapping—especially if the dognapping turned out to be related to the murder attempts. What were the odds of two unrelated crimes happening at the same place in so short a time?

I tried to remember what Mrs. Winkleson had said earlier about the threatening letters she'd received. "Cancel the rose show or else," was all I could remember her saying. And "or else" were the only words left of the note I'd found in Mrs. Sechrest's hand.

Probably a bad idea to point out this coincidence to the chief. He'd probably already noticed it. And in case he hadn't, I'd talk to Horace later.

By midnight, the whole downstairs was in impeccable shape again, and there were only a handful of potential witnesses left. Rob and I were dozing on two of the white brocade couches, along with the caterer and three of her staff. Mother was sitting in one of the ghastly leather chairs, methodically stitching a crewelwork picture of a vase of roses. The brilliant reds, electric greens, and other bright colors of her embroidery thread were the only splash of color in the huge room.

I wondered if she was really being self-sacrificing in waiting her turn, or if she had some reason for delaying her interview. Using the time to work out her story. Waiting to see what really happened to Mrs. Winkleson.

Nonsense. Mother wasn't a poisoner.

But what if she had some inside knowledge of who was? Knowledge she hadn't yet decided whether to share with the chief. . . .

"Tired, dear?" Mother said, glancing over her embroidery glasses at me.

I nodded.

"It looks as if it won't be long now," she said, returning to her fabric. "Oh, and here's your father. What news from the hospital?"

"Mrs. Winkleson is a lucky woman," Dad said, as he sat down heavily in another uncomfortable leather chair. "She'll make it."

"Very lucky," I said. "If I'm ever poisoned, I hope I'll have two doctors standing by, not to mention an ambulance with two well-trained EMTs."

"It also helps to be poisoned with something that's easy to identify," Dad said. "It didn't hurt that both Smoot and I have the genetic ability to smell the characteristic bitter almond odor of cyanide. Not everyone can, you know."

"And how fortunate for her that she was poisoned with something treatable," Mother said. Was I only imagining the slight emphasis on "for her," as if to imply that Mrs. Winkleson's good fortune wasn't all that satisfactory to the rest of us?

"And how fortunate that Chief Burke was on hand," I said aloud. "To investigate the crime from the minute it happened."

"Though it didn't turn out to be murder," Mother said. At least she didn't add "More's the pity."

"I'm sure he's relieved about that," I said. "And it's still attempted murder."

"Plus it's a good bet whoever tried to poison Mrs. Winkleson is the one who killed Sandy Sechrest," Rob said. "So this gives him a whole new bunch of evidence to help solve that crime."

"I suppose," Dad said. "There's no actual proof the two are connected. And the complete change in methods is a little odd."

"I suspect it's only in books that serial murderers have an obsessive need to commit each crime in precisely the same way," I said. "Although I can certainly see that Mrs. Winkleson might have more than one mortal enemy."

"Still rather a lot of people here," Dad said, frowning. "I hope that doesn't unsettle Mrs. Winkleson."

"Unsettle her?" I repeated. "She's in the hospital, isn't she? How would she know how many people are still here, much less be upset by it?"

"She's coming back," Dad said.

Chapter 33

"Coming back?" I repeated. Perhaps I'd been spending too much time around Dr. Smoot. For a moment, I pictured Mrs. Winkleson returning as one of the undead the medical examiner was so fascinated with. "She wasn't poisoned then? Or not that seriously?"

"She was poisoned all right, and it could have been quite serious if she hadn't received prompt medical attention," Dad said. "But she's not really ready to come home. Signed herself out against medical advice, but she insisted she had to come home so she could get up tomorrow morning to get her roses ready for the show. She'll be here soon."

"Is that wise?" Mother said. "Surely it would be better for her to rest for a few days."

"That's exactly what I told her," Dad said. "But when I did, she accused me of trying to knock her out of the competition."

"She didn't," Mother said.

Dad nodded.

"She said that the killer had tried to poison her and stab her in the back without slowing her down, and she'd be damned if she'd let some quack doctor do it."

"The nerve!" Mother exclaimed.

"So she's assuming it's because of the rose show that someone's out to get her?" I asked.

"Seems a reasonable assumption," Dad said.

"Not the only possibility, though," I said. "For example, I don't think the chief should count out Mr. Darby as a suspect. He's very protective of his animals."

"Is she mistreating the animals?" Dad asked.

"Not that Dr. Blake and Caroline have been able to learn," I said. "But I get the idea Mr. Darby isn't happy. So maybe she's doing something they haven't found out about yet. Or maybe he's just upset that she gets rid of all the animals that aren't quite perfect."

"Gets rid of them?" Dad asked. "How?"

"Nothing horrible, as far as I can tell," I said. "Supposedly they're sold to other farms. Most of them are unusual or valuable animals, so there's a good market. But I think Mr. Darby gets attached to the animals, and resents her selling them off."

"Understandable," Rob said. "But is it a motive for murder?"

I shrugged.

"And there's her nephew, of course," I said. When I said it, I saw Dad glance around quickly, to make sure the nephew wasn't still there.

"Don't worry," I said. "He went back to his hotel a couple of hours ago."

"Hotel?" Dad said. "They couldn't find him a bed here?"

"I don't think he felt particularly welcome."

"How sad!" Mother exclaimed.

"Maybe," I said. "Of course, it's possible that he really did hear about the murder on the news, assumed it was his aunt, and immediately set out to get here. But until the chief checks his alibi to see if he really was at home in Warrenton at the time of the murder. . ."

"Because no one pays any attention when I say I spotted him outside the gateway before the murder," Rob said.

"Because they always like to check on testimony from someone who might have a grudge against the intended victim himself," I said.

"Oh, all right," Rob mumbled.

"Besides, they might want to check if he left Warrenton in time to have committed the dognapping," I said. "Don't forget the chief is still trying to solve that as well."

"Yes, Theobald did seem rather eager to take possession of the house when he thought she was dead," Mother said. "No accounting for taste, is there?" She looked around and shuddered.

"Hey, it's not so bad," Rob said. "A few gallons of paint, a few sofas that aren't actually harder than the wood floor, and you'd be amazed how livable this place could be."

"It would take more than a few gallons of paint," Mother said. "But you're right. What a canvas for a competent decorator!"

She meant, of course, what a canvas for her. She took off her glasses, stood up, and began slowly revolving with her hands on her hips and eyes narrowed.

"The first thing I'd do——" she began.

"Mrs. Langslow?"

We all started slightly, and turned to see the chief standing in the archway. A tuxedo-clad waiter was standing at his side. Seeing the waiter, the caterer and the rest of her crew rose and began shuffling to the hallway. The waiter fell in step with them. Apparently they'd all come in the same vehicle and were stuck here until the last of them was interviewed.

"Good news," Dad said to Chief Burke. "Mrs. Winkleson will be fine."

"Great," the chief said. "I'll go down to the hospital tomorrow morning to interview her."

"You can interview her here, if you like," Dad said. "She should be along any minute. Signed herself out. Sammy's bringing her back."

"Splendid," the chief said. He didn't sound as if he thought it was splendid. He sounded dog tired. "Well, in the meantime, Mrs. Langslow? If I could talk to you next?"

"Of course," Mother said.

"But why do you need to talk to her?" Dad asked.

"We're talking to everyone who—"

"After all, she couldn't possibly have poisoned Mrs. Winkleson," Dad went on.

"Why not?" Mother whirled to glare at Dad. "Don't you think I have the nerve? The cunning? The intelligence?"

"Oh, good grief," the chief murmured, closing his eyes. Dad's mouth fell open and he was clearly floundering desperately for words.

"Of course that's not what he meant," I said. "Dad of all people should know that you have the nerve, cunning, and intelligence to do anything you set your mind on. But he also knows you wouldn't stoop to doing this."

Mother looked puzzled but slightly mollified,

"What do you mean, wouldn't stoop?" Rob put in. I glared at

him. Didn't he see I was winging it? Trying at all costs to defuse the quarrel between Mother and Dad? Now I was going to have to explain why poisoning Mrs. Winkleson amounted to stooping when at least half the party guests were in awe of whoever had managed it and probably eager to contribute to the poisoner's defense fund.

The party.

"Do you really think Mother would poison anyone at a party where she was one of the hostesses?" I said. "That would fly in the face of every law of hospitality."

Mother, liking the sound of that, drew herself up even taller and changed her stern look to a slight smile.

"Yeah, and poisoning someone with Dad around? Dumb idea," Rob added. "Everybody knows he's an expert on poisons."

Yes, everybody knew, but did Rob have to remind everybody? And more to the point, remind Chief Burke? Had he forgotten that Dad, too, could have a motive for wanting Mrs. Winkleson out of the rose show?

"Besides," I added, "Mother would never do something this unsubtle."

"I thought poisoning was a subtle crime," Rob said.

"Some poisonings," I said. "But this? Poor Mrs. Winkleson puking all over her own living room within minutes of drinking the spiked drink? Mother's a doctor's wife. If she wanted to poison someone, she could certainly find something hard to detect. Something that wouldn't kick in until long after Mother was gone, and for that matter, all the medical people Mother would know were attending the party."

"Thank you, dear," Mother said. "Of course, there is one thing you didn't think to mention."

We all looked at her expectantly.

"If I were poisoning Mrs. Winkleson," she said, her voice suddenly very stern, "I wouldn't have botched it."

"This is all very interesting," the chief said. "But it's getting late. Mrs. Langslow, if you please . . ."

Mother smiled graciously at him, and sailed toward the archway to the hall.

"Why don't you two go home?" Dad said. "I'll wait for your mother."

"Good idea," I said. "I don't want any more adventures tonight."

"Before you go," the chief said, "just one more thing."

Chapter 34

"Just one more thing," I repeated. "Isn't that what Columbo always used to say?"

"Yes," said Dad, the mystery buff. "Just before he asked the critical question that trapped the killer."

He was beaming with delight at seeing real life echo one of his beloved mystery icons. The chief and I both sighed identical patient sighs.

"All I wanted to ask," the chief said, "was how you knew it was a spiked drink? As opposed to the food, I mean."

"I don't," I said. "I assumed it. After all, everyone was eating the crab croquettes. Everyone who isn't allergic to crab, that is," I added, looking pointedly at Mother, who had paused dramatically in the archway to listen. "It would have been hard to poison one and make sure she got it. And almost everyone knew Mrs. Winkleson always drank Black Russians."

"Yes," Mother said. "You should see the fuss she puts up when someone can't serve her one. The ABC store is perpetually out of Kahlúa these days."

"So any number of people would have known that was likely to be Mrs. Winkleson's glass?" the chief asked.

"Everyone in the garden club," I said. "And all of her staff. And I should think her family, too."

"And we warned the caterers," Mother said. "I'm sorry," she added, seeing the chief's crestfallen face. "Not a very useful bit of evidence, is it?"

"It is what it is," the chief said. "If you don't mind."

The chief indicated the way to his interrogation room and followed Mother out.

I fished Horace's truck keys out of my bag and handed them to Dad.

"Here," I said. "Could you give these to Horace? Tell him I'm sorry about the windshield wipers?"

He nodded, pocketed the keys, sat down on one of the couches, and closed his eyes.

"I'll give you a ride down to your car if you like," Rob said.

"I like," I said. "It should be pretty safe outside, with the whole county police force here, and ordinarily I'd welcome the exercise, but tonight I'm so tired I'd probably fall asleep on the way, in midstride."

Rob dropped me off, waited until I was safely in my car, and then waved good-bye and pulled out.

I dumped my tote in the passenger seat and was about to start my car when I saw a slight flicker of motion out of the corner of my eye and stopped to peer into the darkness beyond the horse barn. What had moved? Then again, what did it matter? Silly to be so on edge at the slightest movement on a farm filled with birds and animals, not to mention police officers. It was probably just one of the vampire horses, being permitted to enjoy the night air in spite of the rain. Or perhaps an insomniac goat. Unlikely to be a marauding black swan at this time of night. Whatever it was, certainly not my problem.

Except that it might be prowling near the barns where I had, at last, gotten everything set up perfectly for tomorrow's show, or possibly in the pasture where Mrs. Sechrest had been killed. That was Chief Burke's problem, not mine, but maybe he'd want to hear about it if someone was sneaking around his crime scene. For that matter, there was still the mystery of the disappearing farm animals. Still, not my problem.

Then a vision popped into my brain of a small dog, soaking wet and hungry, wandering about in the dark. What if I'd spotted Mimi?

I reached under the car seat for the big flashlight I kept there. I didn't turn it on—yet. I wasn't quite sure whether I wanted to use it for light when I located the source of the movement, or as a weapon. I shoved my purse under the seat and made sure my cell phone was in my pocket, in case I needed to call for help or report anything to the police. Then I set out to track down the source of the motion.

No one lurking behind the barn. Only a few huddled shapes at the far end of the goat pasture, where I remembered there being a sort of open shed the goats could use if they wanted shade or shelter from the rain.

Then I spotted something again—this time a brief flash of light from beyond the woods. Was that what I'd seen before? Maybe. I realized that what I'd seen looked like what you'd see if a car passed by on the highway, so fast that its headlights flashed by for a few seconds before disappearing in the distance. But there was no highway for miles and miles in that direction, only the rolling acres and dirt roads of Mrs. Winkleson's farm, and no legitimate reason I could think of for anyone to be driving those dirt roads in the middle of the night. Any additional searching the police did would be done by daylight, so they could be sure of not stepping on evidence.

So I'm nosy. I patted my trusty cell phone, then climbed over the fence and slogged across the muddy ground toward the source of the light.

I didn't encounter any goats, or if I did, I was moving too slowly to arouse their faint or flight reaction. At the other end of the pasture, I climbed the fence again. I spotted what I thought was the bulk of Mrs. Winkleson's rose compound to my left and paused for a few minutes to see if I could detect anything out of the ordinary there. I could see a number of small, luminous white spots where the white roses were blooming, but no sign of movement. I turned back toward the direction the light had come from and trudged through the woods.

Apparently this was only a thin fringe of woods between two pastures, but it was spooky enough, with vine-laden trees looming above and small rivulets of water showering down whenever I shook the leaves overhead. I paused to listen when I got to the point where the woods gave way to open field.

At first, nothing. Then I heard a low moo to my left. I crept forward a foot or two and peered through the drizzle.

A little farther along the treeline I spotted a large, rectangular shape with a small, more rounded shape stuck to one side. After a few moments I realized I was looking at a large truck.

Another moo, and I spotted a cow moving up a ramp into the truck, its white belted middle gleaming faintly.

I doubted Mrs. Winkleson or Mr. Darby had arranged for the Belties to take any midnight outings. More probably, some enterprising cattle rustlers were hoping to take advantage of the confusion following the murder and attempted murder. I felt sure I was getting closer to learning what had happened to the missing farm animals.

"Any more?" a voice said, from somewhere near the truck.

Another voice answered, but too softly for me to make out the words. If I crept closer, perhaps I could recognize the speakers, or at least get a good look at them. Even get the truck's license plate number. Then I could slip back into the woods and call Chief Burke to—

Brrrring!

My cell phone.

Chapter 35

"What's that?" the voice from the truck said.

Cursing silently, I retreated into the woods, fumbling at my pocket to get the cell phone out, dropping the flashlight in the process.

"Leave that and let's get out of here!" the voice said.

The cell phone rang again as I was finally pulling it out. I heard several metal slamming noises—no doubt the ramp being slid back into its slot and the truck's doors slamming closed. A great rumbling motor started up, drowning out the final half-ring my phone made before I punched the off button.

The truck began lurching away. I fumbled around for my flashlight, found it, then thought better of using it. No doubt the truck was already too far away for me to read the license number. I decided to put some distance between myself and where I'd been the last time my cell phone rang, since I didn't know how many people were with the truck or, more important, whether they'd all left with it or whether anyone had stayed behind to silence an inconvenient witness. I dodged through the underbrush for a few yards, then took shelter under the drooping branches of a large cedar tree.

The sound of the truck faded into the distance, and all was

quiet. Nothing appeared to be moving, except for the cedar tree, which dropped large dollops of cold water on various parts of my body at random intervals.

After a few minutes, I turned my phone back on and changed the ring to vibrate. I glanced at the little screen. I'd missed a call from Michael. Not surprising. Despite my reputation as a night owl, most people would hesitate to call me after midnight unless it was an emergency. He had probably forgotten how early I had to be up and called to give me a postmortem on *Millard! The Musical!*

I'd call him back as soon as I could. For now, I needed to call the chief. I figured if he wasn't still up at the house he couldn't have gone far. I dialed his cell phone.

"Something wrong?"

Not the most gracious way to answer the phone, but no doubt he'd seen my name on the caller ID and knew this wasn't a social call. I wasted no time on amenities either.

"I think someone's stealing Mrs. Winkleson's Belties," I said. "I'm up in—"

"Her what?"

"Her cows. The black and white cows. Belted Galloways, or Belties for short. I thought I saw someone out behind the barns, so I looked around, and I stumbled across someone—two some-ones, actually—loading cows into a big truck. They fled when they heard my cell phone ring and realized someone was spying on them."

A brief silence.

"You normally leave your cell phone on while you're spying on people?"

"I was about to call you to report them," I said. It was only a slight exaggeration. "And who expects to get a call after midnight, for heaven's sake?"

"Where are you?" he asked,

"In a pasture somewhere," I said. "Go across the goat pasture, take a right at the rose compound, walk into the woods, and when you come out of the woods, that's where I am. And where the truck was."

I heard him repeating my instructions, and then I heard Sammy say, "Yes, sir!"

"Stay where you are," the chief said to me. "Sammy's coming to find you. And keep this line open. If you see anything threatening, speak up."

"Right."

"Could they have been heading for the back entrance?"

"Since I have no idea where I am or where the back entrance is, your guess is as good as mine," I said. "They were heading away from the house and barns—that's all I know."

I heard the chief giving orders—probably on his police radio, from the occasional snippets I caught of static-laden replies.

Suddenly I saw something moving toward me. I yelped slightly in surprise before I realized that it was two cows approaching me.

"What's wrong?" the chief snapped.

"The cows," I said.

"What about the cows? What's happening?"

I didn't answer because I wasn't quite sure what the cows were up to. Were Belties territorial, like the black swans? Mischievous like goats? Or merely curious? I wasn't sure whether to run or stand my ground, and settled for bracing my back against a tree and staying put. The two Belties stopped about two feet away and stood as if expecting me to do something.

I reached out and scratched one behind the ear. She grunted contentedly. The other cow butted my shoulder gently.

"Meg! What's wrong?"

"The cows were just lonely," I said. "I'm fine."

Though I wasn't sure how fine I would be if I stopped petting the cows. After all, however meek they were, they outweighed me by a ton. And they were beef cows, not dairy. Did that make them more fierce? I figured out a way to hold my cell phone and still keep a few fingers free for scratching. At least it wasn't actually raining, although I had the feeling it was going to start raining again any minute, and hoped someone would show up before it did. I was still petting both cows when Sammy appeared after what was probably only a few minutes but felt like years.

"Meg! Are you okay?'

"I'll be fine if you can convince these cows that the petting zoo is closed for the night."

Sammy, who was raised on a farm, seemed to have no trouble shooing the over-friendly Belties away.

The chief and Horace showed up shortly afterward. The three of them spent quite a while inspecting the part of the pasture where I'd seen the truck loading. At least I hoped I'd pointed to the right part of the pasture. They milled around for fifteen minutes or so, pointing their flashlights this way and that way. I saw multiple flashes of light from Horace's digital camera. Eventually, Horace came back my way.

"Rain's working for us this time," he said. "Enough hoof prints for us to tell that they got away with several other cows, and I should be able to get some very clear tire impressions."

I couldn't see his face, but from his voice I suspected he was smiling ear to ear. He trudged off into the rain as the chief and Sammy strolled up.

"Where's Horace going?" I asked.

"To get the stuff he needs to make some castings of the tire impressions." The chief opened his trunk, pulled out a folded tarp, and handed it to Sammy. "Cover them up good," he said. "In case the heavens open again before Horace gets back."

"Right, chief."

"So," the chief said, turning to me. "You just happened to be wandering around near the back entrance to Mrs. Winkleson's farm in the middle of the night."

"Are we near the back entrance?" I said. "I've never seen it."

"Then what are you doing out here?"

"I was down at the barns, getting into my car, and I just happened to see a light over here," I said. "I think they had the headlights on when they drove up and then realized it was a bad idea."

I gave him chapter and verse on what I'd been doing since I left the party. Midway through, the rain started up again, and we moved into his car. Horace arrived soon thereafter, leaning out the window of his truck to make up for his missing windshield wipers. As I answered questions, I watched him rig up a makeshift tent over his chosen tire tracks.

Another police car pulled up and another officer stepped out and squelched over to where Horace was working.

"I'll leave them to it for the time being and take you back to your vehicle," the chief said, turning on the ignition. "Just one more thing. Does this have anything to do with what your grandfather and Caroline Willner have been up to this afternoon?"

"I have no idea," I said. "What have they been up to?"

"Good question," he said. But he didn't answer it.

"I was wondering myself if this had anything to do with the dognapping," I said. "And if either the dognapping or the cattle rustling had anything to do with the attempts on Mrs. Winkleson's life."

"Also good questions," he said, again without answering.

The whole way back to my car, he carried on a conversation with Debbie Ann, the dispatcher, about where on his desk to find some paperwork he wanted faxed to the State Bureau of Investigation ASAP. He dropped me beside my car and wished me a polite, if curt, good night.

Once I was safely in my car, I dug in the backseat and found one of the cans of Diet Coke I'd thrown in in case I needed a caffeine boost during the day.

I started at a tap on my window. The chief. I rolled the window down.

"Trouble starting your car?" he asked.

I held up the can.

"Trouble starting me," I said. "A little caffeine to get me home."

I popped the top, took a deep swig, and tucked the can in the cup holder. The chief waited until I'd fastened my seat belt, and started the engine before he drove off. Back to the new crime scene, I assumed.

This might have nothing at all to do with the day's first crime scene, I thought, as I turned my car around to head for the gate. Maybe the cattle rustlers just happened to pick tonight for their raid even before the events of today. Maybe they'd picked it for the weather. Even when it wasn't raining, the cloud cover made visibility even lower than at the dark of the moon. Maybe they'd heard about the murder and the poisoning and decided to take advantage of the resulting confusion.

Or did the stolen cows have anything to do with why someone kept trying to kill Mrs. Winkleson?

I'd interrogate my grandfather and Caroline tomorrow. And maybe—

My hip vibrated. I stopped to fumble in my pocket for the cell phone. Michael, of course.

"I didn't wake you, did I?" he said, not even bothering with hello. "I completely forgot how late it was." Behind him I could hear the cheerful babble of voices.

"I was up," I said. "Are you in a bar?"

"Restaurant. We've been celebrating the death of *Millard! The Musical!* On the whole, our protégé is taking it philosophically. Of course, you'd be philosophical too if you'd had six martinis with only a single slice of pizza as ballast. Where are you?"

"In my car, about to head home," I said.

"You haven't been working all this time on that silly rose show!"

"No, I've been up because someone tried to poison Mrs.

Winkleson at the cocktail party, and then I stumbled on thieves attempting to steal her Belties."

"Belties? Is that some kind of geriatric unmentionable?"

"Belties, Belted Galloways. Those black-and-white cows."

"Seriously? You foiled some cattle rustlers?"

"Not really," I said. "They got at least one cow. Maybe more. I have no idea if the police will be able to follow them. But I did rescue two cows."

"Awesome!"

Clearly Michael had been celebrating with a few martinis of his own and was in the mood to talk. Normally I don't drive while on the cell phone, but I decided to make an exception. I put the phone on speaker, used a piece of duct tape from my tote to strap it to the dashboard, and drove slowly home, sipping my soda while I filled Michael in on the events of the past six or seven hours.

In spite of the caffeine and Michael's conversation, I was half asleep by the time I reached the house. Still, before dragging myself upstairs, I went through the kitchen to make sure Spike was safely asleep in his crate. He must have had a lively day. He didn't even wake up when I shoved a dog biscuit through the mesh in the door.

"I hope Mimi—" I began, and then stopped myself. What did I hope for Mimi? I had been about to say "comes home safe and sound as soon as possible." But was Mrs. Winkleson's chilly, forbidding house much of a home for a little dog? Maybe the best thing for Mimi would be to escape her dognappers and find her way to someone who wouldn't know a pedigreed Maltese from a pound puppy. Someone who would take her in and treat her with the kindness and affection that might have been sadly absent from her life so far.

"I hope it turns out okay for Mimi," I said finally. With that vague wish running through my mind, I stumbled upstairs, fell into bed, and slept as if drugged.

Chapter 36

I wasn't fond of five A.M. on normal days, and I liked it even less on the morning of the rose show. Since I hadn't remembered to set my alarm the night before, I wouldn't have seen it at all if Rose Noire hadn't taken her life into her hands by shaking me awake. Later, when I'd ingested enough caffeine to return to civility, I'd apologize for the rude, though heartfelt things I'd said to her.

At least, bless her heart, she'd loaded all the trophies into my car and put on a pot of coffee before waking me, and then disappeared so I could be alone with my morning grouchiness. I filled a thermos full of coffee and drove carefully over to Mrs. Winkleson's farm with who knows how many thousands of dollars worth of gold, silver, crystal, marble, glass, and wood rattling in my trunk and backseat.

A deputy was still on duty at the gate.

"You're not going to keep people from coming in, are you?" I asked. "The exhibitors are coming this morning, and then the show opens to the public at two this afternoon."

"Don't worry, ma'am," he said. "We're not here to keep anyone out, just to keep an eye on who does come in. Challenge anyone who doesn't look like they belong. Maybe make Mrs.

Winkleson feel a little easier after those two attempts on her life yesterday."

"Great," I said. I didn't point out that since whoever had tried to kill Mrs. Winkleson was almost certainly someone who belonged—either to her staff, her social circle, or the garden club—I wasn't sure how useful his vigil would be.

I unlocked the show barn, lugged the trophies inside all by myself, and then locked it up again. Sooner or later someone who knew what to do with them would show up or I'd wake up enough to figure it out myself.

About five minutes after I unlocked the prep barn and plopped myself down at a table just inside, the first of the exhibitors showed up with a bucket of roses in each hand.

By six-thirty, nearly every exhibitor was in place, hard at work. I leaned my chair back against the wall, closed my eyes, and tried not to jump out of my skin every time an exhibitor asked me for sharpies, or entry tags, or programs, or directions to the restroom, or just wished me good morning in a voice that showed they were much more awake than I was.

I'd gotten a call from Michael, telling me that he and his fellow professors were about to set out for home. I'd made one more attempt to get him to bring home a pregnancy test, and then, when yet another rose grower interrupted me in mid-request, ended up asking him for some real New York pastrami and rye. If he brought back all the foods I'd asked for, we wouldn't need to go grocery shopping for at least a week. Maybe a month.

"Good morning, Meg!"

There went another exhibitor, tripping into the barn and

waving gaily as she passed my command post on the way to her prep table. This one, I noted, was pushing a grocery cart full of roses and paraphernalia. Roses, I'd learned, required as much specialized equipment as newborn humans. At least infants eventually learned to take care of themselves.

Throughout the barn, nearly two dozen exhibitors had set up shop on the long cafeteria tables and were diligently preparing their blooms for the show.

I glanced at the nearest table, where Mother was working on her entries. However often I'd seen this process, it never failed to astonish me.

She began by studying the buckets at her feet, each holding a dozen or so varied blooms. She would toy with a bloom or two, frown, and finally pluck one lucky flower from the herd.

Then she studied every inch of the rose and its foliage, both over and through her reading glasses and then with a magnifying glass, saying, "Hmm" a great many times. Sometimes she would eventually shake her head with a small expression of displeasure and put the rose in a water-filled bucket at the other end of her table. Given how perfect all the roses looked, I initially assumed she was displeased with these flowers because she was itching to do some grooming and couldn't find anything they needed. After half an hour of watching, though, I realized that the shake of the head meant that even her skills were not enough to rescue the poor, benighted flower before her. But she placed them all very carefully in the discard bucket all the same, making sure their stems reached the water. After all, there was always the chance that the rest of the roses would be even worse, forcing her to return to a previously rejected rose. The chances of that were much higher given the rain and wind still besieging Caerphilly. Almost all of the exhibitors were muttering about weather damage.

If a rose passed that first inspection, Mother would attack the leaves. Some she removed, while others she trimmed down to a smaller, neater size, using deckle-edged scissors, to imitate the natural serrations along the leaf edges. Any brown spots or irregularities were also snipped away with the deckle-edged scissors. Once she was sure the leaves were in optimal condition, she laboriously buffed each one until it shone like a freshly polished shoe.

"Wouldn't a little wax have the same effect with less work?" I'd asked once, while watching her practice this at home.

"That's illegal!" Mother had exclaimed—by which I assumed she meant against the American Rose Society's rules. "You can take away from the flower, but you can't add anything!"

I was glad I'd asked the question when no one was around, not in a crowded prep room like today's.

Mother was now in phase two—cleaning up the rose itself with tweezers, tiny brushes, Q-tips, little sponge-ended makeup applicators, and a tiny bottle of compressed air.

Soon, she'd nod with satisfaction and begin the final phase— grooming the petals. As with the leaves, some petals she'd pluck out entirely, but more often she would trim the edges of certain petals, using nail scissors or even a scalpel from Dad's medical bag to remove discolorations, irregularities, or other blemishes completely invisible from six feet away where I sat. When all the petals were as perfect as art and nature could make them, she would begin teasing the flower more fully into bloom, again using her Q-tips, makeup brushes, and tiny bits of sponge.

"Why don't you just pick roses that are already open?" I'd asked Mother the first time I'd watched the process.

"Because you can't unbloom a rose," she said. "You can coax a half open rose to open more, but if you pick them already open to the right degree, more often than not, they'll be too fully open by the time the judges see them."

I knew from my work on the program that there was a category for open roses "with stamens prominently showing," but Mother didn't seem too excited about it.

"You know why, right?" Rob had said, when I mentioned it.

"Probably because the roses in the open category aren't eligible to win Queen of the Show," I said.

"Nah, it's deeper than that," Rob said. "Aren't the stamens what produce the pollen? It's all about sex. The open rose category is like full frontal nudity for plants. No wonder she disapproves."

He might even be right. All I knew was that Mother saved her deepest sighs for when she had to consign a promising bloom to the open category.

Apparently it wasn't just Mother's roses that needed major coaxing this morning. Around the room I could see at least a hundred roses sporting one or more Q-tips. Most held over two or three, but Mother was not the only exhibitor whose roses bristled with as many as two dozen. It reminded me of going backstage when Michael was directing *Hedda Gabler* and seeing the women in their elegant Victorian costumes sitting around with their hair in curlers.

Mother had finished ten roses already, and had several dozen more waiting, either in small groups in buckets or already deposited in one of the identical glass vases my volunteers had set out on Friday. I glanced at my watch. No wonder she was so focused. Over half of the four hours of prep time had gone by already, and she had only done a fraction of her roses. I glanced around at the several dozen other exhibitors. She wasn't alone. All up and down the aisles of tables, other anxious exhibitors were preparing their entries with the same obsessive precision, while around them waited enough roses to keep them grooming for hours. Maybe days.

The cumulative effect was . . . well, intimidating. Here I was, bleary-eyed and caffeine deprived, watching the competitors spending more time grooming a single rose than I usually spent on my face in a week. Of course, I was a devotee of the sort of natural look you acquire not by artful application of makeup but by washing your face and applying a few smears of a hypoallergenic combination sun block and moisturizer. Wasn't there a category for the most natural rose? I studied the program. No, not that I could see. That explained why the most neglected rose in the barn was receiving easily twice as much primping time as I'd bothered with the night of my senior prom.

"There." Mother pulled the last Q-tip from a deep red rose and nodded with satisfaction at the results.

"Very nice," I said.

"I just might have a chance to get the Dowager Queen with that one," Mother said, in an undertone.

Get the Dowager Queen? After a few moments, I realized she wasn't hatching some new plot to use the rose as a weapon against Mrs. Winkleson, only expressing her hope of winning the Dowager Queen trophy, given for the best bloom of a variety introduced prior to 1867. But it still sounded faintly ominous. I shoved the thought aside and tried to look suitably impressed with the rose in question.

"Meg, dear, could you get a runner to take this one over to the show barn?"

I looked around, but none of our runners were in sight.

"I'll take it over myself," I said, turning back to her table. "I need to check how things are going over there."

"Thank you, dear.'

Mother was busily tidying her work area, sweeping the little bits of leaf and petal into a trash bag and arranging her tools in perfect order before beginning to groom another batch of roses. I picked up the vase sitting on her table, making sure not to unsettle the rose it contained, and turned toward the door.

"Meg, dear."

I turned back. Mother was looking from a red rose on her table to me and then back again, with a small frown on her face.

"What's up?" I asked.

"This is the one I just finished," she said, pointing to the red rose in front of her. "You picked up the one I was about to work on."

Oops.

"I'm sorry," I said. "I can see that. I'm not sure what I was thinking. I guess I was on autopilot. Not quite awake."

"It doesn't even have a tag yet."

Mother shook her head slightly, took the rose from me, and

held out the one she'd finished. I took it, and lingered long enough to watch her begin peering at the next rose.

I peered too. It already looked fine to me. No better than the one in my hand, but certainly no worse.

Mother shook her head and began snipping vigorously with the deckle-edged scissors. Clearly I had no aptitude for rose showing.

I made sure I had a good grip on the vase and headed for the door. Just as I was about to slip out, I heard a shriek from the other end of the barn.

"Goat! Goat!"

Chapter 37

I whirled back and saw a small posse of shaggy black-and-white forms romping through the open door at the other end of the barn. Around me, rose growers were shrieking and cursing, grabbing buckets and holding them above their heads, throwing random objects at the goats, or just standing horrorstricken, with single roses clutched convulsively to their chests.

"Don't startle them!" Mr. Darby yelled, as he appeared in the doorway behind the goats.

Too late, of course. The goats had keeled over as soon as the shrieking began. Most of them lay stiff-legged on the barn floor, well short of the nearest rose, but one had actually reached an unlucky exhibitor's table before being startled. She'd knocked over several buckets when she fell and lay there, happily chewing one red rose while another hung out of her mouth by its stem. Fallen roses were scattered about her, including another red rose that almost looked as if she'd tucked it behind her ear. A pity we hadn't startled that particular goat a little sooner.

"She's eating my black roses!" the rose grower shouted. "Stop her!"

"Marguerite Johnson! You naughty goat!" Mr. Darby said. But he didn't try to help the rose grower, who was frantically trying to pry Marguerite's jaws open, while the dark red rose inched closer and closer to her mouth. Finally, Marguerite opened her mouth enough to fold in the blossom itself, and the rose grower fell back on the ground nearby and burst into sobs.

"Bad goat," Mr. Darby repeated. "Bad, bad goat."

I could see that some of the goats' legs had begun to twitch slightly. I set the vase with Mother's dowager rose on a windowsill that looked out of reach for even the tallest goat.

"Drag them outside before they can move again," I shouted, taking hold of one end of the nearest goat. "And shut that damned door!"

Some of the rose growers and volunteers leaped into action, grabbing goats by the legs and tugging them toward the door. Mr. Darby picked up Marguerite—evidently one of his favorites—draped her over his shoulders, and carried her out. She was still chewing and eyeing the rest of the roses with interest as she sailed out the door.

Mrs. Winkleson tottered out of the barn door just as we got the last of the goats outside. She looked pale and drawn. Clearly her ordeal at the hospital had taken its toll. I was about to ask how she was feeling and if she needed any extra help, but she opened her mouth and blasted my sympathy to shreds.

"What's going on here? What are you doing to my goats?"

"Taking them out of the barn, so they won't eat your roses along with everybody else's," I said. Everyone else was scurrying back inside, as if eager to avoid accusations of goat abuse. "I thought you took them up to another pasture to avoid precisely what just happened," I said, turning to Mr. Darby.

"I did," he said, sounding uncharacteristically heated. "But someone left a gate open between the pastures. We can't have all these garden club ladies and police officers running around leaving gates open willy-nilly. We have valuable livestock here!"

"I doubt if any of the garden club ladies have been mucking around in the muddy pastures," I said. "They're too busy racing against the clock to get their roses ready. And most of the police officers grew up on farms themselves, and know better than to leave gates open."

"Then who let my goats out?" he said, in a slightly less belligerent tone.

I shrugged elaborately, and then allowed my eyes to fall on Mrs. Winkleson's boots, which were coated with red clay mud. I made sure he followed my glance before I looked away. As I suspected, he got the hint immediately. It didn't hurt that Mrs. Winkleson, looking far less frail than she had a moment ago, was obviously trying to sneak up on a couple of the goats, with her huge black umbrella at the ready.

"I'll take them up to the back pasture," he said. "Where they'll be safe."

With a malevolent glare at his employer, he made a chirping noise and began striding away across the pasture. The goats scrambled eagerly after him, like rats after the Pied Piper.

"I don't want them interbreeding with the inferior stock up in the back pasture!" Mrs. Winkleson called after him.

"They're not interested in breeding this time of year," Mr. Darby called back. Was it my imagination, or did I hear him mutter "stupid cow" under his breath?

"Has Marston brought my roses down?" she asked, turning to me. "There's no time to waste."

"If he has, they'll be inside the barn," I said. I strode back inside and didn't look back to see if she was following.

Three of the rose growers besieged me the minute I stepped inside.

"We lost valuable grooming time!" one shouted.

"That goat ate my darkest roses!" another wailed.

"We need an extension!" the third shouted.

I checked my watch.

"Attention," I boomed, in my loudest tones. "The goats are now being removed to a secure area. Due to the interruption, we will be extending the grooming time by precisely ten minutes. Entries must be completed by 10:10."

Most of the exhibitors looked content.

"But what about my black roses?" It was the poor woman whose table Marguerite the goat had upset.

"I'm sorry," I said. "You have my profound apologies. Please give me a list of the categories in which you would have entered the roses you lost. If we discover that any of your competitors had anything to do with the goat incursion, we'll disqualify them from those categories, if not from the entire show."

She seemed mollified. Mrs. Winkleson, who was near enough to overhear me, frowned, opened her mouth to say something, and then thought better of it. Good. I was more sure than ever that she had something to do with the goat invasion, and I hoped she was on notice that I was watching for any more tricks.

She went over to the table where Marston was waiting with a two-level chrome bar cart full of roses and paraphernalia.

More roses than paraphernalia actually. The cart had obviously been customized for rose show use. Both levels had been fitted with a black-painted wooden frame containing row after row of holes precisely the right size to hold the standard show vases. The bottom rack held Mrs. Winkleson's roses, already parceled out into individual vases the same size and shape as the show vases, only made of black glass. The top rack was empty, no doubt awaiting the finished roses.

It didn't look as if the roses needed much finishing. The roses—all either white or deep, deep red—were arranged with regimented precision, and the black vases already carried the standard tags that had to be filled out for each entry.

Two of the tiny maids stood nearby. One deposited a black metal basket on the table—Mrs. Winkleson's rose-grooming tools, no doubt—then curtsied and hurried out. The other held a black wrought-iron lawn chair.

"Don't just stand there, stupid! Put the chair down!"

The maid hurried to obey, and then scurried out as if afraid someone would strike her. Why did I suspect that if she didn't have an audience, Mrs. Winkleson might well have done just that?

Marston stood by impassively as Mrs. Winkleson seated herself in the chair and made a great show of arranging her tools.

Then she stuck her arm out. He picked up a black vase containing a white rose and placed it in her hand. She brought the rose closer to her face and scrutinized it, though her inspection seemed to lack some of the intensity and passion Mother brought to her rose grooming.

"Vase!" she snapped.

Marston reached out, selected one of the regimented clear glass vases from the table and handed it to Mrs. Winkleson. She pulled the rubber band holding the show tag off the black vase and slipped it around the glass one. Then she moved the rose to the newly labeled vase and handed the black vase to Marston, who replaced it in the bar cart.

She turned the rose around, twitched gently at a petal, flicked an invisible something off one leaf, and then handed it to Marston, who placed it on the top rack of the trolley and handed her the next rose in line from the bottom rack. Mrs. Winkleson dealt with that in equally brisk fashion. At this rate, she'd have no trouble readying her entries in time. Clearly any roses impertinent enough to display imperfections had already been dealt with elsewhere. Why did I envision a basement workshop with two or three captive rose-groomers chained to benches, working on blossoms under Mrs. Winkleson's supervision, perhaps even using forbidden tools or techniques, if there were such things?

Not something I should worry about. Mrs. Winkleson could have broken every rule in the ARS's book without my noticing. But odds were if she did break any, someone would notice. Every other exhibitor in the barn was watching her, some out of the corner of their eyes, others with frank, hostile stares.

Occasionally, between roses, she'd lean back in her chair and close her eyes for a few moments, as if gathering strength. This made sense, actually, given what she'd been through the night before. Anyone else would have had people hovering around, asking could they do anything, imploring her not to overdo it, and clucking in sympathy. Instead . . .

"Look at her, acting as if she can hardly lift a finger," Molly Weston said, looking up as I walked by her table.

"Well, it might not be an act," I said. "I don't know exactly what they do these days to treat cyanide poisoning, but I'm sure it's no picnic."

"She really was poisoned?" Molly asked. "I thought that was just a wild rumor. Or a fit of hypochondria on her part."

"No, she really was poisoned," I said. "Dad took her to the hospital."

"Well, that's different. Poor thing, even she doesn't deserve that."

"But we all reap what we sow, don't we?" I said.

"We surely do," Molly said, and returned to the rose she was grooming.

Just then Chief Burke appeared in the doorway of the barn. I glanced over to where Minerva, his wife, was working on her roses. The chief looked her way, too, but only briefly before striding down the aisle between the tables and stopping beside Mrs. Winkleson.

"Madam, I need to—"

"I can't be bothered now!" Mrs. Winkleson said. "I have less than an hour to finish my roses!"

"Fine," the chief said. "I'll just let my murder suspect go. No problem to have him running around on the loose until you can be bothered to answer a few questions. He probably won't kill too many people in the meantime. Of course, since you seem to be the main one he's trying to kill—well, never mind."

If he really meant that, he'd have stormed off instead of folding his arms and standing by her table, glowering.

"Suspect?" Mrs. Winkleson repeated.

I'd have expected her to look at least a little bit happy at the thought. But she kept looking at her roses and then back at the chief, as if torn. I could tell the chief's temper was near the exploding point.

"As official organizer of the rose show," I said, "I will grant Mrs. Winkleson—and anyone else you need to question—an extension on their preparation time equal to the number of minutes they would otherwise lose by cooperating with your investigation."

"Thank you," the chief said. "Now, madam, if we could go somewhere more quiet?" He gestured toward the barn door.

"Watch the roses," she said to her butler. "And you'd better be counting from when he first interrupted me," she added, turning to me.

"That's fair," I said.

Of course, to be really fair, I should probably give a five- or ten-minute extension to everyone. Not much rose grooming had happened since the chief entered, and I suspected it would be a while before the others put the interruption far enough out of their minds to concentrate on the roses again.

I didn't think there was any way I could concentrate myself.

Chapter 38

"Keep an eye on things," I told Rose Noire. She was at a table nearby, working on Sandy Sechrest's miniature roses under the intense scrutiny of Mother, and for that matter, just about every other rose grower in the room. Apparently Rose Noire's idea of posthumously entering Mrs. Sechrest's roses in the show had so won the hearts of the other members of the Caerphilly Rose Society they'd all put their heads together and donated the equipment Rose Noire would need for her grooming.

But since Rose Noire had no experience whatsoever with grooming roses, I thought it would be a more touching tribute if they'd all pitch in and groom a few. Apparently there were limits to what even the most altruistic of the exhibitors would do when there were trophies at stake and they already had more roses than they could possibly groom by the 10 A.M. deadline—though I'd just extended it to 10:10. I hoped the judges were okay with that.

I looked around outside. Deputy Sammy and Horace were standing outside the horse barn, so I deduced that's where the chief had taken Mrs. Winkleson for their private chat. I strolled over.

"You can't go inside," Sammy said, stepping in front of the door.

"Wasn't planning to," I said. "Just wondering if you had any idea how long the chief's going to be with Mrs. Winkleson?"

"No idea," Sammy said. "Do you need her for something?"

"I could live without her indefinitely, but the rose show can't," I said. "I have to give her a full forty-five more minutes to finish her roses before the judges can start. While I realize arresting a murder suspect is more important than judging the rose show, I have a whole barn full of people back there who might not get it."

"Well, we're not exactly arresting him for murder just yet," Sammy said.

"Who's him, and what are they arresting him for, then?" I asked.

They both glanced involuntarily at a nearby police car. Mr. Darby was sitting in the back seat, while another officer was leaning on the fender, keeping his eyes on the prisoner.

"Mr. Darby?" I exclaimed. "The chief thinks he did it?"

"Why? Who do you think did it?" Horace asked.

"I have no idea who did it," I said. "If I did, I'd tell the chief. I'm just surprised. He seems like a nice man."

"It's always the nice ones you have to watch," Sammy said.

"That's the quiet ones, not the nice ones," Horace said. "And I agree. A very nice man. Look how much he loves animals."

"It's because of the animals," Sammy said. "I'm sure that'll turn out to be the reason he did it."

"I don't think he did it at all," Horace said. "The cattle rustling, yes, but—"

"Cattle rustling?" I repeated. "So this is related to what I saw last night?"

"And what your grandfather and Caroline discovered yesterday afternoon," Horace added.

"We got a lead on the truck you reported," Sammy said.

"From my tire tread impressions," Horace said.

"And we went over to Mr. Darby's place early this morning," Sammy continued. "That's why we couldn't be here to help."

"No problem," I said. "You did plenty yesterday, and what with the murder and the attempted murder, I assumed you'd both be pretty busy today. What happened this morning?"

Sammy glanced behind him, as if to make sure the chief was safely inside, and leaned closer.

"Dr. Blake and Caroline discovered that Mr. Darby and his cousin have a small farm over in Clay County with dozens of those fancy cows and goats on it," he half-whispered. "And his explanation of how he came by them sounded fishy."

"He had a bunch of sale papers, but they were all made out to other people's names," Horace put in. "He claimed it was because Mrs. Winkleson wouldn't have sold the cows and goats if she'd known it was him."

"Which could be true," Sammy said. "You know how she is."

"Lot of work proving anything," Horace said. "Hunting down all those people whose names are on the bills of sale, and finding out if they really did buy goats and cows, and if so, if they really sold them to Mr. Darby, and if not, if they knew Mr. Darby was using their names. And what if it turns out that you can't find those people?"

"Then maybe that would mean the sales weren't legit," Sammy said.

"In other words, he stole them," Horace said.

"And tried to kill Mrs. Winkleson to cover it up," Sammy added.

"Now that's the part that doesn't make sense to me," Horace said, shaking his head. The two of them appeared to have forgotten that I was there, and I was almost holding my breath, trying to keep it that way. "Surely he'd have known that as soon as anything happened to Mrs. Winkleson, we'd be crawling all over the place to investigate, not to mention her attorney taking an interest in all her business records to prepare for probate. If I were him, the last thing I'd want to do would be to stir up a hornet's nest before I'd managed to hide the stolen livestock and cover my tracks."

"But that's because you know how a murder investigation works," Sammy said. "And hindsight is twenty-twenty. Even he probably realizes now that it wasn't the smartest thing to do. Especially since he blew it twice in one day."

"Three times if you count that last cow-stealing trip," Horace said.

"And then finding that hydrogen cyanide in his cottage," Sammy said.

"It's a common pesticide," Horace said. "I bet you'd find it at half the farms in this county."

"Not that common, and how many farmers do you think there are in the county with motive, means, and opportunity to knock off Mrs. Winkleson? And what did he hope to accomplish by stealing her dog?"

"Mr. Darby stole Mimi?" I exclaimed. "Have they found her?"

"Not yet," Horace said. "But they haven't finished searching his farm."

"And the note they found in Mrs. Sechrest's hand came from the same printer as the one they found in Mimi's empty crate."

"*Appears* to come from the same printer," Horace said. "And we haven't found that printer yet. What puzzles me is—"

The barn door slid open, and Mrs. Winkleson emerged. Horace and Sammy snapped to attention.

"The nerve of that man!" Mrs. Winkleson said, over her shoulder. "I shall dismiss him immediately. And I'll have Marston bring you those records as soon as possible."

She headed for the prep barn. The chief emerged.

"Can I help you?" he asked me.

"You need to question any more of the rose exhibitors?" I asked. "If you do, let me send them out to you. It will be less distracting to the rest."

"No, I'm good," the chief said.

"Then I'll go back and log Mrs. Winkleson in," I said. "Thanks."

"You're not even curious what I was questioning her about?" he called over to me.

I turned back. Horace and Sammy looked anxious.

"I can see Mr. Darby in the back of the patrol car. I can put two and two together."

Sammy and Horace relaxed slightly.

"For your information," the chief said, "I am not arresting Mr. Darby on suspicion of murder."

"Then what are you—never mind," I said. "I should know better than to ask. So you're telling me that we should all still watch our backs."

He smiled and nodded.

I puzzled over that as I went back to the barn. Did that mean the chief didn't really think Mr. Darby was guilty of the murder and attempted murder? That he didn't believe the cattle theft was related to the other crimes? Or just that he was enjoying keeping his cards to himself?

They'd found cyanide in Mr. Darby's cottage? I think I'd remember if I'd seen anything of the sort on his shelves. So either it had been hidden someplace I wasn't able to look, or it hadn't been there when I'd searched. Maybe someone had planted it there.

Or maybe when I'd visited the cottage he'd been carrying it around in his pocket, already planning his second attempt on his employer's life.

At least, if Mr. Darby had been the one to steal Mimi, he probably wouldn't have done anything to her. Perhaps they'd find her soon.

But if Mr. Darby was the dognapper, what was Sandy Sechrest doing with a copy of the note left behind in Mimi's crate? Had anyone searched Mrs. Sechrest's house for signs of Mimi?

Not my problem. Not right now, anyway. I had a show to run.

Chapter 39

Back inside the barn, I checked my watch as I strolled up to Mrs. Winkleson's table. Marston was still standing by the tea cart, so I deduced that rose grooming trumped Mrs. Winkleson's promise to bring something to the chief "as soon as possible."

"Okay," I said. "You get an additional eleven minutes to groom, for a total of twenty-one."

Not that she needed them. She was already methodically transferring her roses from her own black vases to the standard show ones, with only a few token attempts at grooming.

"I could use a runner here," one of the rose growers said. Dad leaped to her table.

"And here," another exhibitor called. Dad was now carrying a vase in each hand, and none of the other runners were in sight, so I went to the second exhibitor's table and took charge of two vases, each containing a single elegant tea rose.

"That one's for class 101," she said. "And this one's for 124."

"Right," I said. I stifled the impulse to point out that the class numbers were clearly marked on the tags attached by rubber bands to the vases. I knew that if the roses were placed in the wrong class, the judges would disqualify them, and clearly she was wound a little more tightly than usual, this close to the deadline. I followed Dad into the show barn and then studied the tags on my two vases before carefully placing them in their proper slots.

Then I took a moment to survey the room. It was filling up with brightly colored blooms. The aroma wasn't as strong as I'd expected. I'd gathered from talking with Dad over the last few weeks that a lot of the roses being shown had been bred for looks rather than scent. But at least where I was standing, near categories 124 (most fragrant modern rose) and 125 (most fragrant old garden rose or shrub), the air was filled with an intense and surprisingly complex range of scents. I closed my eyes, inhaled deeply and—

"Meg?"

Dad. I opened my eyes.

"Come here," he said, in a conspiratorial whisper. "I need to show you something."

I took another deep breath near the most fragrant competitors before following him to the next table, where the Winkleson prize candidates were arranged in a semicircle around the little black-and-white tag that said "Category 127."

"Look at that," he said, pointing to one of the roses.

"Very nice," I said. And it was. Like most of the entrants, it wasn't really black but a very dark, velvety red. Still, this one looked at least a shade darker than almost all of the others. I was about to reassure him that yes, his rose was a shoo-in for the Winkleson prize when I realized that the rose in question might not be Dad's.

The entry tags were folded up so the judges wouldn't know

while judging which grower had entered which rose. I could only read the top few lines, containing the name of the rose variety and the category number. Even in as few words as that, I could tell that this tag wasn't in Dad's elegant and unmistakable printing. But then Mother was probably writing the tags. I unfolded the tag on the dark rose and peeked at the exhibitor's name.

The dark rose was Mrs. Winkleson's.

As I closed the tag up again, I was struggling to find something reassuring to say that wouldn't actually be a lie. Unless the judges were blind, odds were good that they might give Mrs. Winkleson the swan. Dad looked around to see if anyone else was nearby before whispering again.

"That's Matilda," he said.

"Matilda that you thought had been eaten by deer?"

Dad nodded.

"How can you tell?"

"She's got it listed as a Black Magic," he said. "That's a very popular dark red rose. From Jackson and Perkins. The majority of the roses here are Black Magic. See?"

He pointed out some of the other tags. I inspected them and nodded.

"Yes, most of them are Black Magic," I said. "But none of them look like this."

"Precisely," Dad said. "I'm quite familiar with Black Magic. I've used any number of them in my hybridizing program. So either it's a sport—a chance genetic mutation of the sort rose breeders dream about—or that's not a Black Magic rose at all. And I'm betting the latter. Look at the shape."

I studied Mrs. Winkleson's rose and then the Black Magic roses entered by all the other exhibitors. There was a time when they'd have all looked alike to me, but I must have begun to absorb a few things from all the rose-centric dinner table conversations I'd heard in recent months.

"It's . . . fluffier," I said. "As if it had more petals packed into the same space."

"It does have more petals," Dad said. "I used some dark red cabbage rose stock in my hybridizing program. And the leaves are different. They're smaller, and lighter in color. And smell it."

I bent down to Mrs. Winkleson's flower and inhaled deeply.

"Now that's how a rose should smell," I said. The spurious Black Magic rose had an intense, almost intoxicating fragrance that tickled my memory. I took another deep sniff.

"Cloves and licorice," I said.

"Good nose. Now smell the others."

I did so. They all smelled nice, though not nearly as strong. And different. Nice, but no hint of cloves or licorice.

"They have the typical moderate damask scent you'd expect from a Black Magic rose," Dad said. "Not that one. That's Matilda. I'd recognize that spicy scent anywhere."

From what I remembered of Great Aunt Matilda and her seven marriages—or was it eight?—spicy was appropriate.

"Has Mother seen this?" I asked aloud.

"Not yet," Dad said. "And don't tell her."

"No, not while Mrs. Winkleson is still recuperating from the last murder attempt," I said. "If you're right, what can we do?"

"I don't know," Dad said. "There may be nothing we can do to prevent her from winning the trophy with a stolen rose."

I studied the competitors again.

"Well, I think that one has a chance," I said, pointing to a rose at the other end of the semicircle from Mrs. Winkleson's.

"That's Cordelia," Dad said. "My other candidate. I wasn't sure whether to enter her or Matilda, until the deer made the decision for me. At least I thought it was deer. Now I'm not so sure."

"Nice name," I said. Dad nodded, growing a little misty-eyed. Cordelia was the name of his long-lost mother. Before Dr. Blake had entered our lives, all we'd known about my paternal grandmother was that she'd left Dad as an infant in the fiction section of a Charlottesville library—which, for a family of readers, seemed just as acceptable as the more conventional method of leaving foundlings on the steps of the church. We still didn't know much about her, but at least we knew her name.

I studied Cordelia and the Matilda rose that Mrs. Winkleson had stolen from several angles. A toss-up. Either one could win, depending on how the light happened to fall at the moment the judges saw them. If anything, Matilda was in slightly fuller bloom, which would give her the edge right now. But by an hour from now, when the judging began, the stolen Matilda might be a little past her prime.

It would be cheating to turn on the heat and hasten the process, I reminded myself.

"Whether we win the prize isn't the important thing," Dad was saying. "We have to prevent her from continuing the fraud."

"How could she?" I asked. "It's not as if she could keep that one Matilda rose fresh until the next rose show."

"But it's not just one rose," Dad said. "I'm sure she has a bush. Maybe two. Remember, last night's deer attack—if it was a deer attack—wasn't the first time something happened to Matilda. I originally had three Matilda seedlings. Early this spring, I thought a deer had completely eaten two of them. It wasn't the flowers. Both plants were pulled out of the ground and eaten whole. Or so I thought. There was a lot of obvious deer damage to the nearby plants as well. But what if the Matilda seedlings weren't eaten? What if Mrs. Winkleson stole them?"

"I wouldn't put it past her," I said. "But how can we possibly prove it?"

Dad thought for a moment.

"Well, I understand they're doing some interesting work on rose DNA," he said. "So far it's mostly focused on protecting patent rights on new cultivars, and possibly on improving resistance to blackspot disease. But there's no reason it couldn't be used forensically. My remaining Matilda bush still has enough leaves that I could sacrifice one. So all we need to do is get something from her so-called Black Magic rose."

We both stared at the flower in question for some moments.

"We can't touch it now," I said. "People would suspect us of trying to sabotage her entry."

"But you'll be coming back in before the general public, right?" he said. "To supervise the runners who move the winners to the trophy table. Or at least to make sure they've done their job right?"

He pointed to the table where we'd arranged all the various plaques, bowls, loving cups, and other prize items, with the giant black glass swan as its centerpiece, looking rather like Gulliver among the Lilliputians.

"The judges won't be moving the winners themselves?"

"No, no," he said. "Judges don't touch anything. Only the runners. So while that's happening, you could find a chance to snag a leaf or a petal."

"I can try," I said.

"Meanwhile, let's check the area around her prep table," he said. "Maybe we can find a few bits of leaf or petal."

"I doubt it," I said. "I think she groomed her roses, or had them groomed, up at the house. All she did in the barn was pop them from her vases into the show vases and admire them a little."

"But there are still the bushes," Dad said. "You could go take a sample from her rose bushes. You know where her garden is."

"I've been to her garden, once," I said. "Finding it again's not going to be simple."

"You can do it," Dad said.

"And then there's getting in. The place is an armed fortress."

"You can do it," he repeated.

He was looking at me with such an expression of mingled hope and wistfulness that I gave in.

"I'll try," I said. "I can't promise anything."

"Thank you!"

"And I can't even try till the judging starts," I said. "I have to stick around until then. But once it does start, we'll have a three-and-a-half-hour window. Find Mrs. Winkleson and keep an eye on her. In fact, keep her in the barns if possible. Call my cell phone if you lose her or if she takes off over the fields. I'd rather not get caught trespassing."

"No problem!"

I hate it when people say "no problem." It's almost always guarantees disaster.

Chapter 40

I returned to the prep barn and strolled up and down the center aisle, glancing at all the exhibitors as I passed. Everyone was racing to finish grooming their roses. All the tables were littered with bits of leaf and petal, tiny brushes, and the Q-tips and bits of sponges they were pulling out of their roses.

Except for Mrs. Winkleson's table. It was immaculate, and she seemed perfectly calm as she methodically moved her roses from the black glass vases into the clear.

No chance of stealing any rose DNA there. I strolled back up the aisle and sat down at my table.

I could see Dad pacing up and down the aisles between calls for his services as a runner, and I suspected he was keeping a medical eye on several of the most frantic exhibitors, the ones who looked on the verge of a heart attack or possibly a nervous breakdown.

The calls for runners were coming faster and faster, to the point that some of them actually were running. And there were still at least ten times as many roses in the prep barn as there were in the show barn.

"Runner!" someone called.

I glanced around. No one else was leaping to answer the call, so I got up again and carried off another brace of vases.

At 10 A.M. I gave everybody ten minutes' warning. At 10:10, I called time for everyone but Mrs. Winkleson, and sent Rose Noire and Molly Weston to guard the door and make sure no one snuck in any entries under the wire. All the exhibitors stood around, tidying their workspaces, packing up their tools, and casting hostile glances at Mrs. Winkleson.

At 10:21, I called time on Mrs. Winkleson, and sent runners to take her last few roses into the show barn.

She immediately slumped as if she had been running a marathon. I tried to summon up a little sympathy for her. After all, even if the dose of cyanide the killer had given her hadn't turned out to be lethal, whatever they'd done at the hospital to treat her poisoning couldn't have been fun. But I couldn't help feeling that she was fishing for sympathy.

And coming up empty. None of the other exhibitors came over to compliment her on her entries, swap stories about how much rain damage they'd had to overcome, inquire about her health, or wish her well in the competition. She watched the cheerful hubbub for a few minutes, her face inscrutable.

"Bring the car around, Marston," she said finally. "I shall go up to the mansion and rest until the judging is over."

Marston immediately vanished. Mrs. Winkleson sat back in her chair and closed her eyes until Marston returned and helped her out of the barn.

Dad went trotting out after her. Did he mean to catch a ride with her up to the house? No, but I saw him walking briskly up the drive toward it.

As soon as she left, everyone seemed to relax and smile again.

Conversations broke out. I strolled up and down the aisles eaves-dropping.

"—hate to see her win after some of the tricks she pulled. Did you hear—"

"—and the damned thing was closed up tight as can be, but I just put it outside for an hour and let nature work on it—"

"—I've got no use for them. I was just going to pull them up and pitch them, but if you'd like them—"

"—supposed to be resistant to blackspot, and instead it's more susceptible than all my other roses put together—"

A lot of rose lore and rose world gossip. A few words about Mrs. Winkleson's dirty tricks. Nothing about the murder or the attempted murder. Or about Mr. Darby's apparent arrest for cattle rustling.

"Meg, dear," Mother said. "I'm having a picnic brunch brought in. You'd think Mrs. Winkleson would have arranged that. It's only common courtesy. But. . . ."

Here she shrugged and smiled, as if acknowledging the irony of using courtesy in the same sentence with Mrs. Winkleson's name.

A pair of delivery men in the uniform of one of Caerphilly's swankier catering services appeared in the doorway carrying stacks of boxes. The exhibitors pitched in to clear space, and within minutes the prep tables were covered with long square plates full of bacon, sausage, hash browns, grits, biscuits, gravy, scrambled eggs, doughnuts, croissants, yogurt, and a dozen kinds of fresh fruit.

I grabbed a croissant in passing and went to check on the

judges. Mrs. Winkleson had set up a brunch for them in the area set aside as their lounge, the otherwise off-limits horse barn. But since her bounty had consisted of a dozen stale supermarket doughnuts and a small pot of weak coffee, all six of them were standing around looking cross and discontented.

I cringed. I should have checked on their accommodations before.

"The show is ready for you," I told them. They filed out, followed by Rose Noire and Molly, who were going to be acting as runners during the judging.

"For heaven's sake, let's bring them some plates from Mother's brunch," I whispered to Rose Noire. "If I were them I'd disqualify every rose in the show after that miserable excuse for a breakfast."

In the prep barn the caterers were now unloading smoked salmon, caviar, and champagne, and setting up a small omelet-cooking station.

"Who's paying for this anyway?" someone said at my elbow.

It was Theobald Winkleson, the unhappy nephew. I hadn't seen him at all while Mrs. Winkleson was here, but apparently he'd been watching from somewhere nearby.

"Don't worry," I said. "It's not costing your aunt a penny."

He frowned as if he wasn't sure he believed me and began loading up a plate.

Rose Noire and I borrowed Marston's silver cart, snagged a little of everything, and wheeled it into the show barn. When I left, Rose Noire was pouring champagne and the judges were starting their work with smiles on their faces.

Time for me to carry out my promise to Dad.

I detoured into the horse barn with a large trash can, on the pretext of cleaning up the judges' largely untouched coffee and doughnuts. When the barn was spotless again, I left the trash-can just inside the front door. Then I snagged one of the heavy black horse blankets and slipped out the back door.

I was halfway across the goat pasture when I heard shrieks from the show barn. What now? Cyanide in the champagne? Marguerite returning for dessert?

I flung the horse blanket over the fence and ran through the goat barn to the front door of the cow barn. I slid the door open a few inches and peeked in.

Rose Noire and the judges were huddled at this end, attempting to hide behind the silver serving cart.

"What's wrong?" I asked.

No one spoke, but several of them lifted trembling fingers and pointed toward the other end of the barn.

I sighed, and slid the door open another foot, so I could stick my head inside.

One of the black swans was standing at the other end of the barn by the prize table with its wings spread out to their full width. As I watched, it flapped its wings and uttered a harsh cry.

On the prize table, the black glass swan remained mute and motionless, but its wings were held in almost the same position as the live swan's.

Damn. By accident or design, my friend, the glassmaker, had modeled his nearly life-sized glass sculpture on what a real swan looked like when it was about to pick a fight with another of its species.

The real swan flapped its wings again, and I could hear a faint tinkle of breaking glass as one of the more fragile trophies fell over.

"Help!" Rose Noire whispered.

"Why don't you all come outside while I deal with this?" I suggested, hauling the door open wide. The judges scurried out, knocking over the silver cart in their haste.

The swan hardly noticed.

"Someone has to protect the roses," Rose Noire whispered. She continued crouching behind the fallen cart.

For some reason, I found myself remembering how hard I'd tried to get the garden club to hold its show downtown in the high school gym, or in one of the college buildings.

"Oh, no," everyone had said. "That would be so boring."

Right now, I'd have loved boring.

I looked around at the crowd outside the barn and spotted a familiar figure. Horace, again wearing his tattered gorilla suit.

"Horace," I said. "Come help me rescue Rose Noire."

He might have hesitated under other circumstances, but Horace had a longstanding crush on Rose Noire—who was, as I kept explaining to non-family members, only his fourth cousin once removed, so it wasn't really unsuitable at all.

"Can I help too?" Sammy asked. He also had a crush on Rose Noire.

"Go to the other end of the barn and open the door there," I said to Sammy. "The one that leads out into the pasture."

Sammy nodded and raced off around the corner of the barn. Horace shuffled over to the door and peeked in.

"What do you want me to do?" he asked.

"Help me scare off the swan," I said. I grabbed a pitchfork that was standing near the barn door. "When we go in, beat your chest and roar."

Horace looked terrified, but he nodded, and followed me into the barn.

The swan was still flapping its wings at its glass rival.

"Come on," I said. I held the pitchfork in front of me and began slowly marching down the center of the barn. Horace shuffled along beside me. When we got within ten feet of it, the swan turned and focused on us.

"Uh-oh," Horace said.

"Don't say uh-oh," I said, shaking the pitchfork in what I hoped was a menacing manner. "Roar and beat your chest!"

"Rrrrr," Horace said. He was doing okay in the chest beating department, but his roaring sounded more like a kitten's purr.

"No," I said. "Roar! Like this!"

I uttered several loud roars. I probably sounded more like a lion or an angry bear than a gorilla, but it sounded plenty menacing to me. Horace, encouraged, beat his chest with greater conviction, but left the roaring to me.

The swan continued to flap its wings for a few seconds, but then it began edging toward the now open back door.

"We've got it on the run!" I said, between roars. "Keep it up!"

Horace and I continued to advance toward the swan, with me roaring and shaking the pitchfork while Horace alternately waved his arms and beat his chest with them. The swan broke and ran for the door. I heard a small gasp from Sammy, and he leaped inside the door and flattened himself against the wall.

"Good riddance," I said, as Horace and I watched the swan make its retreat across the pasture and into the woods. "Sammy, bring the judges back in."

"I think I may faint," Horace said.

"Take deep breaths," I said. He sat down and followed my advice.

The swan had knocked over several dozen roses on the tables closest to the prize table. I picked up the ones that had merely fallen and put them back on the table, and counted how many broken vases needed to be replaced.

"Oh, Horace!" Rose Noire exclaimed. "That was wonderful!"

I knew Horace was beaming inside his gorilla head. Sammy, standing nearby, looked forlorn.

"And good job with the door, Sammy," I said. "Can you fetch three large and two small vases?"

"Right!" Sammy said, and scurried off.

Only one trophy seemed broken, a fragile glass trinket of some sort. We'd find something else to give the winner. Maybe I could get my glassmaker friend to melt the fragments into something even nicer.

I oversaw swapping out the broken vases for new ones, and made sure the right tags were attached to the new vases. I considered calling the exhibitors in to spruce up their entries, and decided that if we waited for that, the judges would probably lose their nerve and leave. Rose Noire swept up the broken glass and Horace and Sammy went to replace the spilled food. The judges shuffled back in, looking anxious.

"Okay," I said to Rose Noire. "I'm off again. Hold the fort

till I get back. And keep the doors closed in case the swan finds reinforcements and comes back to get even."

Since my route lay in the same direction the swan had taken, I was a little on edge about taking off over the fields. I considered commandeering the pitchfork, but Horace still had it, and was striding up and down the courtyard looking bold and purposeful. The judges might find that reassuring. Sammy had to settle for a mere push broom as his weapon, but he was doing his part, too. I grabbed the horse blanket and set off, looking warily to either side.

By now, I almost knew how to get to Mrs. Winkleson's detention camp for roses: across the goat pasture, now fortunately devoid of both hungry goats and combative swans, over the fence into the field beyond. The woods around Mr. Darby's cottage were on my left. I followed the treeline until I spotted the chain link fence.

I slipped into the woods to look around and listen carefully. I didn't see or hear anything. I ventured out again, and crept up to the rose garden, keeping to the edge of the woods as long as I could.

The gate was shut and locked. I checked the padlock to be sure. I'd brought Dad's lockpicking tools, just in case they came in handy, but when I saw that it was a very high-tech Medeco I didn't even bother getting the tools out. According to the genial retired burglar who'd taught Dad a few of his professional skills—just for fun on Dad's part, since he was an avid mystery reader and adored Donald Westlake's burglar books—no lock was unpickable, but Medecos came close enough that I didn't see any reason for me to waste my time on them. So much for plan A, picking the lock. I was expecting to use plan B anyway.

I tied the horse blanket around my shoulders and began climbing up the chain link fence. The horse blanket was for draping over the razor wire at the top, so I wouldn't get cut to ribbons. I hadn't quite figured out what to do if the razor wire turned out to be electrified.

Fortunately it wasn't, and the horse blanket cushion worked. I climbed part of the way down and then jumped, landing lightly beside the first row of roses.

I pulled out the makeshift DNA collection kit I'd assembled from materials available in the prep barn, including a small pair of pruning shears, a box of plastic zipper Baggies, and a black waterproof marker. I drew a quick map of the red rose of them on the first Baggie. The garden contained twenty-three of them in three rows of eight with one empty space near the end of the farthest row, presumably where one bush had died. Then I numbered the bushes on the map and began bagging my specimens, cutting the smallest possible leaf from each bush, numbering the Baggie to match the bush's place on my map, and adding the name or number of the rose from the tags.

Some of them were familiar names from Dad's dark rose collection: Deep Secret, Black Baccara, Midnight Blue, and of course Black Magic. Others were identified only by numbers. Mrs. Winkleson favored a six-digit system beginning with zeroes, and had only gotten up to 000117, which meant she had room to add nearly a million more hybrids before she had to amend her system.

Toward the end of my sample collection, right after the

blank space, I found something interesting. Yet another bush labeled "Black Magic," but it didn't look like the other Black Magics I'd sampled. The leaves were smaller, and instead of the deep, glossy green of the other Black Magics, they had a slight lime or chartreuse cast to them.

While the blossom left on it was only partially open, I could already see that it had more petals than the other Black Magic blooms. This was definitely the bush from which her entry in the show had come.

I snipped two leaves from that bush.

I checked the label again. Yes, the tag hanging from the bush said Black Magic.

Then I spotted something else peeking out from the bark mulch around the base of the bush. I brushed the mulch away to see more clearly.

It was a length of yellow plastic plant tie material, about half an inch wide. Dad used the stuff not only to stake wayward branches but also to label plants temporarily, using a waterproof marker to print on the plastic the name and planting date and any other information he wanted to remember.

In fact, this plant tie had writing on it. In Dad's unique, meticulous printing, so like calligraphy, it said "L2005-0013." Which, if memory served, was what Dad had been calling his new hybrid before christening her Matilda.

The stem of the rose bush had clearly grown since the label had been attached. It had grown around the plastic, so the label was inextricably enmeshed in the plant. Dad never left his temporary labels on the plants long enough for that to happen, but apparently Mrs. Winkleson wasn't as careful.

It was Matilda. Or if not Matilda, certainly one of Dad's hybrids.

It all fell together. The person who'd been arguing with Mrs. Winkleson up at the house—the one who'd said, "I'm tired of covering this up. And if I went public with it, you'd be the one ruined." Could it have been Sandy Sechrest? I hadn't recognized the voice, but I was ready to bet it was—Sandy who had been helping Mrs. Winkleson with her hybridizing. She'd have had ample opportunity to uncover the plastic label the same way I had, and I'd probably overheard her finally confronting Mrs. Winkleson about it. If so, I'd bet anything the killer hadn't mistaken Sandy Sechrest for Mrs. Winkleson. More likely Mrs. Winkleson had killed Mrs. Sechrest, trying to cover up her theft of Dad's rose.

That meant that Mrs. Winkleson had probably poisoned herself last night. We'd all been saying how lucky she had been, to have taken a less than lethal dose of cyanide with two doctors nearby. Nothing lucky about it—she'd been taking a calculated risk to throw off suspicion.

I had to get back to the barn and find Chief Burke. Once he saw this—

"What are you doing in my rose garden!"

I looked up to see Mrs. Winkleson standing outside the chain link fence, pointing a shotgun at me.

Chapter 41

"Taking cuttings," I said, with what I hoped was an inane, innocent smile. "Dad was amazed at your entry for the trophy. And jealous. He begged me to see if I could snoop around and find out more about your methods. Maybe even steal a cutting. But I guess you caught me. I'll just put them back."

"I could shoot you where you stand," she said. Yes, and from the look on her face, she'd enjoy it. I looked around for some kind of cover. Nothing but rose bushes. And while most of them were tall, healthy, and dense for rose bushes, they were still a long way from looking like plate iron or Kevlar or anything else you'd want between you and a bullet. Or a slug, or buckshot. Even if the shotgun was only loaded with birdshot, at this close range I suspected she could do some damage.

"You could shoot me," I said. "But how would that look? It's not as if I was burgling your house. I'm unarmed, and locked inside a chain link fence. Doesn't make a very plausible self-defense case."

"No," she said. "But I have a small revolver in my pocket. After I shoot you, I'll just throw it down inside the fence and claim you were trying to shoot me with it."

Just then my pocket began vibrating. My cell phone. Was it

Dad, belatedly trying to warn me that Mrs. Winkleson had left the house? I hoped so, since Dad did know, at least in theory, where I was. If the call was only from Michael, giving me an update on his ETA, it wasn't going to help me escape from Mrs. Winkleson's clutches.

But if it was Dad, and I didn't answer, and he got worried enough . . . I had to stall.

"No one was trying to kill you," I said. "You killed Mrs. Sechrest. Then you realized what a lucky break it was that she'd started dressing all in black when she came over here. People would assume the killer mistook her for you, especially after you made that big fuss about having received threats."

"I did receive threats," she said. "I get them all the time. And for all I know, she could have been the one who stole my dog, out of spite."

"Did you accuse her of it?"

"Yes," Mrs. Winkleson said. "Of course she denied it."

That probably accounted for the paper in Mrs. Sechrest's hand. Mrs. Winkleson had probably made her accusations by thrusting one of the threatening letters at Mrs. Sechrest.

"And then you arranged your own poisoning," I went on. "You waited until you were sure that Dad and Dr. Smoot were both there, and then you sipped the drink you'd doctored, and collapsed with as much fuss as possible. Doing it in the middle of your argument with me was a nice touch."

She twitched her mouth in what looked more like a grimace than a smile.

"You should have seen your face," she said. "But you deserved it. You were rude."

"I was rude? That's the pot insulting the kettle."

"And it's all nonsense," she said. "What possible reason could I have for killing that poor woman? She was helping me with my roses. My health doesn't permit me to do as much as I'd like."

She tried to look frail and exhausted, as she had while working on her roses, but the arms holding the shotgun didn't waver at all, so I wasn't buying it.

"Mrs. Sechrest was going to reveal that you had stolen some of Dad's prize seedlings and were entering their blooms as the results of your hybridizing program," I said. "I don't know how she figured it out. Maybe she helped you steal them, or maybe she just figured out that they didn't come from any of the crosses she'd help you make. But she knew it, and you killed her to keep her from telling everyone."

I knew better than to mention the embedded name tag with Dad's unmistakable printing on it, which was probably the way Sandy Sechrest had learned about the theft. If Mrs. Winkleson knew about it, she'd either remove it or hurt the plant trying.

"You can't prove it," she said.

"DNA doesn't lie," I said. "And if anything happens to me, my father will be even more suspicious, and will demand that the chief do a DNA test on your roses."

"DNA might prove that my rose is the same as one of your father's," she said. "But DNA can't prove who stole it from whom. By the time they got around to analyzing it, if they ever did, I could prove that the Langslow family were trespassers and thieves. Now stand away from those roses."

I looked down. I was standing beside the stolen Matilda, and in the midst of all Mrs. Winkleson's dark red roses. I didn't know what firing a shotgun at them would do to the roses. Evidently Mrs. Winkleson didn't either.

"I don't think so," I said. I planted myself firmly behind the Matilda rose. "If you want to shoot me, you'll just have to take a few of your roses with me. In fact, why should I wait till you shoot? I'll take out a few right now."

I reached over to the rose bush next to Matilda. It was a Black Magic, from the tag, and therefore replaceable, as long as the tag wasn't a cover up for another theft.

"And I thought Sandy was stupid," she said. "Confronting me with her stupid accusations and demanding that I give some of my prize rose bushes to your father. But at least she had no idea how effectively I could deal with her interference. You should have known better. Now move!"

That sounded to me as if she was confessing to murder, even bragging about it. Did she really think that would make me more willing to release my leafy hostage?

I gave the bush an experimental tug. I'd have to get a better grip, and I couldn't tell without peering closely at it whether it was one of the varieties with pitiful little thorns or one of the ones that would rip your hand open.

"You wouldn't dare," Mrs. Winkleson said.

The complacent sound of her voice was what pushed me over the edge. I braced myself, took a firm hold, encountering only one puny thorn, and gave it a stronger tug. I almost fell down, it came out so easily.

"Stop that this instant!" Mrs. Winkleson bellowed. "Put that back."

I grabbed another bush. Not Matilda. I was still hoping to save that for Dad.

"Unhand that rose or I'll—*eeeeeee!*"

Mrs. Winkleson shrieked and leaped into the air, and as she did, the shotgun went off with a roar. I flattened myself and peered through the rosebush to see what she was doing.

After a second or two, I could hear a sort of rustling, pattering sound as something hit the rose leaves. I assumed it was the pellets from the shotgun. One of them landed on me, but fortunately not on my bare skin, so it didn't sting too much.

"Take that you wretch!" she shrieked. I flinched, but she wasn't talking to me. Apparently her sudden leap hadn't been voluntary—Algie, the belligerent goat, had snuck up behind her and butted her hard. She was flailing at him with the now unloaded shotgun, and he was backing away warily.

Time to move. I leaped to my feet and sprinted for the part of the fence where I'd made my entrance. The horse blanket was still draped over the razor wire. I didn't know how fast Mrs. Winkleson could load a shotgun, but even if she was some kind of champion at it, she had to fend off Algie before she tried, and he now appeared to be circling her and looking for an opening to butt again.

"Stop that! Don't you dare!" Mrs. Winkleson shrieked. I wasn't sure whether she was objecting to Algie's actions or my escape attempt. I didn't stop to ask. Motivation really is everything—it was amazing how much faster I made it over the chain link fence on the way out.

Mrs. Winkleson was using the shotgun as a stick to heave

herself up, which would have been a lot easier if she didn't have to keep turning to keep her eyes on Algie.

I heard a harsh cry from behind me. I glanced over my shoulder and saw one of the black swans approaching, wings outstretched in a menacing fashion. I ducked aside and it ignored me and headed for Mrs. Winkleson. She waved the shotgun at it. The swan stopped, but didn't retreat.

"Give up," I said. "People are bound to have heard that shot. Someone will be here any minute and—"

She made the mistake of paying too much attention to the swan. Algie charged, knocking her over again. The swan, not to be outdone, waded into the fray, and I dived in to grapple for the shotgun.

Algie got in a few good butts before retreating from the superior ferocity of the swan. When the dust settled, the swan was sitting on Mrs. Winkleson and I had the shotgun in my hands.

When Mrs. Winkleson saw me holding her weapon, she began scrabbling at her pocket. I realized she was reaching for that small revolver she'd mentioned earlier. Unfortunately, the swan didn't seem to notice—it just stood there flapping its wings in triumph. My first instinct was to put some distance and a whole lot of trees between us, but then I realized that if I wasn't around, she'd be free to turn the revolver on the swan, or even on Algie, who was lurking nearby, hoping for another shot at revenge. I couldn't let that happen to either of my rescuers, even if they'd been motivated by spite instead of good Samaritanism.

I pointed the shotgun at her.

"Don't even try reaching for that revolver," I said. "Or I'll give you the other barrel."

I had no idea whether the shotgun even had a second barrel—it didn't look as if it did. You could put what I knew about shotguns in a thimble and still have room for your finger. But I was hoping Mrs. Winkleson didn't know much about them, either. The revolver seemed more her style.

She froze, so maybe I was right. The swan settled down. Algie stiffened and keeled over. What now?

"Meg! Are you all right?"

Horace. I couldn't see him yet, but it sounded as if he was coming along the treeline toward us.

"I'm fine," I said. "And I have Sandy Sechrest's killer here."

Horace appeared from behind some trees. He stopped dead when he saw me holding Mrs. Winkleson at gunpoint.

"Oh, my," he said. "Let me call the chief."

"You'll never prove a thing." Mrs. Winkleson's voice was probably too soft for Horace to hear, though I could, quite clearly. "I'll charge you with trespassing, and attempting to shoot me, and . . ."

"No, you won't," came a voice from the other side of the chain link enclosure.

Mrs. Winkleson and I both started as three of the rose growers stepped out of the shrubbery—Molly Weston, the lady who'd worn the pink suit to last night's party, and one of the three volunteers who'd been making blots on the programs.

"We saw what happened," Molly said. "Meg may have been trespassing—heck, we snuck out here ourselves to see if we could do a little spying on your rose garden, but none of us were spry enough to climb that fence. And we saw who was trying to shoot whom."

"And heard what you said," the lady in pink said.

"I got pictures on my cell phone," the blot lady said, holding it up.

"I got video on my iPhone!" the lady in pink said.

"That little thing does video?" the blot lady asked.

"Yes—of course, I have no idea how good the quality's going to be," the lady in pink said. "Maybe we should take a look and—"

"Silly me," Molly Weston said. "I just used *my* cell phone to call 911." She sounded a little exasperated with her photo-happy companions.

"So," I said, turning back to Mrs. Winkleson. "You really think you're going to get away with—"

"Everybody drop your guns and put your hands in the air!"

It was Sammy. I obediently dropped the shotgun, making sure to throw it well out of Mrs. Winkleson's reach. She didn't drop anything, and was very slow to put her hands up. By contrast, Horace and all three of the rose growers threw their hands up instantly, and the lady in pink and the blot lady dropped their cell phones to boot.

"What in blazes is going on here?"

The chief.

"Meg? Are you all right?"

And Michael, back safe and sound from New York.

"I'm fine," I said.

Though I didn't really breathe easily again until Sammy carefully checked Mrs. Winkleson's pockets and fished out a small but lethal-looking black-handled revolver.

Chapter 42

"I'm still having a hard time believing that Mrs. Winkleson killed someone over something as silly as roses," Michael said.

"Don't let them hear you call roses silly." I said, gesturing toward the other end of the prep barn where the rose exhibitors were waiting with visible impatience for the judges to finish.

"I don't mean that roses are silly in general," he said. "But as a motive for murder?"

"Wasn't really about roses," I said. Though it came out sounding more like "Wf neenee bah woz," since I was talking through a mouthful of pastrami on rye. I hadn't minded missing Mother's brunch to go snooping at Dad's request, but for some reason, after I'd answered all of Chief Burke's questions and seen Mrs. Winkleson arrested and hauled off for further questioning, I'd suddenly found myself shaking with hunger. Maybe it was a side effect of realizing how close I'd come to never eating again. So we'd commandeered a table at the far end of the barn, and I was sampling a few of the food delicacies Michael had brought back from New York.

"Then what is it about?" Michael said, a little muffled himself by the chocolate cheesecake he was nibbling.

"Pride, maybe," I said. "She wanted everyone to think she

was an expert rose grower and hybridizer. And maybe control. She ruled her little world with an iron hand, and even tried to impose her own color scheme on nature, for heaven's sake. You think she'd sit still while Mrs. Sechrest ruined her plans for glory?"

"I guess not," he said. "But allow me to change my adjective. Silly's not the word. It's stupid. However lovely roses are, they're a stupid reason for murder. Stupid, and maybe even crazy."

"Now that I won't argue with," I said. "And I doubt anyone else in this barn would either. Do you think—"

"Hey, Meg, Michael, did you hear the good news?"

It was Rob, being dragged along by the Small Evil One, with Dr. Blake and Caroline following more slowly.

"If you mean the good news that Mrs. Winkleson did not manage to shoot me and is under arrest for murder, then yes, I have," I said. "I can't think of any good news that would top that."

"Mind if I have some," Rob said, pointing at the deli spread. Michael indicated the litter of brown paper parcels with a sweeping gesture, and Rob wasted no time before making himself a supersized sandwich.

"Actually, I meant the good news about Mr. Darby," Rob said.

"We've figured out what he's been up to," my grandfather said. "He wasn't stealing cows and goats after all."

"Then who was?"

"No one. You came across him and his cousin loading up cattle they'd purchased quite legitimately."

"So why were they loading them in the middle of the night?" I asked. "And why did they run away like thieves when they heard me? Some boyish fondness for playing cowboys and rustlers?"

"They were afraid you were Mrs. Winkleson," Caroline put in. "She refused to sell to Mr. Darby."

"So he had a friend buy them at a fair market price," Dr. Blake explained. "Then the friend turned around and sold them to Mr. Darby for the same price."

"But he still had the problem of getting them off the farm without Mrs. Winkleson realizing that he was the purchaser," Caroline said. "She'd have stopped selling to the friend if she'd figured it out."

"The chief's pretty provoked," Rob said. "To hear him talk, you'd think Mr. Darby deliberately set out to complicate his murder investigation."

"Champagne?" It was Marston, accompanied by a tiny maid carrying a silver tray. On the tray were a dozen or so champagne flutes, already filled from the bottle of Dom Perignon that stood in the middle of the tray.

"Did Mother arrange for this?" I asked. Even for Mother, it seemed a bit extravagant. I took a glass with the rest, and had a token sip. If my suspicions were correct, I wouldn't be doing much drinking in the immediate future, but no use giving the gossipmongers anything to play with.

"This is from Mrs. Winkleson's cellars," Marston said.

"Aren't you afraid she'll fire you if she finds out?" I asked.

"I suspect she won't be the one doing the firing," Marston said, with a shrug. "I doubt if her nephews will feel the need for a butler, and I understand that this weekend's events have convinced the Warrenton police to reopen the file on the late Mr.

Winkleson's death several years ago. At the time, it was thought to be food poisoning, but his nephews have always been dubious. His symptoms much resembled those we observed when Mrs. Winkleson poisoned herself."

"And you're not allowed to profit from murder," I said.

"So the nephews may get the farm sooner than they feared," Rob said. "I hope Mr. Darby and his cousin can afford to buy a whole lot more animals, because I don't think the nephews are keen on keeping the designer livestock."

"Speaking of the nephews, did the chief ever figure out what Theobald Winkleson was doing lurking about on Friday?" I asked. "Because that almost convinced me he was the killer."

"As it happens, the chief was well aware that both nephews were in the habit of lurking about," Marston said. "I have no idea why. Their uncle's death occurred at Mrs. Winkleson's old home, in Warrenton, so it's not as if they could hope to find evidence here. Nor was their presence apt to discourage Mrs. Winkleson from making what they considered frivolous purchases."

"Maybe they were just trying to annoy her," Rob said. "That I can understand."

Marston smiled slightly as if he agreed.

"Is there any news about Mrs. Winkleson's missing dog?" Marston asked.

Rob and I shook our heads.

"They didn't find her at Mr. Darby's farm," I said. "And now that we know Mrs. Winkleson was the murderer, it makes the dognapping more of a mystery than ever."

"I'm sure Mimi's fine," Caroline said. "And if she isn't found—well, isn't it really for the best? I'm sure such a sweet, affectionate little creature will have no trouble finding a happy home wherever she is."

"Yes," Marston said. "All the staff are very fond of Mimi. We all wish her the best."

He was looking at Caroline with a peculiar intensity.

"Don't worry," Caroline said.

I had the sinking feeling that Caroline wasn't just trying to be reassuring—that she knew very well that Mimi was fine because she knew exactly where Mimi was.

She and Marston smiled at each other. The tiny maid was beaming with delight. I realized exactly what must have happened. Marston and the maids had rescued Mimi from her unhappy home with Mrs. Winkleson. Caroline and my grandfather had used me to get onto the property so they could smuggle Mimi out. I'd probably actually witnessed the handoff in the gazebo.

"Mimi's not bad for a yappy little dog," Dr. Blake said. "We were originally thinking maybe Spike could use a mate."

"If and when they found Mimi," Caroline said, giving him a sharp dig in the ribs.

"What? Oh, right," my grandfather said. "If and when."

"And then, no doubt, you remembered that Spike has been fixed, and wouldn't be much of a mate for poor Mimi," I said. "Not to mention the fact that Spike lives in Chief Burke's jurisdiction. Somehow I doubt if the chief will give up on finding Mimi quite so easily. After all, dognapping's a felony."

Marston and Caroline looked at me as if I'd thrown a large toad into the center of an elegantly set table.

"Only so much time and money he can afford to spend on one missing dog," my grandfather said. "Especially when the one person who wants the dog found will have a few other things on her mind."

And especially since the chief, a dog lover himself, might be in sympathy with Mimi's liberators. I just hoped the new home they were planning for Mimi was far enough away to be safe. And that someone who could easily afford it, like my grandfather, found some way of conveying to Mrs. Winkleson a sum of money that far exceeded even her most inflated notions of what Mimi was worth. I'd tackle him about it later, with no eavesdroppers.

"Speaking of the chief, what's he doing still here?" Dr. Blake said. "Shouldn't he be down at the station, putting thumbscrews on Mrs. Winkleson?"

"His wife's an exhibitor," I said. "He's probably waiting to see how she did. The judges shouldn't be too much longer."

"I hope not," Dr. Blake said, glancing at his watch. "We should hit the road. Long drive ahead of us."

"We can spare a few more minutes to see how the young people did in their show," Caroline said. By young people, I realized, she meant my parents.

"True," my grandfather said. "But let's not stand around here wasting time. We could inspect the goats again."

They strolled off arm in arm.

"A long drive?" I echoed. "He got his license back?"

"I'm taking them," Rob said. "Do you know a town called Abingdon?"

"Yes," I said. "That should be far enough."

"Far enough for what?" Rob said.

"Far enough to qualify as a long drive," I said.

"How far is it?"

"At least six hours. It's almost in Tennessee."

"Yikes," he said, reaching for the rye bread. "I'd better pack provisions."

"Get them to take you to a nice restaurant," I said. "Abingdon has several. What are they rescuing now?"

"Dunno," Rob said. "They didn't say. Maybe they just want to do a little sightseeing. Hey, what's in that one?"

He was pointing to yet another brown parcel, indistinguishable from the deli packages that littered the table, except that Michael was keeping this one on his lap.

"Special surprise for Meg," Michael said, moving it under the table and out of Rob's reach.

"Sorry," Rob said, sounding unrepentant. "If it's anything good, save me some, will you?" he added to me. "I'll try to guilt trip Gramps into some good meals on the trip. Come on, Spike, let's go bark at the goats one last time."

With that, he and Spike strolled off.

"Sightseeing?" Michael repeated.

"I wouldn't bet on it," I said. Should I tell him about Mimi? Probably better not share my guesses, however accurate they were. No sense making him yet another accessory after the fact. "They're off to rescue some other kind of animal. Just remember, in case they ask, we're way too busy with the llamas to take on any more animals."

"Just the llamas?" Michael asked. "Or am I wrong in guessing that maybe we might be needing this?"

He handed me the paper bag he'd been withholding. I peeked inside to see several home pregnancy tests.

"You're a mind-reader!" I exclaimed. "Exactly what I would have asked you to bring back if someone hadn't been eavesdropping every single time we talked on the phone. Well, except for the middle of the night, when I wasn't really thinking well."

"Oh, is that what was going on?" he asked. "I just thought you were having rampant food cravings and made an optimistic guess at why."

We both burst out laughing.

"Meg, dear." Mother, of course. "I'm so glad to see that you've recovered from your shock."

"I'm fine," I said. "Any word from the judges?"

"I think they'll let you know directly when they're finished," Mother said. "After all, you're the organizer. And an excellent organizer if I say so myself. In fact, everyone says so."

"Thank you," I said. Then I braced myself. Mother so often used compliments to sweeten completely unreasonable requests.

"You had to cope with so many unfortunate events, and still managed to pull off a wonderful show."

Translation: in spite of all obstacles, she was optimistic that she might win a satisfactory number of trophies.

"Everyone's so impressed," she said. "The good job you've done is such a contrast to what's happening with next month's garden show."

Uh-oh.

"I know it's a lot to ask, dear," Mother said. "But if you could see your way clear to taking over organizing the garden show—"

"Sorry," I said. "But no."

"We had an informal meeting of the board just now, and everyone thinks it's a splendid idea, so as soon as we can convene an emergency meeting and take an official vote—"

"No thanks," I said.

"And I'm sure we can get all the nice volunteers who helped with the rose show to pitch in."

"Except me," I said. "No."

"But dear," Mother said. "It would be such a help—"

"No, Mother."

"Won't you even think about it?"

"No."

"But dear—"

"No."

Mother and Michael were looking at me as if they'd never seen me before.

"Sorry, but much as I'd love to organize the show. I can't," I said. "I have a few other things I need to be doing in the next month. But don't worry. I know someone who would be a much better organizer."

"Who?" Mother said, sounding dubious.

"Rose Noire," I said. "She really enjoyed working on Mrs. Sechrest's roses. I heard her say so. The one thing that has really hampered me in organizing the rose show was that I didn't really know that much about roses. But here you have someone who's already a keen gardener and very interested in expanding into roses. Who could be more perfect?"

"She doesn't have your organizational skills, dear," Mother said. "Now all you have to do—"

"That's because she hasn't had you guiding her," I said. "But now she will. Go ahead. Ask her."

"But it would be so much easier if you'd do next month's show," Mother said. "Then you could start training Rose Noire if you think she has promise and—"

"No," I said. "Go ask Rose Noire."

To my relief—and, I admit, my surprise—Mother frowned slightly, and then sighed, and sailed away, presumably in search of Rose Noire.

"Wow," Michael said. "That was—"

"Horribly rude," I said. "You don't have to tell me. But I just can't deal with organizing something else so soon, and I don't think anything short of rude would have gotten the point across."

"I was about to say amazing," he said. "I don't think you've ever stood up to your mother like that before. Well done!"

"We'll see," I said. "I hope Rose Noire—"

"Meg? Is your father in here?"

Horace had appeared in the doorway behind us.

"He's over there, fretting with the rest of the exhibitors," I said. "Why?"

"I have something for him," Horace said.

I peered out the door. He and Sammy were standing on either side of a large plastic pot containing a rose bush.

"Michael, can you find Dad?" I called over my shoulder.

I reached down and parted the branches. Yes, there was the plastic strip, still imbedded in the stem.

"Matilda!"

I think Dad and I said it simultaneously. Dad stepped forward and squatted down beside the bush to finger the plastic strip.

"We've photographed it in situ," Horace said. "So the chief said it was okay to dig it up and give it back to you."

The chief appeared behind them.

"Meg convinced me that we should get Matilda out of Mrs. Winkleson's reach before she gets out of lockup," he said.

"Thank you," Dad breathed. "She looks all right. A little spindly, but nothing a few good feedings of manure can't make up for."

We all beamed as Dad examined every inch of Matilda's foliage with the same intensity he'd have used on a human patient.

"Let's take her to your car, then," Michael said.

"We'll take her," Horace said. He and Sammy hoisted Matilda up again. Spindly or not, it took a fairly large pot to hold her. Dad went running ahead to open the car, while Michael followed.

"Just one more question," the chief said.

"Fire away," I said. I was tucking the brown paper bag into my tote and trying to decide if I had room for cheesecake.

"When you found the rose bush—"

Just then two of the exhibitors came running up.

"The judges are finished!"

"Look, chief," I said, "I know you probably have a million more questions, but—"

"But the judges are finished," he said. "You have responsibilities."

"Thanks," I said, and headed toward the barn.

"Besides," he said, falling into step beside me, "Minerva will skin me alive if I don't come see how her blasted dwarf roses did."

"Miniature roses," I said.

"Whatever."

We arrived at the doors of the barn. One of the judges was looking out. The exhibitors had crowded around the door, trying to see over his shoulder.

"Looking for me?" I called out.

"Ms. Langslow," he said. I slipped inside the door and slid it closed behind me. The judges gathered around me.

"We're still writing up our results," the tall judge said. "I'll have them for you in a few minutes. Meanwhile, we've had the runners move the winning blooms to the trophy table."

I glanced over to the far end of the barn where the trophy table stood. Now, along with the trophies, it also held several dozen glass vases of brightly colored blooms.

"Great," I said. "Ready to let the public in?"

The judges all nodded. They seemed to be waiting for something. Was there some point of etiquette I'd overlooked?

"Thank you very much," I said. I shook hands formally with each of them. Apparently that was what they'd been waiting for.

"Let's go get some more coffee," one said, as they all turned away.

"Beastly weather," another said.

I waited until they left the barn by the back door. Then I hauled the front door open and let the public in.

Not that big a crowd. Maybe a hundred people, most of

them either the exhibitors or their friends and family. Most of them stampeded up to the trophy table, and I could hear exclamations of delight and dismay.

One of the last through the door was Dad, and unlike the others, he didn't make a beeline to the trophy table.

"I'm too tense to look," he said. "How did Cordelia do?"

"I haven't looked myself," I said.

We both glanced at the trophy table. People were crowded around it three deep.

"It'll be a while before that crowd clears out," I said. "Let's go see who didn't win."

He nodded and followed me as I walked over to the table where the entries in category 127 were displayed. We stood side by side a few feet from the entries and studied them.

"Cordelia's not here," Dad said, with a note of rising excitement in his voice.

I stepped closer and examined the remaining entries one by one. Many Black Magic roses . . . a couple of numbered seedlings . . . but no 2005-427, which was still the official name for Dad's Cordelia rose.

The last rose, Mrs. Winkleson's so-called Black Magic, had the letters DQ written on the top of the tag.

"What's DQ?" I asked Dad.

"Disqualified," he said. "Who's disqualified?"

"Mrs. Winkleson's entry. The stolen Matilda."

"That's impossible," Dad said. He hurried to my side and peered down at the rose. It was as beautiful as ever, and a full shade darker than any of the others—maybe two shades. Hard to believe it hadn't won.

Rose Noire came running up.

"Meg! One of my roses was a runner up! Well, Mrs. Sechrest's roses, but I groomed it! And your Mother won Queen of the Show!"

"Splendid," I said. "Not Dowager Queen?"

"No, Mrs. Burke won that. Even the chief's in a good mood. And Uncle James! Your Cordelia rose won the black swan!"

"Wonderful!" Dad exclaimed. "But why did the judges disqualify Matilda? She's just as good as Cordelia any day."

I reached down to Mrs. Winkleson's stolen entry and lifted up the tag so we could see it better.

"Ooh," I said. "The judges have sharp eyes."

Written beneath the DQ were the words, "This is NOT a Black Magic rose!!!!"

"No," Dad said softly. "It's a Matilda Hollingsworth. And now that I've got her back, she'll be winning a few shows herself."

With a broad smile on his face, Dad marched to the other end of the barn to inspect his trophy.